I0593161

SILVERBELL
SHORE

Never Let Me Go

DL GALLIE

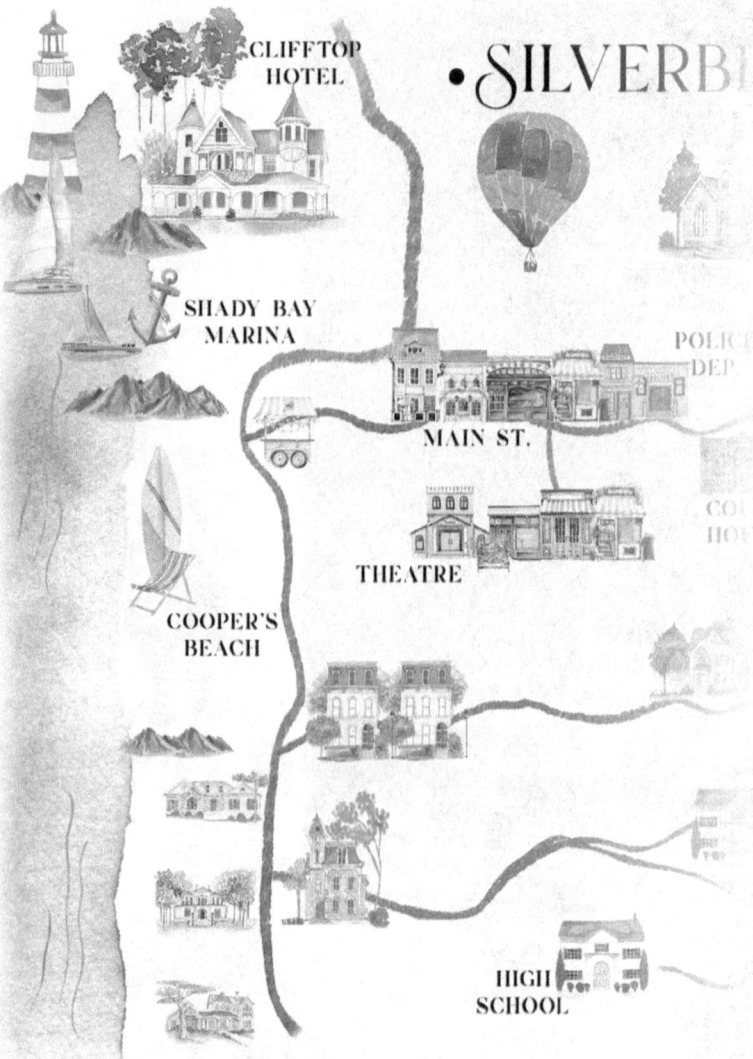

CLIFFTOP
HOTEL

SILVERB

SHADY BAY
MARINA

MAIN ST.

POLICE
DEP.

THEATRE

CO
HO

COOPER'S
BEACH

HIGH
SCHOOL

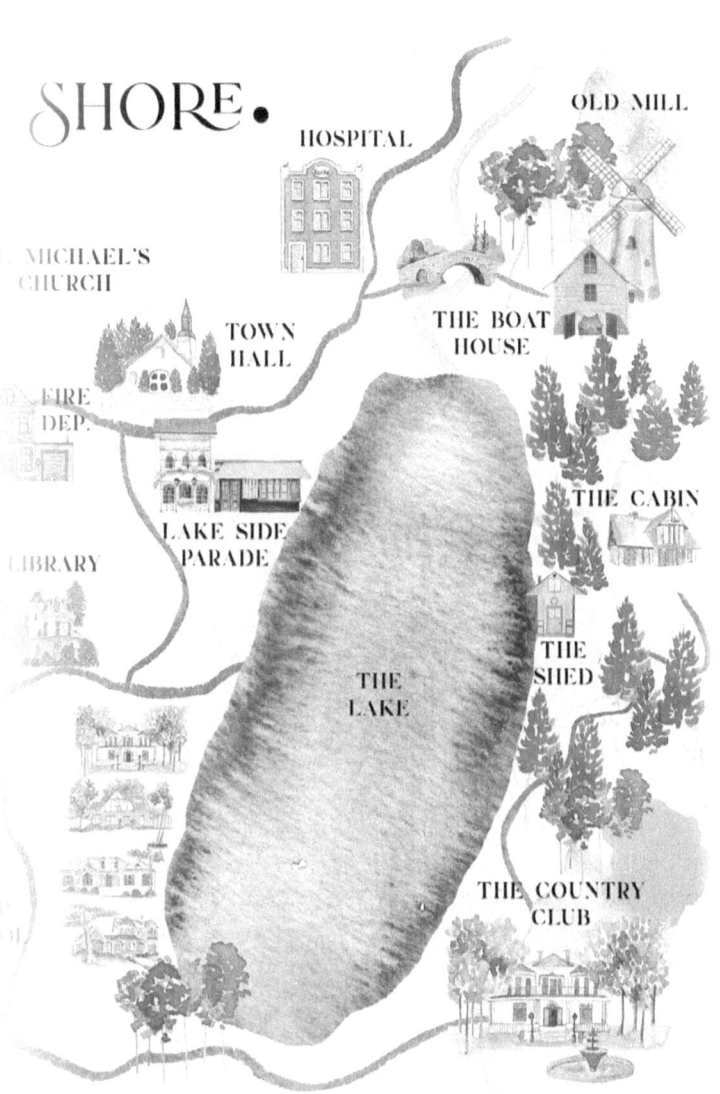

SHORE.

HOSPITAL

OLD MILL

L. MICHAEL'S
CHURCH

TOWN
HALL

THE BOAT
HOUSE

FIRE
DEP.

THE CABIN

LAKE SIDE
PARADE

LIBRARY

THE
SHED

THE
LAKE

THE COUNTRY
CLUB

Edited by Karen Hrdlicka, Barren Acres Editing
Proofread by Gemma Woolley, Gem's Precise Proofreads
Cover Design by Alexandra Silva
Interior Design & Formatting by LJDesigns

Series Information

Silverbell Shore is a (fictional) town on the East-Atlantic coast where the sea meets the rolling hills. Founded shortly after the Civil War as a fisherman's town, it's home to billionaires with private beaches, hotels and country clubs. As well as your everyday person—doctors, cops, EMTs, firefighters, farmers, teachers, students, etc.

Whether you're sunshine or grumpy, light or dark, the seemingly quiet and quaint town of Silverbell Shore welcomes you and all your deepest, darkest, forbidden secrets.

DL GALLIE

DEDICATION

To Alan the Asshole Appendix
You may have knocked me down and threw emergency
surgery at me, but Bradford, Fern, and I won 'cause I got
the book done...eat shit, asshole.

PS. Bradford is yours, Sophie...sorry, Alex, she claimed
him first.

DL GALLIE

PROLOGUE

My adventure in California didn't quite pan out how I imagined. I had dreams of making it as a big-time, Hollywood makeup artist. Instead, I became a secretary and started dating my boss … my much older, sexy, silver fox boss and became a stepmom to his fur baby, Mr. Woolley.

It was perfect in every way, even if he was my boss and old enough to be my dad, but he promised to never let me go and I was okay with that. Bradford Manning was everything I dreamed my Prince Charming would be and more. He was the first man to send me flowers and after that first time, once a month, on any given Thursday, he sent me a gorgeous bouquet of sunflowers and every Sunday, we'd have breakfast on the rooftop terrace of his Venice Beach house. The meal would end with multiple orgasms, and then we'd spend the rest of the day naked together.

But in an instant, my Hollywood fairy tale fell apart after I nearly lost my life in a car accident. Bradford was by my side as much as he could be through my recovery. Then one day, out of the blue, he did the one thing he said he wouldn't, he let me go.

Now, I'm returning home to Silverbell Shore, heartbroken and a failure.

CHAPTER 1

Fern

"I can't believe it's all about to end," I tell Cali and Raven, as we sit in the country club having brunch together. The three of us made this a monthly thing when Raven got his license at sixteen and his parents bought him a Honda Civic. He thought he was an extra in *Fast and Furious* when he drove that car but Raven knew how to handle it, and Cali and I have never felt unsafe with him. With graduation just around the corner, it's just hit me that the three of us are about to embark on separate journeys. Cali is off to the Big Apple to study marketing at Fordham

University, or FU. *Is that not the best university name ever?* Worst part about FU—he he—is being so far away from her. I'm going to miss her and her crazy antics so much. While she heads north to the Big Apple, I'm heading to the West Coast to pursue my dream of becoming a makeup artist for the movie stars. And our third amigo, Raven, is off to Chicago. Currently he's undeclared, but he has always wanted to live in Chicago because of deep dish pizza and the Cubs. So come fall, the three of us will be scattered across the country. "All our catchups will be via FaceTime and a screen. It's just not going to be the same."

"Are you getting all emotional, Fern Halstead?" Raven teases me, but from the somber look on his face, he's feeling this too. Out of the three of us, Rave is the most emotional and in touch with his inner feelings and all that shit. Me? I'm a stone. There's no getting through my emotional walls.

"I think she might be," Cali pipes up with tears in her eyes.

"Says the one who's about to break down," I tease my bestie.

"Am not," she hisses, "there was a bug."

"Mmmhmpf," I reply, giving her the eye.

"Okay, fine, what you said really hit home. I'm going to miss you guys when we all head to different parts of the country shortly. Fern, you're gonna become this amazing Hollywood makeup artist and, Rave, you're going to be awesome at whatever you finally decide to do in life, and me, well, I'll be the best marketing bitch there ever was."

"To us being the best of the best." Rave raises his glass of iced tea for a toast.

"To being the best of the best," Cali and I repeat.

After our deep moment, we fall back into conversation and talk about Aria Thomas's party this weekend. We aren't cool enough for that crowd so while everyone will be partying it up at the beach, the three of us will be at my place for a movie night.

Out of nowhere, Rave declares, "I need a piss," and hops up to 'take a piss,' leaving Cali and I shaking our heads, staring after him as he sashays toward the restrooms.

"That boy is so crass sometimes," my BFF complains, saying exactly what I'm thinking, hence why she's my BFF. My ride or die. The PB to my jelly. But we also have Raven, the one with no filter … or tact.

"True," I agree, "but we wouldn't have him any other way." She nods and then just like Raven's pee declaration, I screech, "OMG, Cali!" I reach across the table and grab her arm, just to make sure I have her attention. I'm pretty sure my screech got her attention since the people at the table next to us are currently scowling at me, but my eyes are locked on the man walking in, Kane Heatherington. He's Cali's dad's best friend and the hottest man in Silverbell Shore.

"What?" she hisses, but my eyes follow the delicious specimen who just so happens to be the man of my best friend's dreams, and a dream is all it ever will be since her dad is his best friend, this isn't an age gap romance. Stuff like that doesn't happen in real life, and it sure as shit does not happen in Silverbell.

Vaguely, I hear her saying something about talons but my focus is on the silver fox walking this way, that is until she pinches my arm and stares at my hand on her arm and I realize what I'm doing. "Shit, Cal, I'm so sorry," I tell her, releasing my grip on her and then rubbing the indents on her arm. She's giving me her 'what the fuck' look but I can't form words. Mr. Heatherington gets me all flustered, not like he flusters Cali but he gets me in a tizz and today he is looking mighty fine. I'm pretty sure he's the only man on Earth who Cali and I both agree is H O double T, hot. Hell, even Raven agrees with us … and he's a dude.

"What caused you to go all grabby-grabby, stabby-stabby with your fingers just now?"

I utter two words I know are going to make her day, "Mr. Heatherington."

At the mention of his name, she turns into a flustered mess. Inwardly I chuckle but if I could wish anything for my bestie, it would be for her to get the man of her dreams, however controversial that would be. I can only imagine the gossip train around here if sweet little Calliope Fischer hooked up with her dad's bestie.

The man in question stops by our table. "Calliope. Fern," he says in greeting and by the look on my bestie's face, she can feel the timbre of his voice vibrate through her body, much like I just did. This man could seriously narrate the phonebook and I'd happily listen from A to Z. If this was a cartoon, she'd have pulsating hearts in her eyes and birds would be tweeting teeny tiny hearts around her head.

"Hi, Mr. Heatherington," we both singsong like schoolgirls, which technically we still are since we don't graduate 'til next week from Silverbell Shore High.

"Congrats on your upcoming graduation, girls."

"Thanks, Mr. Heatherington," we both reply in unison, causing us both to laugh at how in sync and school-like our thank-you is.

"Calliope, I heard you got into Fordham. That's no easy feat."

"Thank you, Mr. Heatherington. It was tough but worth the effort."

"Please, call me Kane, we're all adults now. When you're done at FU…" I can't help but giggle when he says FU. His lip lifts to chuckle too but he schools it quickly, he is an adult after all. "…get in touch and I'll be sure to create a position at The Clifton for you."

"Thanks, Mr. Heathre—I mean, Kane, I'll keep that in mind. But I want to get a job because I earned it, not 'cause the boss is best friends with my dad."

He nods and smiles. "I admire that, speaking of your dad, he must be so proud."

"He is and I'm pretty proud too."

"As you should be. I wish Michael had your determination and tenacity. Instead, he's failing and likely never to graduate."

"He'll get there, Mr. H."

Sitting here I watch the two of them converse, and I'm so proud of my girl. She's actually forming words rather than just grunting like usual. My little Calliope is growing up so fast, and then she shocks the absolute shit out of me when she reaches out and squeezes his hand.

Cali.

Touched.

Mr. Heatherington.

Willingly.

Have I drifted into *The Twilight Zone*? They are STILL talking and I could not be prouder of her right now, but the moment is broken when her dad arrives.

"You harassing my daughter?" her dad teases Mr. Heatherington when he joins us. "Princess." He greets his daughter with a kiss to her head and nods at me in the fatherly way he does and says my name. Garret Fischer is my second dad, but he doesn't even come close to how amazing my dad was. Alex and Sophie Halstead were the best parents a girl could ask for, God rest their ever-loving souls. They passed a few years ago in a freak gas leak at home and I was left in the care of my nanna, but at almost ninety, raising a teenager was the last thing she wanted to do so I became an honorary Fischer.

"Hi, Mr. Fischer," I greet him before I reach over and pick up Cali's iced tea and take a sip. She eyes me stealing her drink. I ignore that glare and drink her drink while she chats with her dad and Mr. Heatherington, but the conversation is halted when Raven returns. "Man, if pissing was an Olympic sport, I just won a gold medal," he announces, dropping down into his seat after using the facilities.

"Raven," I whisper-hiss, smacking him up the side of the head. "You are so crass ... and loud."

"Yet you love me." He blows a kiss at me and that's when he realizes we have company. When he sees who our company is, his eyes widen, his cheeks darken in embarrassment, and he sits up straight as if his posture will take back the crassness of his Olympic piss declaration.

Even though he's lived next door to Cali since he was three, he's intimidated by her dad. Hell, he was even scared of mine and Alex Halstead was a gentle giant. The reason for his fear of Mr. Fischer stems back to when we were eleven and he caught Cali and Raven practice kissing one weekend.

"Mr. Fischer." He nods at him and then quickly looks to Mr. Heatherington, "Mr. Heatherington, how are you both?"

"I'm fine," Mr. Fischer snaps through clenched teeth. He didn't ignore Rave this time so that's a step up from the usual ignore he gets.

"I'm well, Mr. Mitchell, thank you for asking," Mr. Heatherington, I mean, Kane drawls. It'll be hard to call him Kane after knowing him as Mr. Heatherington since forever. "How's your mom and dad?"

"Dad's well," Raven replies, stealing a fry from my plate and popping it into his mouth, chewing loudly. Then he adds, "Mom just finished chemo but the doctors are hopeful they got it all this time."

"Good, good," Mr. Heatherington says, resting his hand on Raven's shoulder. He gives it a squeeze in that loving parental way and I can see it reassures Rave that his mom is going to be okay this time round. "I have everything crossed for her. Please pass on my best wishes." Raven nods and then Mr. Heatherington looks to Mr. Fisher. "Ready to go?"

They both say their goodbyes and walk off. Cali's eyes follow them across the room. A bomb could go off right now and she'd be none the wiser. He's clearly out of view because she turns her attention back to us.

"Hey, Cali, you got a little something on your chin," I tell her, pretending to wipe.

She lifts her hand and wipes then furrows her brows. "There's nothing there."

"You've got drool on your chin," I tease her.

"Hardy har har, Fern." She picks up a fry and throws it at me. Not one to let a good fry go, I grab it and pop it into my mouth. The rest of the afternoon flies by and it is another happy memory to add to the million others I have with Fern and Raven.

Summer is almost over and the last few months have flown by, but the time has finally come. Today is the day. Today is the day Cali, Raven, and I scatter ourselves across the country. I thought I was okay with this, but now, standing in the Fischers' driveway as Garrick packs the last of Cali's things into the car, not so much.

"I'm going to miss you so so much," I tell my best friends as I pull them in for another group hug.

"Wow, Fern, you're really emotional over this," Raven states. "I thought it was going to be this one"—he flicks his thumb toward Cali—"who broke down like a baby."

"Shut it, asshole. There—"

"Was a bug," the two of them singsong in unison, and this causes the three of us to fall into laughter.

"I really am going to miss you guys. It's going to be weird not seeing your faces every day," I honestly tell them as another bug flies into my eye. *Damn bugs are super bad today.*

"Weeeeeeell," Raven says as he turns around and grabs two boxes and hands them to us. "This might help."

Cali and I each take a box and when I lift the lid, a

swarm of bugs lands in my eyes and I can't see through the bug-induced water leaking out of them. Before me is the photo of the three of us from prom. We are all dressed up and laughing, this picture incapsulates our relationship perfectly. "Rave," I cry, "this is so thoughtful." Looking up at him, I smile through the tears. "Thank you." I pull him in for a hug and Cali comes to join us.

The three of us stand in the driveway hugging and crying. I feel the moment Cali see's Mr. Heatherington because she stiffens in my arms. "He's here," she whispers.

"As if he wouldn't be," I tell her. "Just think of the reunion you two will have when you reunite. You'll be all grown up and he will throw all judgment out the window and, before everyone, he will declare his undying love for you."

"You are such an asshole," she says, pinching me.

"And you are just too easy to rile up, and that's one of the many, many things I love about you, Calliope Fischer."

"One of these days, Fern Halstead, you are going to have a crush on someone you shouldn't and when that day comes, payback will be a bitch."

"Yeah, that's never going to happen, babe. No one man will ever tie me down." But they were famous last words because when I met *him, Bradford Manning,* I had to eat humble pie.

CHAPTER 2

Bradford

...twelve months later

There is no better feeling than starting the day with a ten-mile run along the beach with my best four-legged friend, Mr. Woolley, by my side. Especially since I know as soon as I get into the office I'm going to have to deal with my sister-in-law, Britney. Ever since Carlton brought her in as a joint partner, the zenness of the office has disappeared and the joy I used to get going into the office vanished.

My brother and I started Manning Tech almost twenty

years ago. We started in the back bedroom of Mom and Dad's house while we both attended MIT and now, Manning Tech is a Fortune 500 company and we own a building in Long Beach. And last year, for the first time since we set up the company, we cracked a billion dollars profit. A billion-fucking-dollars. We're officially billionaires. If you'd told me that when we first started, I would have told you that you're crazy. But with Carlton's genius technical mind and my business skills, together we made something amazing … but then he went and fell in love. I don't begrudge him for that, what I'm struggling with now is her being a part of our business. Don't get me wrong, I love Britney as much as I love my brother, but she has zero knowledge of software development and she doesn't have a business mindset. Yes, her PR skills are great and business has boomed since we rebranded, but her people skills are lacking. If she keeps treating the staff the way she is, we will have none and all we have worked for will be gone. I don't want to see her ruin what Carlton and I have worked hard for.

Returning home, I smile when I see my house come into view. This was my first big purchase, but as soon as I saw the three-story, three-bedroom, four-bathroom, sun-filled beachfront masterpiece, I had to have it. The four-car garage was also a bonus since I have my G-Wagon, a Ducati Streetfighter, and a Camaro. Kicking off my shoes in the entryway, I walk sock-footed into the kitchen and grab a bottle of water from the fridge. Mr. Woolley heads to his water bowl and while he laps up the cool liquid, I chug mine down. Wiping my mouth on the back of my hand, I pop the empty bottle into the recycling bin and make my way to my room to shower and change for the day ahead.

Pulling my shirt over my head, I drop it into the laundry basket, along with my running shorts, briefs, and socks. Reaching into the shower, I turn the water on and while I wait for it to heat up, I brush my teeth.

Twenty minutes later, I say goodbye to Mr. Woolley, lock up, climb into my black G-Wagon—a treat to myself when we made our first ten million—and head into the office. Metallica begins to play as soon as I start my baby up. With opening notes of "Fade to Black" coming through the speakers, I crank it up and begin my drive ... which takes nearly two hours due to an accident on the 405. The trip should only take thirty-five to forty minutes tops, but when dickheads don't pay attention, it takes for-fucking-ever.

"What time do you call this?" Britney growls at me as I walk into my office.

"Good morning to you too, Britney. I'm fine, thanks for asking. Wasn't traffic a bitch this morning?"

"Don't take that tone with me, Bradford."

"And don't take that tone with me, Britney. I'm the owner—"

"Part owner," she interrupts.

"Fine, I'm part owner of this company. The company which my brother and I started together almost twenty years ago and as part…" I place emphasis on this word. "OWNER, I can come in when I please. And for the record, I was here 'til after midnight last night, finalizing the contract for the Neal Group."

"But that's not due for another week?"

"And now it's done so I can focus on the next one."

"That just seems excessive."

"No, it's good business sense to stay ahead. Now, what can I do for you?"

"I … ummm, never mind." With that, she storms off and I have no doubt she's going to run to Carlton and whine that I'm being mean to her. Not even ten minutes later, he comes into my office. "Really? It's not even eleven and you two are at it again?" he complains, dropping into the seat across from my desk.

"She started it," I huff in response, and I realize I sound like a five-year-old, but this time, she really did start it.

"Bradf—"

Raising my hand, I stop him. "We are not discussing this again, Carlton, unless you want to tell me that she's out." He looks at me in that 'you know that's not happening' kind of way. "Look, you know I love Britney, she's the best thing to happen to you, but she has no business being here. She has no IT skills, she can't even make a coffee without setting off the smoke alarms, and she's rude to the staff." That's a side of her I never knew existed. When you first look at Britney, you see this blond-haired, blue-eyed Amazonian. She's not dumb, she's quite smart, she just has no tact or people skills. She'd be more suited to, hell, I don't know what but Carlton wanted to bring his wife on board. They want to share this together, I get that. They are partners in life and after she came up with the PR proposal to makeover the company, I thought *why not?* Sure, her rebranding idea was brilliant but at the same time, it was a big mistake bringing her in. "Now, what can I do for you? But make it quick because I have a call with a potential new client in thirty minutes." He gives me the 'give me details' look with just a tip of his head. "Frazier Inc. is wanting to overhaul their system, their WHOLE system for their WHOLE worldwide company." Carlton's eyes widen at this.

"That'd be huge if we score that contract," he confirms.

"I know, hence why I wrapped up the Neal Group's contract last night. It's ready to deliver, we just need to arrange a time with Margaret."

"She'll be pleased."

"She's always pleased with our work. This is the fifth time we've worked for her. You know, her drive reminds me of you and I when we first started this place."

"She does, hey?"

For the next half hour, Carlton and I discuss options for this next bid. When he leaves, I feel confident we can secure this account and I'm less agitated about Britney. That is until I walk into the supply room later that afternoon and find her bent over the copy machine being nailed from behind by my brother. "Ugh, really?" I protest, covering my eyes. "You know you both have offices? With door locks? Or a bed at home? Fuck, I'm gonna have to go bleach my eyes."

"Please," Carlton scoffs, while still balls deep inside his wife, "how many times have I found you with someone bent over your desk?"

"It's not my problem you don't knock before walking in," I defend myself. "We were behind closed doors." I pause. "Closed. Doors."

"As are we," Britney says breathlessly.

Why the fuck am I still standing here? Without a word,

I turn on my heel and walk out, looking for bleach to wipe that vision from my mind.

Leaving them at it, I walk into the kitchen and grab a drink of water. Leaning against the countertop, I start to think about my love life. It's been a revolving door of women over the years, love and marriage isn't in the cards for me. I'm meant to be an eternal bachelor for the rest of my life, where Mr. Woolley and I will grow old together and that's enough for me ... or so I thought until *she* walks into my life.

CHAPTER 3

Fern

Being an adult sucks!

It sucks donkey dick: big, fat, hairy, shriveled donkey dick.

I did every makeup course there was, paid my California registration fee and then it was a small job here, nothing there. Thanks, but we want someone with experience. Well, give me a flipping job so I get experience, dickhead.

I'm a failure, a big, fat, hairy failure just without the fat and hair; thank you laser treatments and my fast metabolism keeping me skinny.

Everyone back home thinks I'm living the glam life here in California but in reality, I live in a shared apartment with three other girls. My diet consists of ramen noodles, coffee, and boxed wine. If it's a good week, it's mac and cheese and a cheap bottle of vino. Things are hopefully starting to look up because today, I'm starting a temp job at Manning Tech as one of the CEO's PA. His long-time PA recently passed after working for him since he and his brother started the company, which was around the time I was born, according to the Google search I did. According to the temp agency, I will be the fifth one to be his PA since his long-time one died, which isn't giving me hope that it'll be a long-term gig. Is he an asshole? Did his OG PA die or is it something more sinister? I really need to stop watching *Law and Order*.

My search did not find anything personal regarding Bradford Manning, which makes me wonder what kind of sleazeball he is. Everyone has a virtual footprint in this day and age but then again, he does own a tech company. He probably erases all the salacious stuff before it has a chance to air. I'm guessing as the older brother, he's an old, wrinkled, fuddy-duddy whose looks are declining as he gets older. But going by the pics I saw of his brother, Carlton, he can't be that fugly. Carlton and his wife, Britney, seem to be the opposite to Bradford, they are everywhere and quite often featured on *TMZ*.

The pay they are offering is pretty good and it's the only reason I took it. I'm not an office bitch, I don't do the coffee run, unless it's to get me one, but Momma needs to pay the bills so here I am in a black pencil skirt, white blouse, and heels ready to get my PA on.

Staring at my reflection, I shake my head as a wave a discontent washes over me. "How is this my life?" I mumble to myself as I flick open the top button, a PA can look sexy. She doesn't need to look like a librarian from the sixties. Right?

Walking into the kitchen, I grab my to-go coffee mug, fill it with the liquid gold sitting in the pot—thank you whichever babe in this house made a pot this morning. Quickly, I throw a banana into my purse, check my hair and makeup one final time, and once I'm happy, it's time to get to the office. Ugh! Locking up, I head out with my coffee in hand and walk down the street to the bus stop for my first day at the Manning Tech office. Thankfully, the building is also located in Long Beach so it's only a twenty-minute bus ride away.

After checking in with security, I'm given a temporary ID badge—in which I look like a serial killer—and then I make my way up to the executive level on seven to meet Mr. Manning. Stepping into the waiting elevator, I push the number seven button and the doors begin to close. Nerves suddenly take flight in my stomach. *Why am I nervous right now?*

The doors open and I step out onto the executive floor. It's open and airy and not stuffy like I was expecting. I follow the corridor around like the security guy said, and I almost stumble when my eyes land on the hottest man I have ever seen. Move over Mr. Heatherington, there's a new silver fox in town. The man before me has on black slacks that hug his ass in that ohh so perfect way. A white button-down, rolled up to the elbows. His hair is short on the sides and shaggy on the top, there are flecks of gray in amongst his luscious dark locks, reminding me of silver sprinkles. He looks up and when his eyes land on mine, my panties disintegrate as the most gorgeous set of hazel orbs lock on to me. He begins to walk toward me and my heart starts to race erratically within my chest cavity. *Can a twenty-two, almost twenty-three-year-old have a heart attack?*

"Yes, they can but it's usually due to a genetic condition or just shit luck," he says, his voice deep and gravelly.

"Huh?" I question like an idiot.

"You asked if a twenty-two, almost twenty-three-year-old could have a heart attack, I was answering your question."

"Ohh," I reply like the idiot I am, and then my eyes widen when I realize I asked that out loud. *Great first impression, Fern.*

"It's a pretty good one from where I'm standing," he says, his gaze raking over me. My body heats as he peruses me and from the slight smirk on his face, I think he likes what he sees.

"Shit, I did it again," I mumble to myself and this causes him to chuckle. He throws his head back, elongating his neck, and I get the urge to run my tongue from his collarbone up the muscular column, along his jawline before I slam my lips to his, kissing him deeply. He stops in front of me and stares intently at me. *I'm totally going to get fired before I even start.*

"No, you won't be getting fired."

"Ohh fuck." My eyes widen when I realize I swore.

"Shit, fuck, ugh." Lowering my head, I take a deep breath. Schooling my facial features, I lift my head and smile. "Good morning, I'm Fern Halstead, your new PA … if you'll still have me."

"Bradford Manning." He offers me his hand. "Boss and definitely happy to have you."

Somehow my brain kicks into gear and I lift my hand, placing it into his. When our palms touch, a spark jolts between us causing my eyes to widen. I've never felt that 'spark' before. I thought it was just a myth romance authors came up with, but it seems I was wrong. "It's a pleasure to have you on board, Fern." He holds the shake longer than is appropriate but I don't mind at all.

Not.

At.

All.

Fuck me, is this what Cali has felt like all her life? I've been here for less than five minutes and I already have a crush on this man. I need a FaceTime with Cal and I need it now. As soon as I get a chance, I'm texting her and locking it in for tonight.

"It's a pleasure to be here, Mr. Manning."

"Please, call me Bradford. Mr. Manning is my father and, God rest his soul, he was the asshole of all assholes and I don't wish to be painted with that same brush."

"Bradford, got it," I tell him and I have to admit, I love the way the word Bradford rolls off my tongue. "So, where do you want me?" My eyes widen when I realize how sexual that sounded, but it seems I'm the only one affected because he's in business mode.

"First stop, the kitchen for coffee."

DAMMIT, I am just a glorified coffee bitch I think as I follow my new boss toward the kitchen but I have to say, following behind him isn't too bad, his ass is divine. "And for the record, unless you're getting yourself one, there's no need to get me one. I'm quite capable of getting my own drink and food, but if we have a client meeting, I'll need your help to set up the conference room."

"Got it," I reply, inwardly high-fiving myself and as I follow him into the kitchen, I think I'm going to like it here.

I'm definitely going to like this assignment at Manning Tech.

CHAPTER 4

Bradford

When I looked up and saw her for the first time, I nearly fell over and then, when I saw her walking toward me, I knew she was my new assistant. And after just one conversation, I'm enamored with her. Fern Halstead is a breath of fresh air on a smoky LA day. Never have I ever had this reaction to the opposite sex before. Nothing can come of it for many reasons, but the biggest is our age. She has to be at least twenty years my junior, ohh, and I'm her boss. Albeit a temporary one but still, you never mix business with pleasure. Case in point, Britney and Carlton. Ever since she came on board, I'm seeing that statement in a whole new light. I'm not saying Fern is like Britney, I don't get that vibe at all. I'm just saying keep your personal life and your business life separate.

"Are you listening?" Britney snaps, taking my attention from thoughts of my new assistant and back to her and her asinine idea.

Turning my gaze to her, I nod. "Mmmhmpf, I am. You want to reorganize, restructure, and reduce staffing levels to increase our profit margin, but I think it's a bad idea for many reasons."

"Ohh, and what might they be?" Britney sits back in her chair, crossing her arms and scowling. She was positive Carlton and I would be on her side, but both of us are against her plan, Carlton just doesn't have the balls to stand up to his wife. I really hope when we put it to a vote that he uses his head and not his dick. "I'm waiting, Bradford," she sneers.

"Okay, here goes. One." I lift my thumb up. "Every staff member here is a valued employee. Two." My index finger goes up. "We're spread thin as it is, and with the upcoming projects locked in, we need all-hands-on-deck. Three." My middle finger flips up, going with the other two. As tempting as it is to lower the other two and flip her the bird, the other two digits stay up, even if it feels like a subtle fuck you bird flip. I do everything I can to hold back my smirk but Carlton, the fucker, knows exactly what I did there and he's trying hard to hold back a grin of his own. "It's an asshole thing to do just to make us richer, and finally, I don't want to let anyone go. Everyone here is an integral member of the

Manning team."

"But—"

"No," I interrupt her, "no buts, we are not restructuring and we are definitely not firing anyone. Profits are on the rise, why would we jeopardize that balance?" She stares at me blankly, this is nothing more than a power trip for her. "Exactly, there is no benefit to the company in doing this."

"It will increase profits," she shouts, slamming her hands down on the conference room table, making everything jump and rattle.

"Profits aren't everything," Carlton pipes up and, in this moment, I'm so proud of him for standing up to her. "If we fire people, the rest of the staff will be on edge and when people are on edge, they won't perform to the level they can. In saving a few bucks on wages, we will lose business because we will no longer be the best."

"You're siding with him?" The word *him* is laced with venom.

"No, I'm siding with what's best for business. What's best for the company. You know I love you, Britney, but this is not the right decision."

"Is this because I'm a woman?" she sneers through clenched teeth.

"No, I just said it's because it's not the right business decision," Carlton defends himself and his, our decision. "If it was what I thought was the right choice, I'd back you. If it was Bradford who suggested this, I would be saying the exact same thing."

She just sits there, scowling and shaking her head. "Why am I even here if you don't listen to my ideas?"

Lately, I've been wondering that myself. If I had a do-over when Carlton asked about bringing his wife on board, I would have said no.

"We listen, this is just a case that you need to listen to us."

"Whatever." She throws her hands up in frustration. Kicking her chair back, she rises and rests her palms on the table and stares at us but turns her focus to me. "One of these days, you will regret bringing me on board." *I already do*, I think to myself and before I can reply, she storms out, slamming the door behind her.

"Did she just threaten me?" I ask my brother.

"No, it wasn't a threat, per se. She's just upset that we shot her decision down."

"It really isn't what's best for Manning Tech," I tell him.

"I know." He nods. "It's why I sided with you. Why tempt what's working well? If anything, I think we need to hire a few more people. If we get this new contract, it's going to spread us thin."

"You wanna be the one to tell her that? Maybe soften the blow with an orgasm or three."

"I don't need to seduce my wife to get her to see what's best for the business."

"You sure about that, Brother?"

He just sits there and stares blankly at me and then he shrugs. "I will never understand women."

"The day we do will be a fucking miracle."

"The day we do is the day the world ends."

I laugh at his response. "Is there anything else you wanted to discuss?"

"Nah, we've covered it all."

"Good, why don't you take your wife out for lunch, smooth things over."

"A lunchtime quickie might be good."

"Duuuuude, I don't need to hear about that."

"Duuuuude," he says mimicking myself, "you literally just suggested an orgasm or three to fix this."

"Suggesting and knowing, two very different things. It's like Fight Club, you don't discuss it."

"Showing your age there with that reference."

"Fuck off, I'm not that old."

"Yeah, you are, but don't worry, I'm not far behind." Carlton turns forty next month, joining me in the middle-aged club. I thought I would have settled down by now. Be married and have kids. Give Mr. Woolley a human brother or sister, but I've been so focused on the company I forgot about it. Now, I'm too old for that. Well, not the wife part, but if I'm honest I don't see myself settling down. Ever. That ship has passed, I'll be a bachelor for the rest of my life.

Looking up, I smile when I see Fern walk past the conference room, but that smile vanishes when I see her with tears in her eyes. "Excuse me," I tell Carlton as I push myself up and race out of the conference room. "Fern," I call out. She stops, wiping at her face before she turns to look at me, but when my eyes land on hers, I can tell she's been crying. "What's wrong?" I ask, coming to a stop in front of her.

"It's ... it's nothing." She wipes at her eyes again. "I'm fine."

"Fine? Really?"

"Yes. No. I'm … look, I need this job, I don't want to cause any issues."

"I never said anything about your job. What happened?"

She shakes her head. "It's nothing, I'm just a little emotional today. Must be that time of the month." Her eyes widen as soon as the words are out. "Shit. Fuck. Crap, you don't need to know that." She closes her eyes and mumbles, "I'm gonna get fired on the first day. I can't lose this job."

"Fern," I demand, she opens her eyes and stares at me. "Your job is safe, now, tell me what's got you so upset so I can fix it." And I mean it, I can't explain it, but I really want to wrap this woman safely in my arms and make everything better for her.

She takes a deep breath and nods. "Can we just forget this whole conversation?"

"No," I vehemently state. "Manning Tech does not tolerate workplace bullying."

"No one's bullying me, I just want to do my job."

Staring at her, I nod. I want and need her to do her job too. "Okay, we can forget the period talk and losing job nonsense on one condition?"

"What's that?"

"You need to tell me why you're so upset?"

She stares at me blinking. Then she bites her bottom lip and the urge to pull it free and run the pad of my thumb over her lip is strong, but I refrain. We don't need our temp filing a sexual harassment suit on the first day. "Fine," she hisses through clenched teeth, "some Britney bitch came barreling toward me, uttering something about assholes and men thinking they are the rulers. I asked her if she needed anything and she laid into me. Telling me not to get too comfy because I'll be out soon, and when she takes over things will be changing."

"What?" I snap, causing her to flinch at the harshness of my tone. "Sorry," I quickly tell her. Reaching up, I rest my hand on her shoulder to reassure her I'm not angry with her. "I can assure you, your job is safe. No one is getting fired and as for her taking over, she's delusional. Carlton and I are the owners, the head of PR cannot make decisions like that."

"Ohh," she utters, relief washing over her, "that's good to know. What crawled up that bitch's ass?"

"That bitch is my sister-in-law." Her eyes widen at that revelation and I chuckle at her response.

"Shit, I ummm, she's really your SIL?"

"Yes, she is, and she has no right to speak to people like that. And she certainly has no right to threaten your job."

"You really mean that, don't you?"

"I do." My agreement shocks her, going by the look on her face. "These people aren't just employees, they're family. My business family. When one hurts, we all hurt. Ignore her, but I promise I'll speak with her, and I assure you, one hundred percent, your job is safe, Fern."

"Thank you, Mr. Man—I mean Bradford, I appreciate it. I know I've only been here half a day, but I like it here. The atmosphere is fun and the staff, all bar one, is great."

"That's good to hear. Now, why don't you take an early lunch?"

"Are you sure?"

"Yep." I nod. "Pretty sure in the staff handbook there's a clause that when your job is threatened you get an early lunch."

"I'd much prefer a bunch of my favorite flowers but an early lunch also works."

"Good," I affirm, "and out of curiosity, what's your favorite flower?"

"A sunflower, they are just so bright and cheery and can put a smile on the grumpiest of faces … Maybe we should send Britney a bunch, might loosen her up a bit. Or maybe she just needs to get laid." Her eyes widen. "Shit, sorry, that's your sister-in-law I'm being a bitch about."

"Hey, if the bitch shoe fits, run with it, but personally, I wouldn't waste flowers on her."

"They'd probably shrivel and die in her presence. Shit, I really need to lay off the woman, I'm sure she's lovely."

"She is," I confirm, "she's just…"

"A bitch," she adds with a laugh. "And before I put my foot in it further, I'm going to take my lunch. I'll see you in an hour, Mr. Manning."

"What did I tell you to call me?"

"Sorry, Bradford, I'll see you after lunch."

With that, she turns and walks away, no longer sad, and I find myself staring at her ass when from inside the conference room, Carlton yells out, "Stop staring at her ass, we need to work on this Frazier Inc. proposal."

Once she turns the corner, I head back into the conference room, grinning like the cat who got the canary. "Not one word," I tell my brother when I see the look on his face as I take my seat again.

"I didn't say anything but I will say, I have never seen you worry about a woman like that before. I think you've found her."

"You got all that from a five-minute conversation?"

"Yep," he cockily states, "don't let that one go."

Furrowing my brows, I process his words. I think he's right, after only a few hours, I never want to let her go.

CHAPTER 5

Fern

I've been working at Manning Tech for one month now and I have to say, I'm loving being Bradford's assistant. It's not the glitz and glamor of being a Hollywood makeup artist, but there's no backstabbing and bitchiness. Well, except for Britney, but since my run-in with her on the first day, it hasn't been that full-on but when no one is around, her bitch gaze is on point. What Carlton sees in her, I will never know.

The guys are in high gear at the moment, schmoozing the Frazier Inc. people, and it's all-hands-on-deck as the guys work on the proposal of all proposals. Well, that's according to the rumor mill in the break room. I thought gossip was rife in Silverbell, but Manning Tech gives my hometown a run for its gossip money. I have no idea what they are talking about half the time, and when they get all technical and talk about adaptive design, magnification, or backend—FYI, they are not referring to anal—I have no fucking clue. After that embarrassing moment, I now keep my mouth closed unless it's to ask who wants what for lunch or offering to get coffees. Yep, I've become the coffee lady but, thankfully, everyone here takes a turn at being the coffee bitch.

Bradford is an amazing man and a fantabulous boss. My little crush on him is heating up and he is currently the number one star in my fantasies. The things fantasy Bradford can do with his tongue is enough to make a porn star blush.

Sometimes it feels like he's flirting with me too, but it's all in my mind. What would a forty-plus-year-old billionaire ever want with me? I could always ask my bestie how she deals with her older man issues, since she's sneakily struck up a secret friendship with Mr. H. Personally, I think more has happened between the two of them, and she's just being tight-lipped about it 'cause it's so taboo. You can't get more scandalous than hooking up with your dad's best friend.

Since it's my one-month anniversary of working at Manning Tech, I decide to treat myself to lunch out today. So I head to the coffee shop on the corner and grab a chicken and bacon ranch wrap and an iced tea. Since it's a gorgeous day out—most days are gorgeous here in California but that's moot—I decide to eat in the park across from the office.

Bradford exits just as I'm finishing up and like a stalker, I watch him stroll down the street. *He really is hot* I think to myself as I watch a group of women ogle him. He's oblivious to them and their flirting, and then I begin to wonder if maybe he's gay. I haven't seen him with a woman since I started, actually, I haven't seen him with anyone. Surely, someone like him has a voracious sex drive. I know I do, and recently it's only been me and Clifford the Big Red Dick.

The alarm on my phone beeps, letting me know my lunch break is over. Why does your lunch break always go so fast? Dropping my garbage in the trash can, I head back to the office. When I walk toward my desk, I see the most stunning bouquet of sunflowers I have ever seen sitting there.

Walking up to them, I notice the card and my eyes widen when I see my name on the envelope. Picking up the card, I flip it over and read.

> HAPPY ONE MONTH AT MANNING TECH
> HERE'S TO MANY MORE.
> BRADFORD MANNING

Holy shit, these are from Bradford, but what's even more holy shit, he remembered I mentioned sunflowers were my favorite. Poking my head into his office, I frown when I don't see him and then I remember he's out getting his lunch.

Sitting down at my desk, I sit here and stare at my

flowers. No one has ever sent me flowers before, ever. I mean sure, I buy myself a bunch when they're discounted but this is different.

"We don't pay you to sit there staring into space," Britney growls.

"I'm not," I defend myself. "I'm waiting for my computer to boot up, thing keeps crashing."

"So get IT to fix it, we are a tech development company," she sneers. "Where's Bradford?"

"Out," I rudely tell her.

"Some PA you are. Like seriously, why are you still here?"

"Because I need her," a deep baritone voice says from behind her. Britney spins to face him and her back straightens. "Now, stop harassing my staff, what do you need, Britney?"

"I don't need anything from you," she hisses at him. I don't know what this woman's problem is, but she needs to remove the stick up her ass.

"Then run along, we have work to do." She huffs and storms off, stomping her feet and swinging her arms back and forth like a petulant child. Unlike my first run-in with her, I keep my thoughts to myself. Looking up at Bradford, I smile. He returns my smile and continues on to his office. Just before he steps in, he says my name, "Fern?" Spinning to face him, I crane my neck to look up at him. "Are you okay to stay late tonight?"

"Sure, I don't have any plans."

"Great." He nods. "I'll order Thai as a way of thanks," and then he adds, "Nice flowers." He winks and walks into his office, closing the door behind him. That one little eye twitch shoots straight to my clit, and I have to swallow back the moan wanting to slip free. *What is this man doing to me?*

For a few moments, I just sit here and stare at the closed door to his office. The ringing of my desk phone snaps me from la-la land and I get back to it.

✳

"Thanks so much for your help with this tonight, Fern. I really appreciate it," Bradford says as we finish up the dinner he ordered in. That was the best Thai I have ever had and I think the most filling meal I've had in weeks. Yes, I've had a few paychecks already, but LA is expensive. Once I take out my rent and bills, there's not much left for food.

"Just doing my job," I tell him.

He laughs and I implore him with my eyes to explain. "The replacement before you, she told me I was an egotistical asshole for asking her to stay late."

"She does know she could have just said no, right?"

"Apparently not, she wasn't the right fit anyway but after that outburst, I called the agency and they sent me the angel of all angels."

"Where is she?" I ask, looking around knowing very well he's referring to me. "I don't see an angel." *But I do see a sexy silver fox.*

"You clearly don't see what I see," I scoff again at him

"You want to know what I see?" Nodding, I stare at him and wait for him to tell me. "I see an amazing woman who is going to go far in life. I see a woman with an infectious smile, a big heart, and someone who makes a killer coffee."

"It's not hard to make a black coffee."

"You'd be surprised," he jokes and an unladylike snort comes out of me.

My eyes widen in embarrassment at my snort and I jump up so I can hide said embarrassment. As if things couldn't get any worse, my heel catches on the leg of my chair and I begin to fall. The conference room table is coming toward my face at a fast pace and I can't stop the inertia pulling me down toward it. At the very last second, a muscular set of arms slide around my waist, saving me from face-planting, but the addition of his arms and the downward motion causes me to fall sideways and I bump into Bradford. He begins to stumble and he falls backward, bringing me down on top of him, where I come face-to-face with my boss.

We're both breathing deeply as we stare into each other's eyes. He lifts his hand and brushes a tendril of hair behind my ear and cups my cheek. His thumb gently runs along my jawbone and over my lips. Closing my eyes, I lean into his hand and swallow deeply.

"Fern," he whispers my name and my eyes fly open. Staring down at my boss, I feel every ridge of his muscular body against mine. I know I should climb off of him, but I'm quite comfortable where I am. For the first time in my life, I'm thankful I'm clumsy because it ended with me on top of Bradford.

He lifts his other hand and cups my other cheek. "Bradford," I murmur and before I can say anything else, he leans upward in a crunch and presses his lips gently against mine. My eyes widen and I freeze.

My boss is kissing me.

My sexy as fuck, older boss is kissing me.

He goes to pull back but I cover his hands with mine and press my lips back to his, harder this time. His tongue pushes against the seam of my lips and I willingly open. He slips his into my mouth and it languidly slides against mine. Around and around our tongues caress in an erotic dance.

Closing my eyes, I give myself over to Bradford and the kiss. I give myself over to the best kiss of my life. My nipples harden and they painfully press against the fabric of my bra. I moan into Bradford's mouth when he slides his hand up into my hair and then I hear it, a vibrating from above.

We both freeze and I open my eyes. Frozen, I stare down at Bradford as the vibrating stops. Only for it to immediately start again and I realize it's a phone. *My* phone. "Shit," I hiss, pushing myself up to my knees so I'm straddling his legs. I reach up onto the table and blindly move my hand trying to find the device. Finally, I touch it and I'm relieved to feel it still silently vibrating.

Picking it up, I don't look who it is, I just answer, "Hello," I breathlessly say into the receiver.

"Hey ho," my male best friend sings down the line.

"Raven," I breathlessly say, "what's up? I'm still at work."

"You sound breathless, you okay?"

"Yeah, I was—" *Making out with my boss on the conference room floor.* "On the other side of the office, can I call you back?"

"Yeah, sure, chat soon."

Just like that, he hangs up and that's when I feel a hand

tap my hip. Looking down, I see Bradford's hand there and I smile. I like having his hands on me, that is until he tersely growls, "You mind hopping off me?"

"Ohh, yeah, sure."

Pushing myself off him, I stand up and brush down my skirt. He's still lying on the floor and I stand above him, anxiously looking at him there like the sexy silver fox that he is.

"You can go now," he hisses, his demeanor completely different from before my call. Nodding my head, I stand here, staring down at him. "Now," he hisses. His tone puts me on edge, but I can tell when someone regrets something and I don't want to have the 'that was a mistake' conversation. So I turn on my heel and race out of the conference room.

Stopping by my desk, I grab my things and hightail it out of there. Thankfully, the elevator doors open as soon as I press the call button. Finally, fate the bitch is on my side, but where was she five minutes ago before my boss kissed me?

Stepping in, I punch the ground floor button and walk farther in. Spinning around, I lean against the back wall and when I lift my head, I see Bradford standing in the corridor staring at me. I can't read his expression but going by the way he acted after the best kiss of my life, he regrets kissing me.

My eyes well with tears and, thankfully, the elevator doors close before the first tear falls. Never will I kiss my boss again.

CHAPTER 6

Bradford

One minute I'm kissing Fern, feeling a high like no other, and the next, I'm listening to her answer a call from Raven, her tone full of guilt. I'm guessing this Raven is her boyfriend, and I realize I just made my assistant cheat on her boyfriend.

I'm still lying on the floor when I see her race past the conference room to the elevators. I need to apologize for kissing her and being such an asshole, but when I step into the corridor and see her, I feel nothing but guilt for making her feel like shit. Even from where I am standing, I can tell she is about to cry.

Racing into my office, I log into the security system and bring up the elevator feed. When I see her standing there crying, my heart hurts. I caused that, all because I gave in to temptation. From the moment I laid eyes on Fern, four weeks ago, I was enthralled. If it wasn't for the encouragement of my brother last night, who by the way I'm now going to disown because this all blew up in my face, I would have never made the first move.

"Dude, what's up with you?" Carlton asks as we sit out on the terrace, staring out at the ocean while the steaks cook on the grill.

"What do you mean what's up?"

"I don't know, you seem different. What's on your mind? Let your baby brother fix it."

Letting out a sigh, I bring my glass of Jack Daniels Single Barrel to my lips and take a sip, the smoky liquor burning as it slides down my throat. "You ever been attracted to someone who is the complete opposite in every way to everyone else you've ever been with?"

"Ummm, hello, have you met my wife? She's the total opposite of everyone I dated before I met her."

I chuckle and nod my head because he's right. Before Britney, Carlton dated the librarian-type. The quiet and shy one and Britney, well, she's the life of the party and doesn't know how to be quiet. Throwing back the rest of my drink, I slam the empty tumbler down. Sensing my unease, my brother refills my glass and nudges it toward me. "Okay, spill? Who's got your balls into a twist?"

"I'm not naming names but—"

"It's your new PA, right?"

My eyes widen, how the fuck does he know? Quickly I school my features and play it cool. "What?" I scoff, trying to play dumb but from the look on my brother's face, he knows I'm lying. "No. You've never met her."

"Okay, so there's a chick I've never met before and you're attracted to her, but she's different than your usual type."

"Correct," I affirm with a nod.

"So what's the issue?"

"She's different."

"Different can be good. Look, if I hadn't taken a chance with Britney, I never would have found the love of my life. Maybe you need to take a chance like I did, what could go wrong?"

"What could go wrong?" I murmur to myself as I continue to stare at the computer screen and watch her cry. "So fucking much has gone wrong, Brother, so fucking much," I mutter as I rewind and watch her fall apart. Shaking my head, I lean back in my chair. Why did I have to kiss my PA? My PA who just so happens to already have a boyfriend. I'm an asshole. No, I'm a predator. I'd bet my left nut that tomorrow I'll be issued a sexual harassment suit for accosting my unavailable, in a relationship PA in the conference room. "Fuuuuuck," I growl out in frustration.

Knowing I won't be any good now, I head back into the conference room and pack up what we were working on. I place the dinner containers into the trash and switch off the lights. Grabbing my things from my office, I lock up and head to the elevator.

Climbing into the metal car when it arrives, I stab the button for the lobby and it whisks me down. Exiting the elevator, I make my way across the lobby, nodding at the night guard. I step out into the hot, humid evening air and make my way around to the parking lot, but I pause mid step when I see Fern sitting at the bus stop. The last bus for the day has already left and it's not safe for her to be alone at this time of night. Without thinking, I walk over to her. "Fern," I utter her name, her head snaps toward me and I see her tear-stained cheeks in the streetlight and that 'you're a fucking jackass' feeling slams back into me. "What are you doing?"

"Waiting for the bus," she timidly says.

"Umm, the last bus left an hour ago."

"What?" She jumps up to look at the timetable and I see the moment she realizes she's missed the last bus. "Shit," she hisses, "can this night get any shittier?"

"Would you like a lift home?" I ask her.

"I … ummm … I'll just order an Uber."

"Fern, please, let me take you home. It's the least I can do for keeping you back late and for …" I don't say 'for kissing you' because it's implied. Going by the look of unease on her face, she really doesn't want to be around me and really, can you blame her? She silently stares at me. "Please?" I beg again and thankfully, she nods. "Thank you," I tell her. Stepping aside, I wait for her to join me and then silently we walk toward the parking lot. Our steps fall into sync and when I notice that, a smile appears on my face.

We reach my car and I click the fob to unlock it. Being a gentleman, I open the door for Fern. She smiles gratefully at me and when she climbs in, I see the sunflower charm on her bag and I remember her flowers. "Your flowers," I say, "do you want me to go get them?"

She shakes her head. "No, it's fine. I'll get them next week. Anyway, I need to get a vase."

"You don't own a vase?"

Again, she shakes her head. "Nope, I've never received flowers before."

"Not even from your boyfriend?"

Another head shake, *what an asshole*. If she was my girl, I would send her sunflowers once a month, but she's not so it's a moot thought.

Closing her door, I round the hood and climb into the driver's seat. "Where to?" I ask her.

She rattles off her address and starts to give me directions as I pull into traffic. The car ride is silent but not awkward like I was expecting. Pulling up in front of a run-down apartment complex, I look over at her. "We have arrived." She nods.

"Thanks for the lift, I appreciate it. Had you not come, I would have sat there for hours and then it would have been super late before I got home."

"You're welcome."

We stare at each other, the overwhelming urge to kiss her again slams into me but the moment is interrupted when her phone rings. She pulls it out and I see the name 'Raven' on the screen, the boyfriend. "Hey, Rave, give me a sec." He says something and she nods, holding her phone to her chest. She smiles over at me. "Thanks again for the lift, Bradford. Enjoy your weekend."

Before I can say anything, she jumps out. Lowering the window, I go to apologize for the kiss but then I hear her say, "Rave, babe, it's been a long-ass day, thank fuck it's the weekend."

An irrational rage wells inside of me as I sit here and watch her walk inside. Not only does she have a boyfriend—a boyfriend who doesn't send her flowers—but she's going to quit on Monday and then charge me with assault. And that's what I did tonight, I assaulted her ... with my tongue. But if I only get to kiss her once, it was worth it because kissing Fern is worth any wrath thrown my way.

Once I see she's safely inside, I pull away from the curb and head home, wondering what next week will bring.

CHAPTER 7

Fern

"**O**h. My. God, Rave," I sing into my phone when I get inside, "you will never guess what happened to me tonight."

"You saw that dude from those car movies and the chick from the Cinderella movie making out on Venice Beach at work today?"

"Ummm, no," I tell him, confused as to why he would think I'd get excited over that. I'm not a celebrity gossip junkie like he is. "And I live and work in Long Beach, not Venice Beach."

"Beach schmeach," he nonchalantly says, causing me to chuckle. "Well, what is it then?"

"I kissed someone and then he or me, or maybe both of us freaked out but before the freak-out, it was the best fucking kiss of my life. And even though we both freaked out, I think I'm now in love with him but I'm going to have to leave LA becau—"

"He's married with five kids?"

"No, I, what? Were you dropped on your head as a baby?"

"Yes, you know I was. I'm starting to think you might have been too. But head dropping aside, tell me all about the kiss. What's his cock like?" This is what I love most about Raven, he can ask one question, one inappropriate question, and it calms me. I'm no longer at DEFCON freak-out level over what happened tonight. One of these days, he is going to make some lady, or man, very happy.

"I don't know what his cock is like, we just kissed, but going by what was digging into my stomach, it's big."

"Why was his cock in your stomach and not your hoo-ha?"

"You sound like Cali right now," I tell him with a smile as I think of our third amigo. I really hit the friend jackpot with these two.

"Then I sound awesome, now explain why his cock was in your stomach and not in your—?"

I interrupt him before he can finish that sentence … again. "Well, I tripped and he caught me and then we both fell."

"Yeah, for each other."

"After one kiss, I think not."

"Well, considering you're leaving LA to go to Mongolia to live with the monks after one kiss, I'd say you're smitten."

"I'm not moving to Mongolia."

"But you are smitten," he throws back at me. I process his words and I think he might be right. I mean yes, I've had a mini crush on Bradford since I started at Manning Tech but I'm not smitten. Never in my wildest dreams did I think anything like this would happen, but what's going to happen now? Will he fire me? Will he bend me over his desk and fuck me six ways to Sunday? Or will he pretend nothing happened and it will be business as normal on Monday? When I finish my rant, I realize I zoned out on Raven when he yells, "Hello, Fern, you still there?"

"Ohh, ummm, yeah, sorry, I was—"

"Imagining the good kisser bending you over his desk and fucking you six ways to Sunday?"

"How the fuck did you know that?"

"Please, I'm your brother from another mother and it's exactly how Cal thinks about Mr. Heatherington, except it's in the hall closet of her childhood home."

This causes me to snort and then I grin because it was my snort that started all of tonight's shenanigans. Shaking my head, I flop down onto the sofa and lift my feet up onto the coffee table.

"I do have one question?" he asks.

"Shoot?"

"Why are you being a PA?"

"It's just to keep funds coming in, this makeup gig is tough, Rave. I thought once I was trained, Paramount

Pictures would snap me up and I'd be working on Chris Hemsworth in his next big blockbuster movie, but alas that hasn't happened so far."

"Well, they're dickwads."

"I think the term is dickhead," I tell him.

"Wad. Head. Fucker, whatever fits the dick. But Fern, babe, you were born for this."

"I'm not a Maybelline ad," I snap, hating how angry I am about this. Then I voice my biggest fear, "Maybe I'm not cut out for this after all."

"I wish I was there to give you a big hug and then smack you up the side of the head. You're no quitter, Fern Winifred Halstead—"

"Ohh, you middle named me," I tease him.

"And I will continue to Winifred you until you believe in you like I believe in you. Fern, babe, you just need to give it a little more time."

"When did you get so wise?"

"I've always been wise but you've only just realized it, and FYI, I'm registered at Starbucks for the thank-you."

Sitting here, I shake my head, only Raven would say something like this. "Okay, my shitshow of a life aside, how's Chicago? AAAAAND," I quickly tack on, "I don't want to hear about the new pizza place you found and how it's the most orgasmic pizza you have ever had. I want real stuff. Juicy gossip-type stuff."

"I'm offended you think I would just call to tell you about pizza but for once, that isn't why I'm calling. I … I think I'm in love with my professor."

"Okay, so we are going with the juicy gossip-type

stuff." He grunts in agreement. "Okay, so, which professor is it, the athletic one? The bald one with an amazing ass?"

"None of the above but, Fern, Oh My Fucking God! This man is everything I have ever dreamed of. He's funny and gorgeous and so knowledgeable and …"

"And what?"

"He's the guy I'm TAing for."

"And fraternization with staff is forbidden?"

"He's my professor, Fern. I'm in love with my teacher and kinda sort of boss."

"Why do I get the feeling that you and he have already crossed a line?"

"Because he and I smashed that line and left it for dust."

"Could you get kicked out of school?"

"Yes. No. I don't know but, Fern, I'd throw it all away for him. I'm like hook, line, and sinker gone for him, but that's not the most shocking part."

"There's more?"

"Mmmhmpf, there's, umm, also a girl."

"You're cheating on your hottie professor?"

"Noooo, we're, ummm…"

"Holy fucking fuckballs, are … are you telling me you're in a throuple?"

"Yep," he replies, letting the 'p' pop.

"Oh My God, I'm not getting any and you've got it on tap."

"Sounds like you're about to be getting some but, Fern, what do I do?"

"Are you happy?"

"Deliriously so." I can tell by the tone of his voice how

happy he really is.

"Then follow your heart."

"Is it really that simple?"

"When it comes to love, nothing ever is simple."

Ain't that the truth? Not that I love Bradford, this is nothing more than a crush. A crush that cannot go anywhere because I need this job. I need it more than I need love, so my vagina will just have to suffice with Clifford the Big Red Dick and visions of Bradford Manning.

"Maybe you should take your own advice," he throws back at me.

"We aren't talking about me anymore, we're talking about you. Now, you need to tell me everything."

For the next half hour, Rave tells me all about Abi and James. I'm so happy for him. After yawning for the millionth time, we say our goodbyes and hang up. I change into my pjs and then I grab Clifford the Big Red Dick and bring myself to orgasm with a vision of Bradford and the memory of our kiss.

I'm thankful I have the weekend to process all of this, but regardless of that, come Monday, work is going to be interesting, very, very interesting.

CHAPTER 8

Bradford

Two long freakin' hours later and I finally pull into my garage, it seriously would have been quicker to park in a lot along the way and walk back here. There was a seven-car pile-up on the 405 and traffic was at a standstill for what felt like an eternity. And each time we stopped, my mind drifted to Fern, the kiss, and her douche boyfriend, Raven.

What am I going to do next week? Do I ignore it like I did in the car on the way home? Or do I take her aside and discuss it? Neither, because what I really want to do is kiss her again before I sink my cock inside of her and fuck her six ways to Sunday, but that's not going to happen for a variety of reasons.

I'm forty-three, she's twenty-two, almost twenty-three.

I'm her boss, she's my assistant.

I'm old enough to be her father.

Pouring myself a glass of red, I grab the bottle and head upstairs. Walking through the gaming area, I step out to my private rooftop terrace and a calmness immediately washes over me. I love this time of night up here, it's quiet and peaceful. The beach is void of people and the only sound to be heard is the waves gently crashing onto the shore.

Falling onto the outdoor lounger, I lift my feet and rest them on the edge of the coffee table, staring out into the dark abyss of the night. Taking a sip of wine, I drop my head back and close my eyes, but as soon as I do an image of Fern on top of me kissing me enters my mind. My cock comes to life, but I refuse to acknowledge it. I cannot be lusting over my assistant like this, but there is something about Fern Halstead that's captivated me. As soon as she enters a room, the atmosphere comes to life. She has a bubbly personality that's contagious and she's smoking hot. Sure, I'm old enough to be her father but in the big scheme of things, age is just a number, right? But what would someone like her want with an old guy like me?

Mr. Woolley wanders out and the pitter-patter of his feet on the flooring garners my attention. Lifting my head, I smile at my four-legged best friend. "Hey, buddy," I coo, scratching him behind the ears when he reaches me. He nuzzles my thigh saying hello, and then he looks up at me. From the look in his eyes, it's almost as if he can sense my inner turmoil. "I met someone," I tell him. He lifts his head and stares at me in that 'well go on' kind of way. "She's amazing in every way, but it can never be." He lets out a sad whine, mimicking what I feel. "I'm old enough to be her dad but for the first time in my life, I want to explore something with a woman. But after tonight, I don't know if that will be possible." He just stares up at me, not offering me any words of wisdom, not that he could, he's a dog and this isn't *Scooby Doo*. Dogs don't talk or solve mysteries or give sage advice to their owner about their love life.

Patting the cushion next to me, he climbs up and rests his head in my lap. Sitting back, I continue to stare out toward the ocean, sip on my wine, and scratch my dog behind his ears. Finishing the glass, I know I need to shower and head to bed but I'm wide awake, sleep will not come easily tonight.

Pouring myself another wine, I sit back and play that kiss over and over in my mind. It's my new favorite home movie but as is my life right now, it begins to rain. Before it turns into a downpour and I get soaked walking inside, I maneuver myself out from my sleeping dog. "Night, buddy," I whisper before I head inside, leaving the door cracked a little so he can come back in if the rain gets too heavy. Pulling the sheer curtains across, I flip off the lights and head toward my bedroom after dropping my wine glass into the sink.

Stripping off my clothes, I throw them at the hamper and walk naked into my bathroom. Reaching into the shower, I turn the faucets on and close the glass door. While I wait for the water to heat, I turn to the mirror and stare at my reflection. For a forty-three-year-old, I'm in excellent shape. I'm not your typical old man, well, except for the grays appearing in my hair, but they make me look distinguished, so I tell myself. *Maybe I should dye my hair so I don't look so old.* Shaking my head, I notice steam billowing out of the shower so I open the door and step under the rainwater head. The steaming droplets of water hit my skin and cascade down my body, easing the ache in my muscles.

Grabbing my body wash, I squeeze some into my hand and soap myself up. When my hand brushes over my cock, it springs to life and there's one name on the tip of my tongue, Fern. Gripping my shaft, I begin to stroke myself. Resting my other arm on the cool tiles, I drop my head to my forearm, close my eyes, and I beat off like a teenage boy to images of Fern. I imagine it's her dainty hand wrapped around my cock. Her yellow-colored fingernails shining in the bathroom light as she pumps my dick up and down. Squeezing the mushroom head 'til it turns purple. My balls tighten and I murmur Fern's name as the first rope of creamy white cum paints the black tiles in my shower.

"You're a dirty old man, Bradford Manning," I berate myself before I quickly rewash and rinse off. Climbing out, I grab my towel and dry off. I'm disgusted with myself for what I just did so I avoid looking at my reflection in the mirror. Once dry, I slide naked into bed and lie on my back, staring up at the ceiling.

After tossing and turning for a few hours, I climb out of bed and pull on my running gear. Grabbing my shoes, I sit on the bottom step and slip them on. Snatching up my phone, I bring up my angry music playlist and with "Shortest Straw" by Metallica blaring in my ears, I take off to clear my head from the sexy dirty thoughts I'm having about Fern.

FYI, I still have the sexy dirty thoughts when I return an hour and a half later, after an eleven-mile run, and those thoughts only intensify over the weekend.

CHAPTER 9

Fern

It's the start of a new workweek and I'm a nervous mess the whole bus ride to work. Actually, I've been a nervous mess all weekend long. How I managed to get ready and look somewhat professional this morning is beyond me. My mind kept drifting to my sexy as hell boss, wondering what will happen when we see each other this morning. Absence over the weekend only made me fonder of him.

Tightening my ponytail, I run my hands down my black slacks and readjust the collar of my white silk blouse as we approach my stop. I stand up, ready to hop off the bus. And my mind fills with question after question, scenario after scenario.

Is it going to be awkward with Bradford after our kiss?

Is he going to fire me?

Will he bend me over his desk and devour me?

And the question of all questions, will it happen again? I wouldn't mind if it did, and I really wouldn't mind if any of the above, or more, happened too. I'm no prude when it comes to my sex life, sure, I'm going through bit of a dry spell at the moment but thankfully I have fingers, Clifford the Big Red Dick, and a photographic memory of Bradford and our kiss.

I'm lost in thought about our kiss when I step out of the elevator and bump into something hard and begin to fall. Arms reach out to grab me and when I look up, I see Bradford. His hand is around my waist, his fingertips dig into my skin, and his breath tickles my face. We're staring intently at each other and our breaths are labored.

"Are you okay?" he asks me.

Nodding, I lick my lips. His gaze drops to my mouth and he watches as my tongue slides over it and then I gently bite down. He lifts his hand and pulls my lip free from between my teeth. For a simple move, it's very erotic and I really, really want him to replace his thumb with his lips but it can't happen here, and it definitely won't happen now because the ding of the elevator pops the bubble we find ourselves in. Like I'm suddenly contagious, he jumps a foot backward from me.

"Morning, Fern," Carlton sings out when he steps out of the elevator. "Bradford," he says with a head nod and then he strides down the hallway toward his office.

"Can I see you in my office once you're all settled?"
Did he just growl that?

Nodding my head, I swallow deeply but I don't say anything. I just stand here and keep nodding like a bobble head. He too nods and then spins on his heel and walks away. Normally I'd take the opportunity to check out his ass but today, I'm too nervous so I drop my gaze to my feet.

A few minutes later, I'm standing outside Bradford's office door. Raising my hand, I knock. "Come in," his deep voice echoes through the door and causes goosebumps to prickle my skin. Taking another deep breath, I push down on the door handle and step in. "Close the door," he demands before I've even taken my first step.

Closing the door behind me, I walk over to his desk and sit down in one of the chairs across from him that I always sit in. Silently, he stands up and walks around his desk and leans against it, right in front of me. He crosses his feet at the ankles and rests his hands on the wooden edge, gripping it tightly, causing his knuckles to turn white.

Lifting my gaze to his, I smile up at him. "You … you wanted to see me?"

"I did," he roughly says, "I wanted to discuss—"

"It's fine, I can leave," I quickly interrupt him.

"Huh? What are you talking about?"

"I thought, well, it doesn't matter what I thought. You were saying …"

"Yes, it does matter, Fern. Now tell me, what's going on in that pretty head of yours."

"You, you think I'm pretty?"

"Extremely and I wouldn't have kissed you Friday night if I didn't think you were, but in all honesty, you are fucking gorgeous, Fern. How I've gotten any work done since you started here is beyond me. You light up a room when you walk in and not only are you stunning, but you have a heart of gold too. Any man would be lucky to call you his."

Holy fucking swoon, Batman, but what does this mean? "That night—"

"Was amazing, but as your boss it was highly inappropriate. And there's the fact you have a boyfriend."

"I don't have a boyfriend," I refute.

"I thought your boyfriend called you…"

"Raven?" I ask and he nods. "He's not my boyfriend, but he is a boy who is a friend. One of my best friends actually."

"So my kissing you didn't make you cheat on anyone?"

Shaking my head, I smile. "No, no cheating and I … I liked it, it just took me by surprise. Things with your crush never eventuate but for the last two days, all I've done nonstop is replay that kiss and the thought of never feeling your lips on mine again is …"

"Is what, Fern?"

"Is something I don't want to happen," I quietly reply, but then I shock myself, and him, when I push myself up. I grip his cheeks in my palms and cover his mouth with mine. My tongue licks along the seam of his lips before I push it into his mouth. His tongue tangles with mine as he slides his hand up into my hair, holding me tightly to him. His other hand slides around to my behind and he squeezes my ass cheek. I yelp into the kiss and he just chuckles, but we never stop kissing.

Kissing Bradford is just as amazing as I remember and I want more, so much more from this man but we are at the office so, reluctantly, I break the kiss. Resting my forehead against his, I stare into his eyes and we both breathlessly pant. Catching our breath after making out, again.

"We, we need to stop before we can't and I think we need to discuss this further. I … I like you, Bradford, and I'm thinking you like me too, if those kisses are anything to go by. But we need to set some ground rules. I need this job, I can't let us ruin that."

"Sweetheart, I'd never jeopardize your job because of whatever this is between us. All I know is I can't stop thinking about you, and I know without an ounce of doubt I want to explore this further too. Does my age and the fact I'm your boss scare the shit out of me, hell fucking yes, but I want to explore this with you."

"I want that too," I honestly tell him, and I mean it. I want to explore this, I want to jump headfirst into this and see what happens. Is it crazy? Hell yes, but life's too short not to take risks.

He smiles at me and I feel it deep in my soul. "Will you have dinner with me tonight so we can discuss this further?"

Nodding, I smile back at him. "I'd love that, Bradford."

"Good, now, give me one more kiss and then we have to get back to work."

"So bossy," I tease.

"You ain't seen nothin' yet, baby."

Wow, my insides quiver with what he could possibly mean and excitement simmers. Exiting his office, I feel lighter and I can't help the grin on my face. I'm looking forward to tonight and our first date.

CHAPTER 10

Bradford

I've not been able to concentrate all day. All I can think about is tonight with Fern. I can't remember the last time I was excited for a date. Actually, I don't think I've ever been excited for one. I've been on the occasional date here and there, but I'm more of a casual hookup kind of guy, until her that is. There is nothing casual about Fern, and I'm okay with that.

As soon as Fern left my office earlier, I called my favorite Italian restaurant, Lonny's, and booked a table for two tonight. Lonny, the owner, was thrilled when I asked for the most romantic table he has. He opened Lonny's when he and his wife of fifty-four years, Isabella, first came to America in the late seventies. It's funny to see a German man running and owning an Italian restaurant, but he opened it in his wife's honor. Those two are so in love with one another and they want everyone to have a love like they have. Hence the excitement for a table for two rather than one.

"Are you having a stroke?" my brother asks from the doorway to my office just after lunch.

"No, why?" I ask him confused as he waltzes into my office and takes a seat in front of me.

"'Cause you're smiling, like happy smiling."

"I smile," I snap at him, "sometimes."

"Dude, you have the male equivalent of resting bitch face."

"Resting asshole face?"

"That's it. You never smile except for that time when we hit the billion-dollar profit and when Joey and Pacey finally got together on *Dawson's Creek*. So either we are multi-billionaires now or you got laid or—"

"Or it's none of your business," I growl. "Now, how can I help you, dear brother of mine?"

"Hmmmm, changing the subject, interesting." He scratches his chin, deep in thought, and then his eyes widen and he points accusingly at me. "You're seeing someone," he screeches like a teenage girl who just got the latest hot gossip from *TMZ*.

"I'm ... shut up," I snap at him.

"Soooooo," he drawls out, leaning back in his seat, looking like the cat who got the canary. "Who is she?"

Staring at my brother, I wonder if I should tell him. We

don't have an office fraternization policy so I'm not breaking any rules, apart from the one where I'm old enough to be her father. However, before I can answer, the object of my affection knocks on my door.

"What's up, swee—I mean, Fern?" I nearly called her sweetheart in front of Carlton and I'm positive, from the bewildered look on his face right now, he's guessed who I'm enamored with.

"Sorry to interrupt," she hesitates and steps into my office, "but, Bradford, I have Helen from the bank on the line for you."

"Take a message," Carlton states. "I need to have a discussion with my brother." The emphasis he places on the word 'discussion' confirms my thought from moments ago.

"Yes, please take a message, Fern. Can you please close the door on your way out? And hold all calls and visitors until I tell you otherwise."

"Sure." She nods, spins around, and walks out of my office. My eyes drop to her delectable ass and I find myself licking my lips. She closes the door behind her and the sound of the latch slipping into place echoes through my office.

No sooner has the door closed and Carlton is on me. "Oh my fucking God, you're fucking your sexatary."

"I'm not fucking her." The word yet is silently alluded to. "And she's my assistant, not my sexatary." *But I wouldn't mind her being my sexatary.* And then I'm assaulted with an image of bending her over my desk as I fuck her from behind; hard and fast. That image morphs into her hiding under my desk, blowing me while I'm on a Zoom call with a potential new client. Shit, I need to clear those thoughts before I give my brother more ammunition.

"Secretary. Sexatary, same-same," he states matter-of-factly.

"Not the same at all. One does office tasks, the other does—"

"Dick tasks, in the office. Out of the office. On the way to the office. Now, spill the beans, Romeo."

"You are like a fifteen-year-old-girl wanting all the gossip."

"Well, it's not often the king of resting asshole face smiles. Now, give me all the juicy details about you and your sexatary."

Staring across at the brother, I know that until I give him something, he's going to keep pestering me. I also wouldn't put it past him to go straight to Fern for details. I can't let him do that, he'll scare her off and then I'll be screwed—and not in the good way.

"Fine," I relent, shaking my head. Leaning back in my chair, I lace my fingers behind my head, and tell him about the kiss on Friday night and our plans for dinner tonight.

"You constantly surprise me, Bradford. And for what it's worth, I think you're doing the right thing. Sure, she's younger, like you stated, but age is just a number. If she makes you happy, then that's all there is to it."

"You really believe that, don't you?"

"Yeah, I do. Call me a romantic sap, but when you find the one that person becomes your everything. You miss them when they leave the room, even if it's just to take a piss. They are your first and last thought each day. They consume you while still letting you be you."

"Wow, Carlton, that was very poetic. Well, except for the pissing part. No wonder Brit fell for you."

"It was that and my big dick," he informs me and unluckily for me, I'd just taken a sip of my water and I proceed to spit it all over my desk.

"Ugh, dude, really? I don't need to be hearing about your dick."

"Dude," he snarkily utters, "we used to bathe naked together, I've seen yours and you've seen mine."

"Dude," I reply in the same tone, "we were five. I'm sure you and I have both grown since then, BUT in saying that, I don't want to be thinking about your dick. Now, get out of my office and let me get some work done."

"You just want me gone so you can flirt with your sexatary."

"This is the office, Fern and I have a professional relationship here."

"Yes, and the kiss here Friday night proves that."

Well dammit, he has me there. "That won't happen again."

"Mmmhmpf," he nonchalantly replies. He stands up to leave but before he does, he looks me straight in the eyes. "For the record, it's nice to see you smiling."

"It's nice to be smiling for once," I honestly tell him.

"I hope it all works out with your sexatary," he says, and I shake my head as I watch him walk away. When he opens my office door, I see Fern at her desk and I sit here and stare at her. She looks over her shoulder at me and when our gazes connect, I feel my smile widen.

If I keep this up, I'm going to get a cheek ache but I don't mind because I have a feeling, Fern is worth any ache.

CHAPTER 11

Fern

The door to Bradford's office opens and when Carlton walks past my desk, without stopping he murmurs, "You're good for him, don't fuck it up," and keeps on walking, leaving me stunned at his words but also grinning.

Turning my head, I look into Bradford's office and see him staring back at me. Our gazes are locked and when he smiles at me, it lights up his already gorgeous face, and I find myself returning said smile. We sit here, grinning at one another, but the phone rings and I have to turn away from him and get back to work.

The rest of the afternoon is a blur. One minute it was just after lunch and the next, it's dark outside and Bradford is escorting me to his car for our date.

"So, where are you taking me?"

"It's a surprise," he tells me.

"I'm not really a fan of surprises."

"Well, luckily for you, we're almost there but I promise, you'll love it. This is my most favorite restaurant and I eat here all the time. Lonny was stoked when I booked a table for two."

"Who's Lonny?" I ask as we pull up to a red light.

"The owner, he and his wife opened the restaurant when they first arrived in America and it's been a staple here ever since. Mom and Dad use to take Carlton and me here when we were little and we'd have monthly family dinners here. It was the one time that Dad was a part of the family and not the business focused asshole he was most of the time. After Mom and Dad passed, Carlton and I kept up the tradition but once he met Britney they didn't come very often, but I still did."

"I love that," I tell him. "My parents and I did something similar but after they passed, it was too hard to go back there by myself."

"I'm sorry to hear that, who raised you after they died?"

"I was left with my nanna, but at almost ninety she didn't want to raise a teenager so I was left to my own devices. If it wasn't for my best friend, Cali, and her family, I probably would have starved to death before I graduated."

"I'm sorry you that happened to you."

"Don't be, it made me who I am today and it's made me

appreciate things all that much more."

"That's a good way to think of things."

"There's no point dwelling on the past, it is what it is. All I can do is look to the future and not make the mistakes my nanna did."

"You are amazing, Fern," he tells me as we pull into the parking lot of the restaurant.

"I'm not amazing, I just live life for what it is. I think it's why I refuse to go back to Silverbell."

"What do you mean?"

"I, well, I wanted to be a makeup artist to the stars but it's a cutthroat industry, and I just don't have it in me to walk over people and stab them in the back to get ahead. Even though I studied my ass off and paid the license fees, it just wasn't for me. I took this job to make some money and decide on what I want to do in the future."

"And what do you want to do?"

You, is my immediate thought, but I can't tell him that so I just shrug. "Not sure, but I'm young and still have my whole life ahead of me."

He nods at me but his demeanor has changed. "What's wrong?" I ask him. "You just curled into yourself, and I swear I saw the life in you dwindle."

"You still have your life ahead of you, and me, well, I'm old—"

"You're not old," I interrupt him.

"Yeah, I am. Fern, I'm forty-three and I'm grumpy and old. Whereas you, you're young and vibrant. What could you possibly want with an old geezer like me?"

"Age is just a number when you think about it but,

Bradford, from the short period of time I've known you, I see someone who is young at heart. You have a heart of gold, you're a decent man with a nice ass, and you care about those around you. Therefore, you can't be all that bad … for an old guy."

He laughs. "You are something else, Fern Halstead."

"Thank you, and you know what else I am?"

"What's that?"

"Hungry, now, let's go eat so we can get your old ass home and to bed."

He chuckles and we climb out of his car. I meet him by the hood and he takes my hand, lacing our fingers together. Glancing down at our joined hands, a warm and fuzzy feeling develops in my chest. I'm not usually a hand-holder, but mine fits in Bradford's as if our hands were cast from the same mold. We make our way across the lot and when we step into Lonny's, I can see why he loves this place. It has a homey feel to it and the smells permeating the air have my mouth watering.

An older lady comes toward us. She's smiling brightly but her smile widens when she realizes it's Bradford and me. "Bradford, I was so excited when Lonny said you were bringing a lady friend here tonight." She hugs him tightly and he hugs her back one-armed because he's still holding on to my hand. It's as if he doesn't want to let go. She pulls back from him and looks to me. "And who might you be?"

"I'm Fern," I tell her. She grips my cheeks in that grandma kind of way. "You are gorgeous, I can see why Bradford is smitten with you."

Looking to Bradford, I smirk. "Smitten, hey?"

He just shrugs but before I can tease him, an older man joins us. "Leave the boy alone, Isabella, we don't want to scare away the lovely young lady and ruin this for Bradford."

"There's no chance of that," I tell them both. "He's a pretty great guy and I hope this is the start of something special."

"I like her," Lonny says, then he looks to Bradford. "Don't fuck it up."

"Language, Lonny," his wife admonishes him and slaps him on the upper arm. Lonny blows his wife a kiss, and without a word he shuffles back to the kitchen. Isabella ushers us toward our table. Bradford holds out my chair for me and then Isabella and Bradford discuss wine. A few moments after seating us, she returns with a bottle of white wine, two glasses, and a basket of what looks like homemade bread.

Bradford pours us each a glass of wine and when he hands me my glass, our fingers brush and I feel an electrical current course through my veins. "A toast," he proposes, picking up his own glass.

"What should we toast to?"

"To the start of something beautiful."

"I like that, to the start of something beautiful."

We clink our glasses and then watch each other over the rim as we sip. My eyes widen when the citrus flavor dances over my tongue. I wasn't sure what to expect since I don't usually drink white wine, I'm more of a cocktail or a beer girl so I'm pleasantly surprised.

"You look surprised," Bradford says, snapping my attention to him.

"I don't usually drink white wine—"

"I'm sorry, I probably should have asked."

"Don't be, I really like this. What kind is it?"

"It's a Chenin Blanc."

"It reminds me of a lemon drop."

"I've never had one of those."

"There's this great cocktail bar near where I live, I'll take you there sometime and you can try one."

"Talking about a second date and we haven't even ordered yet."

"What can I say, I know what I like and, Bradford, I like you."

"I like you too, Fern, more than I probably should."

CHAPTER 12

Bradford

I've never been this honest with a woman before but then again, I have never met a woman like Fern before. There's something about her that lowers my guard and causes me to word vomit everything I'm thinking and feeling. It's refreshing to not have to be guarded with someone.

"And is that a good thing or a bad thing?" she asks me, taking a sip of her wine.

"Good, it's definitely a good thing. You are a breath of fresh air, Fern, and when I'm around you, all my stresses and worries fade into the background." Her cheeks turn pink at my comment and I love seeing her blush, but now I'm wondering what she'd look like after an orgasm. Would it be the same shade of pink? Or would it be darker? "I like seeing your cheeks stained pink like that." Her cheeks darken at my words and my cock twitches in my pants. Thankfully, Isabella returns with our appetizer.

"We didn't order," Fern whispers to me after Isabella leaves us.

"You don't order here. Lonny cooks what he wants and Isabella has a knack of delivering exactly what you want."

"I like that," she tells me. "They seem like such a lovely couple."

"They are so in love with one another it's disgusting at times."

"I hope to have a love like that one day."

"Me too," I agree with her, and I hope I have found that with her. The idea of settling down has never appealed to me before but for the first time ever, I can picture that with Fern. I can see the two of us sitting on my rooftop terrace, her tummy swollen with our child, and Mr. Woolley watching on protectively.

"What are you grinning at?"

"Nothing," I quickly reply. I can't tell her that just yet, I'll come across as a crazy person. The world *old man* hits home. I'm old, she's young. Will that be an issue for us?

We eat our appetizer and from the moans coming from Fern, I think she likes the food. I like hearing those sounds coming from her. As does my cock, it's rock-hard right now and I'm thankful for the cover of the table. I need it to go down before we leave because I cannot walk out of here with my dick threatening to bust through my zipper.

After five courses and a bottle of wine, Fern sits back and rests her hands on her flat stomach. "Oh my God, that was the best meal I've ever had."

"There's still dessert to go," I tell her.

Her eyes widen. "I don't think I can fit another bite in."

"Well, how about we get dessert to go and I take you back to my place? We can sit on my terrace and watch the waves while we have dessert."

She looks intently at me and smiles brightly. "I'd like that. I'd like that very much."

As if Isabella is a mind reader, she arrives at our table with a takeout container. "Dessert for you two when you get home." She places the box down, kisses each of us on the cheek, and walks away without another word.

Lifting the lid, I smile when I see cannoli inside. "You are in for a treat when we get to dessert," I inform Fern.

"What is it?"

"It's a surprise," I say, pulling the container away from her.

"You know what I think about surprises."

"I do and I don't care, now, let's go." Standing up, I offer her my hand. Her gaze flicks between my hand and my face.

"Why thank you, Sir," she says and hearing her call me Sir does something to me. "We better not forget this." She drops my hand and reaches for the dessert box, but I'm quicker and slide it away from her.

"Uhh-uh," I admonish her, "I've got that." Pulling out my wallet, I place a couple of fifties down on the table, pick up our dessert, and offer Fern my hand again. She places hers in mine and hand in hand, we walk out. As we reach the door, I turn and wave to Lonny and Isabella before we step out into the balmy night air.

Unlocking the car, I open the door for Fern and once she's seated, I close her in. Walking around to my side, I open the back door and place our dessert on the seat. Climbing into the driver's seat, I start the car and "Never Let Me Go" by Florence + The Machine begins to play. Fern quietly sings along as I pull out of the parking lot. I keep flicking my gaze from her to the road and before long, we reach my street.

"Holy shitballs," Fern hisses when I turn into my driveway, "you really live here?"

"Yep," I reply, letting the 'p' pop. Clicking the button on the remote attached to the sun visor, the garage door begins to lift. Once it's open, I ease my car into its spot and turn off the engine. She climbs out, I reach into the back and grab the dessert container and then climb out too. Walking toward the internal door, I open it and usher for Fern to go ahead of me.

"Well, aren't you gorgeous," she sings, dropping down to pat Mr. Woolley. "And who might you be?"

"That's Mr. Woolley," I inform her. "Mr. Woolley, this is Fern."

He nuzzles into her neck, already smitten but I can't blame him. I'm smitten too. The three of us walk farther into the house. We head up to the second floor. "Wow," Fern says in amazement, "this place is gorgeous, and not at all what I pictured for you."

"What did you expect?" I question, as we continue up the stairs to the top floor.

"I expected a penthouse in a high-rise, not a beachfront condo. I also expected it to be sleeker and more modern with black and gray accents."

"That would be Carlton."

"No shit," she states. "I would expect this for him." she waves her hand around the room.

"I don't know if I'm offended by that or not."

"Ohh, I didn't mean to offend you, Bradford. I just—" Putting my index finger to her lips, I shush her.

"I'm not offended at all."

"Don't just say that," she mutters against my finger.

Shaking my head, I continue, "Most of our friends think the exact same thing." She nods but I still keep my finger pressed to her lips. "He and Britney live in a penthouse apartment in downtown LA, but I find it too busy and peopley." Removing my finger, I slide it down her neck, across her collarbone, and down her arms until I take her hand in mine. Goosebumps prickle her skin and she shivers. Hand in hand, we head out to the terrace. "I like it here by the beach," I tell her, placing the container on the table and walking over to the edge. "Sure, the weekends are busy and it's crazy during the summer, but this time of night is always quiet and peaceful, no matter what time of year it is."

"It's absolutely stunning, Bradford," she whispers, resting her palms on the railing. I step behind her and cocoon her in. She leans back into me and we stare out at the ocean before us.

"It sure is," I voice, but I'm referring to her and not the

view. She spins around in my arms and drapes hers over my shoulders. We stare into each other's eyes, I'm just about to lean forward and kiss her but she beats me to it. Her lips press against mine. Her tongue pushes into my mouth, caressing mine. Everything fades around me, it's just Fern and I kissing under the moonlight and as far as second first kisses go, this one is stupendous.

CHAPTER 13

Fern

"**O**h. My. God," I groan. The sweet crispy shell crunches between my teeth as the rich creamy filling assaults my tastebuds. Closing my eyes, I savor the flavor and when I open my eyes again, I see Bradford intently staring at me. "What?" I question. "Do I have cannoli on my face?"

"No." He shakes his head. "I'm just watching you fall apart eating that cannoli."

"Well, it's the best cannoli I've ever eaten. I can see why you love Lonny's so much. Not only is the food phenomenal but the service is great and their desserts are orgasmic." She pauses. "And I just love Isabella and Lonny."

"I've never taken anyone there before."

"Really? You've never taken a girlfriend there before?"

He shakes his head. "Nope. I usually dine alone or with Carlton and Britney. Hence why they were shocked when I booked a romantic table for two."

Holy shitballs, I'm the first? How is that even possible? And how the hell is he still single? He's a silver fox with a heart of gold, or is that just a front? Is he secretly a monster hiding under a sexy exterior? "You are full of surprises, Mr. Manning."

"Good ones I hope?"

"Very good ones but I think I should get going, I don't want to overstay my welcome."

"You could never do that, sweetheart," he states matter-of-factly. "How about we have a nightcap before I drive you home?"

She smiles brightly at me. "I'd like that."

He kisses me on the tip of my nose and heads inside. Leaning back against the railing, I watch him walk toward the bar and step behind it. He goes about getting our drinks and I take the moment to observe him. His movements are fluid and graceful, not an ounce of regret or nerves are present. Me, on the other hand, my heart is racing, my palms are sweaty, and my panties, well, they're soaked and all we've done is kiss, twice, and have dinner together.

Bradford starts coming outside and I meet him halfway. He passes me my glass and like in the restaurant earlier, when our fingers brush, a spark ignites between us and jolts through my body. Bringing the tumbler to my lips, I take a sip. The smokiness of the bourbon dances on my taste buds and burns a fiery path into my stomach.

We both take a seat on the outdoor lounger and turn to face one another, our knees brushing. He reaches over and takes my hand in his, resting our joined hands on his thigh. We fall into easy conversation and I tell him all about growing up in Silverbell and my besties, Cali and Raven. I laugh when he tells me he was jealous of Raven the other night, thinking he was my boyfriend. "Yeah, nah, that hasn't and never will happen. Rave is my brother from another mother." Another laugh escapes me as he thought that about Rave. "I can't wait to tell him all about this, he'll get a chuckle."

"Great," he deadpans, "what an awesome first impression for your friends."

"Trust me," I reassure him, "he'll get a kick out of that. They both will."

"I hope so."

We fall quiet and finish our drinks. When our glasses are empty, he takes mine and places it down on the table. "Come here," he demands and spins his finger in a circle. He wants me to turn around and lean back on him. Snuggling with Bradford is definitely appealing, so I comply.

Spinning around, I shuffle back into him and he wraps his arms around me, gently running his fingers back and forth over my forearm. "This is nice," he whispers.

"Mmmhmpf," I nod in agreement.

Silently we lie here, listening to the sounds of the waves crashing onto the shore. My eyes get heavy and they droop closed. I drift off to sleep snuggling with Bradford and the next thing I know, the sun is shining brightly above and my skin is hot. It takes me a few moments to register my surroundings, and when I realize where I am, I find myself smiling.

"Good morning, gorgeous," a deep, sleep-addled voice says from behind me.

Looking over my shoulder, I take in the man before me and my smile widens. "Morning," I murmur. "I guess we fell asleep."

"I guess we did." He kisses my temple.

Pushing myself up, I turn to face him and I cross my legs, crisscross applesauce-style. He reaches out and grips my chin. Holding my head up, he leans forward and goes to kiss me on the lips, but I shake my head and pull away from him. I scooch along the lounger, away from him, and cover my mouth. He reaches for me again but I shake my head. "I have morning breath," I tell him from behind my hand. "I can't kiss you."

"I don't care."

"I do. No mouth kisses until I've brushed my teeth."

"So you'd be open to other kisses?" He waggles his eyebrows at me and a laugh breaks free.

"And no to that as well, I haven't had a shower."

"Is that an invitation for us to shower together?"

"No," I screech, "I … ummm, fuck—"

"I'm only teasing, Fern, but for the record, I will shower and kiss you anytime you're ready."

Staring at him, I'm at a loss for words. My stomach, on the other hand, decides to make its presence known and rumbles loudly. "Sounds like I need to feed you again."

"Looks like it but, I really think I should get going. I didn't mean to fall asleep and I have to be at work in fifteen minutes."

"It's fine, Fern, I'm sure your boss will be okay with you being late, but I have to say, waking up with you in my arms was a pleasant surprise. I lay here watching you sleep for a few moments before you stirred."

"That's not half creepy," I tease.

"It's not creepy when I do it."

"Sir, let's agree to disagree, but I do agree to the feeding me part."

"And I do agree to the you calling me Sir part. I really like it when you do that."

Looking intently at him, I bite my bottom lip. "Feed me, please … Sir."

The air around us thickens and before I know it, I'm on my back and Bradford's body is covering mine. His tongue is plunging into my mouth and he cups one of my breasts in his hand. I know I said no to before teeth-brushing kisses but this kiss is making me light-headed, and I forget all about the grossness of kissing before my teeth are clean.

Wrapping my arms around his neck, I hold him to me as our tongues battle it out. His knee slips between my thighs and I find myself rubbing against his leg. I'm dry humping him in the morning sunlight and I could not be happier. That tingly feeling begins to build low in my belly, never have I ever reached a climax just from kissing before but then again, I've never kissed anyone like Bradford before.

As if he can read my body, he increases the pressure

of his knee against my clit, moving his knee in sync with the swivel of my hips. "Come for me," he demands, but I'm a stubborn woman and I refuse to come when he says to come, no matter the pressure is building by the second. "Fern," he growls against my lips.

"I'll come when I fucking want to come," I hiss, but the universe is a fickle bitch and no sooner have I finished yelling at him and I'm yelling for a completely difference reason. My eyes close. My back arches and I moan into his mouth as I come, and boy-o-fucking-boy do I come. My body draws close to release and when my orgasm blasts through my system, it buzzes to life as I ride out the explosive climax.

Sated, I fall back to the lounger, breathing as if I've just run a marathon. Cracking my eyes open, I stare up into his hazel eyes that are more green than brown this morning, and I notice he has a smug expression on his face. "I didn't come 'cause you demanded me to," I whine and the asshole just chuckles at me.

"Sure you didn't," he teases, "but for what it's worth, you are stunning when you explode. I can't wait to see and feel you explode all over my dick one of these days but for now, I need to feed you—"

"Your dick?"

"Food, Fern, I need to feed you food. And just so you know, the first time we fuck, it will be after I've worshipped your body from head to toe and you've come at least three times, and only then will you get my dick."

Biting my bottom lip, I process his words and even though I just came, I'm ready to combust again just from his words. Bradford climbs off me and offers me his hand. Placing mine in his, he pulls me up. Before I step away from him, I reach up and cup his cheek. We don't say anything but our eyes convey it all, we're both falling and I never want him to let me go.

CHAPTER 14

Bradford

After showing Fern to the guest bathroom for her to freshen up, I grab my phone and text Carlton to let him know Fern and I are working out of the office today. My brother, the asshole that he is, immediately texts back.

CARLTON: *I really hope working is code for fucking your sexatary*

CARLTON: *Take the day off and enjoy yourself but remember, wrap it before you tap it.*

Flipping my phone the bird, I climb into the shower—alone—and get ready for my day, with Fern.

After a quick shower, I change into black cargo pants and a charcoal short-sleeve button-down shirt, and once we are both ready, I take Fern out for breakfast.

We head to my favorite café on the boardwalk and once we've eaten, we grab two to-go coffees and return to my place. Taking our coffee upstairs, we sit out on the terrace and talk again. And like always with us, the conversation flows and the laughs are plenty. Fern and I have so much in common, despite our age difference. She has an old soul and it calls to me in a way I've never felt before. Last night I didn't mean for us to fall asleep out on the terrace, but waking up with her in my arms is bliss and something I could quite easily do every day for the rest of my life.

It's almost lunchtime when I drive her home. Pulling up to her place, we make plans to catch up again later that day. Before she climbs out, she leans over the center console and kisses me goodbye. What started out as a quick goodbye kiss turns into a full-on make-out session. I feel like a teenage boy with a crush again and not the forty-three-year-old billionaire I am.

Watching Fern walk toward her building, my heart fills with joy and that feeling skyrockets when just before she steps inside, she blows me a kiss. And being a fool, I reach out, pretend to catch it, and pop it into the pocket of my shirt.

The rest of the week flies by and before I know it, it's the weekend again. Fern spends Friday night at my place and apart from some hot and heavy kissing, the blow job of all blow jobs, and some sixty-nining, we don't have sex. I'm not sure why we haven't taken that step yet but for the first time in my life, I'm excited about getting to know a woman before we jump into the sack together.

The next morning, I drop Fern at her place because she has a video date with Raven and Cali locked in. She apologizes profusely, but I tell her she can make it up to me later that afternoon by escorting me to dinner with Bradford and Britney tonight.

Pulling away from the curb, I wonder what I should do for the day. Being the workaholic I am, I head into the office to catch up on some things I didn't get done this week because I've been preoccupied with my assistant.

When I arrive at the office, I notice a random black suburban in the visitor parking lot but think nothing of it. Entering the building, I head up to the office and when the elevator doors open, I hear raised voices. One of the banshees sounds like Britney and my curiosity is piqued, so I head toward her office rather than mine. There's a dark-haired man with his back to me and from the murderous look on Britney's face, she doesn't seem happy with this stranger.

Britney notices me and her eyes widen. She snaps at the man to "shut the fuck up" and exits her office. Closing the door behind her, she walks over to me. "Bradford, what are you doing here?" Her voice is high-pitched and panicked. Her eyes are darting around and she's biting on her bottom lip, something she does when she's angry.

"I came in to catch up on some work, what are you doing here?" I look around her toward the man in her office but I can't see his face. He's still turned away from me but from the hunch of his shoulders, he too is angry. "Is everything all right?"

"It's fine," she says, but we both know she's lying. I raise my eyebrows at her in that 'really, do I look like a fool' kind of way. "An old friend popped by, surprising me, but he and I are about to head out for lunch. I'll leave you to it so we don't disturb you." Before I can say anything, she walks back to her office and says, "Let's get to lunch." The man nods at the sound of her voice, stands up, and leans down to pick up the bag at his feet, but once again, he keeps his face obscured from me. He pulls the bag over his shoulder, picks up a briefcase from the desk, and waits while Britney grabs her bags. Once they both have their belongings, Britney ushers her friend out. He still keeps his head down and I can't get a clear look at his face. *Why is he hiding from me?*

Britney follows behind him, only stopping to lock up her office. She walks toward me. "See you Monday," she calls out, bumping me in the shoulder on the way past. The two of them silently walk toward the elevator, the tension between the two of them is thick. Turning around, I watch them step into the elevator. Finally her 'friend' looks up and our gazes meet. A shiver runs through me at the murderous look in his eyes, but there's also a familiarity I can't place. The elevator doors close and I stand here for a few moments, staring at the shiny silver doors.

Knowing there's nothing I can do and really not wanting to be lured into more Britney drama, I turn around and head toward my office and get to it. I don't know what it is, but I love being here on my own. I get so much more done … and since a certain brown-haired, green-eyed angel started working here, I've been burning the wick at both ends. When

Fern is here, my mind is on her and she's very distracting but then again, even when she isn't here my mind is on her. I hope now that we are whatever the hell we are, I can get back to being the professional I am. But I have a feeling, having Fern close by and knowing what her lips taste like, it'll be even harder to concentrate now.

I'm just finishing up when my phone pings with a text and when I see her name on the screen, I swear my heart skips a beat.

FERN: *What you up to…Sir*

Seeing the Sir at the end of her text has my cock coming to life. This woman is going to be the death of me, but death by Fern would be an amazing way to pass over into the afterlife.

BRADFORD: *Sir loves hearing you call him that … and you are going to pay for leaving me with a rock-hard dick when you aren't here.*

Her reply comes in immediately.

FERN: *You need to have better control, Sir. And for the record, I'm soaked thinking about you*

Yep, I've died and gone to heaven. I've never met a girl like Fern before and now that I have her, I'm never letting her go.

BRADFORD: *Be ready and waiting for me in ten minutes.*

FERN: *Or what???*

BRADFORD: *I'll spank that sexy ass of yours.*

I've never been into the whole smacking thing but texting with Fern right now makes me feel alive.

FERN: *You realize that's not a threat?*

"Fuck me," I mumble out loud to myself as I reread the message three times.

BRADFORD: *You are trouble, Fern Halstead.*

FERN: *You have no idea, Sir… now hurry up and come get me… I need a spanking*

"Fuck me," I groan again. Quickly I shut down my computer and I'm just about to head out when another text comes through.

FERN: ***picture***

FERN: *Waiting for my spanking*

"Fucking hell," I hiss as I stare at an image of Fern's ass. Fern's sexy as fuck ass. Her dress is up over her hips. She's wearing a skimpy yellow G-string and I so want to sink my teeth into her flesh, biting and marking her skin. *Where the hell is this side of me coming from?*

BRADFORD: *You're in for it when I get there.*

FERN: *I hope so*

FERN: *See you soon … Sir*

This woman is going to be the death of me but as I've said before, death by Fern would be an amazing way to go.

CHAPTER 15

Fern

I've never been so brazen before but Bradford makes me do crazy things and, to be honest, that pic of my ass just now was hot. My ass is fine, F I N E... fine. I still have no clue what possessed me to do it but from his subsequent replies, I'm glad I took a chance.

I'm lost in my head thinking of dirty things happening between Bradford and me when my phone pings with a text. I smile when I see it's from the man I have been sexy dreaming about.

BRADFORD: *You're late, Ms. Halstead, you know*

what that means?

FERN: *It means, we are going to have so much fun when we get to your place*

Feeling brazen once again, I quickly slip off my G-string and scrunch it up in my hand. Grabbing my handbag, I lock up and make my way downstairs to meet Bradford. Carefully, I climb into his car, not wanting to flash my neighbors or spoil the surprise I have. When I'm seated and buckled in, I look over to him and smile. "Hi," I breathlessly say. Never has that word sounded so erotic before.

"Hello, Fern," he says in reply.

Before I lose my confidence, I turn in my seat to face Bradford. "I have something for you."

"You didn't need to get me anything."

"I know but…" I finish it with a shrug. My tongue slides across my bottom lip and I dig my teeth into the plump skin. His eyes watch the motion and they fill with desire. He reaches out and pulls my lip free, sliding his thumb over the indents left from my teeth.

"Here," I quickly say, lifting my hand, still keeping my panties clenched in my fist. He removes his from my face and holds it out for my gift. I immediately miss the contact but we have the rest of the day and hopefully evening to touch and fondle one another.

"I believe you have something for me?" he croons when I don't give my panties to him, the timbre of his voice causes goosebumps to appear on my skin.

Nodding, I stare intently at him and then I drop the yellow material onto his palm. He scrunches his eyebrows in confusion and I see the moment he registers what I gave him. His gaze flicks from them to my legs to my face, and back down to my legs again. The intensity of his gaze causes me to shuffle in my seat. He lifts his eyes back to my face and then he shocks me when he cups my panties in both of his hands and brings them to his nose and inhales. He sniffs my panties and I really wish I was wearing them now because I'm soaked. Who knew watching a man smell your underwear could be so arousing?

"Fuck, Fern," he hisses, "you smell divine. I'm trying to take this slow but between this, you calling me Sir, and the picture of your delectable ass, you're making it hard."

"I hope I'm making you hard, no one wants a soft cock."

He shakes his head at me but at the same time, he's smiling brightly. He reaches up, cups my cheeks, leans across the center console, and kisses me. My panties are still clutched in his fist as his tongue presses into my mouth. Closing my eyes, I give myself over to the kiss and I have to say, someone holding my panties to my face while we kiss is something new, but before I can ponder on that thought, he pulls away from me. He doesn't utter a word, he just stares at me. "You are going to be the death of me, Fern Halstead, but for the record, two can play the kinky game and you have just met your match." He pockets my panties and without uttering another word, he pulls out into traffic and we drive toward his house. He rests his hand on my thigh and my skin sizzles from the contact. He doesn't try anything as we make our way over to Venice Beach and the anticipation of what's to come has me on high alert.

He pulls into his garage and turns off the engine. He opens his door and just as I go to open mine, he shakes his head and demands, "Wait there."

"Yes, Sir," I cheekily reply and I notice him trying to hold back a smirk.

He comes around to my side, opens my door, and offers me his hand. Placing my hand in his, that spark ignites once again, causing my heart to pitter patter within my chest. He pulls me up and slides his hand around my waist. "What am I going to do with you, naughty girl?"

"I don't know, Sir." I emphasize the word 'Sir' and his eyes fill with hunger and my pussy, well, she weeps for what's to come. "Maybe you should spank me."

"My naughty girl would like that and that's not really a punishment, but the thought of seeing your ass pink from my hand has been playing on my mind since you sent me that picture earlier, so why don't you spin around. Then I want you to put your ass out with your hands on the doorframe."

Nodding, I swallow deeply and spin around like he asked me to. Placing my hands on the frame, I thrust my butt out and impatiently wait. His hand lands on the back of my thigh. He bunches my dress up and then, ever so slowly, skims it up my leg and under the material of my dress. His fingertip brushes over my ass cheek, and I have to hold back the moan wanting to slip free. I have never been this turned on before, arousal is dripping down my leg. He steps closer to me and continues to circle his finger over my ass cheek. He leans in closer and I can feel his breath on my neck. Tilting my head, I give him access to my neck. He places a featherlight kiss just under my ear, and I can't help the shudder that runs through my body.

"Fern," he whispers my name.

"Yes," I pant like the wanton hussy I am.

"We should take a walk." Just like that, he removes his hand from under my dress and steps away from me. He walks to the internal door and whistles, a few moments later, Mr. Woolley pads into the garage and Bradford attaches a leash to his collar.

"You coming?"

"Not anymore," I snap and my reaction causes the bastard to laugh. "That wasn't nice, Bradford."

"Now you know how I felt when I got that text."

"All's fair in love and war and, Mr. Manning, you just declared sexually frustrated war with me. Be prepared to go down."

"Going down on you would be my pleasure, Ms. Halstead, but first we need to walk Mr. Woolley."

"You're lucky I like your dog." And because we are in a sexually frustrated war, I walk over to them and take the leash from his hands. Mr. Woolley and I walk out of the garage and before I step into the sunlight, I bend over and lift my dress, giving him an unobstructed view of my ass. Sliding my hand over my ass cheek, I slip it between my thighs and into my slit. My finger effortlessly slides between my folds and I moan. I think this might have been a mistake 'cause I've worked myself up again. Standing upright, I look over my shoulder and bring my finger toward my lips but before I can slide it into my mouth, he's right behind me gripping my wrist. He pulls my finger toward his lips and with his eyes locked on mine, he sucks the digit into his mouth. We both moan and I'm ready to throw myself at him when Mr. Woolley barks, cockblocking me.

Bradford pulls my finger from his mouth and looks down at his dog. "Cockblocker," he sneers and I giggle since I was just thinking that. Bradford presses a button and the garage door begins to close. Then he takes my hand in his and we head out to walk Mr. Woolley.

There's something refreshing, and sexy, about walking along the beach with a cockblocking dog, wearing no panties, and holding hands with a man that you're falling for. I love this feeling and I don't ever want to let it go.

CHAPTER 16

Bradford

That was the hardest—pun intended—walk I have ever taken Mr. Woolley on, and he and I have hiked Mount Lee and the Hollywood sign via the Brush Canyon Trail many times before. My dick has been hard ever since we left the house and Fern, the sexy little minx she is, did everything she could to remind me she's wearing no panties.

At one point, I couldn't control myself and I pulled her into my arms, lifted her up and slammed my lips to hers. All the beachgoers around us faded away and it was just Fern, me, and Mr. Woolley. He wasn't impressed that we'd stopped, but he'd already cockblocked me so a pause for a make-out session is the least he can do. Fern wrapped her arms around my neck, holding on tightly as I assaulted her mouth with my lips and tongue. I made sure to keep her bare ass covered because no one gets to see her perfect globes except for me.

It wasn't until we returned home I remembered, her G-string was IN MY FUCKING pocket. I could have saved myself the stress of baring her ass to everyone and just made her put it back on … and yes, I'm just as shocked that I wanted her to put her underwear back on.

"Water?" I ask when we step into the kitchen after our walk.

"Please." She nods and jumps up onto the kitchen counter.

Grabbing two bottles from the refrigerator, I hand one to her and before I drink mine, I grab Mr. Woolley's bowl and fill it up.

Twisting off the cap, I bring the bottle to my lips and watch her do the same. Who knew drinking water could be so sexually arousing? The way her lips wrap around the bottle has me imagining her wrapping them around my shaft. My cock once again twitches in my pants, a common occurrence these days when Fern is around. Never have I been so physically attracted to a woman before, but it's not just her looks. Fern has this aura about her that brightens the darkest of days and makes the sunniest day shine brighter. She's the breath of fresh air I needed and even though I'm two decades older than her, I'm not as scared as I was before we gave into our attraction.

"What's got you thinking so hard over there?" The sound of her voice has me focusing on her again and not my inner feelings or my dick.

"You," I honestly tell her.

"Me, how?" She places her bottle down and removes her hair thingy, she runs her fingers through her dark locks, the strands cascade over her shoulders and she's never looked more beautiful.

"Well, a gentlemen never tells—"

"But you're not a gentleman," she says, jumping off the counter. She looks over at me and smirks. "You, Sir, are a dirty dirty man and guess what?" There's that word again, Sir. Whenever she says it, something happens inside of me and I want to dominate her in every way possible. I want to wring every morsel of pleasure from her body.

"What?" I somehow manage to get the word out as she sashays over to me. She rests her hands on my chest and leans into my ear and whispers, "I'm a dirty dirty girl and I think I need to be spanked … Sir."

"Is that so?" I place my bottle of water on the counter behind me and rest my hands on her hips, pulling her into my body. She nods and bites her lip in her seductive way that has my cock standing at attention and pressing into her stomach.

She takes a step back.

And another.

I mourn the loss but she surprises me when she spins around, leans forward, presses her hands to the counter, and pushes her ass out. Removing one hand, she looks over her shoulder and lifts her sexy dress up, exposing her delectable naked ass at me. She implores me with her eyes to take what I want, and who am I to deny her.

Like a bull to a red flag, I push off the counter and saunter over to her. Licking my lips, my gaze roams over her bare flesh. Running my hand gently over the globe of her cheek, my skin sizzles and she shudders under my touch. She lets out a yelp when I pull my hand back and slap her cheek. The crack of my hand colliding with her skin echoes through the kitchen. I repeat the process three more times, and between each strike I gently rub her heated skin. Seeing her cheeks turn red is hotter than I could ever have imagined.

She drops her head to the counter on the last hit. Both of us are breathing heavily and I start to wonder if I hit her too hard and she didn't enjoy it when she doesn't move. "Are you okay?" I ask because the longer she doesn't move, the more I begin to internally freak out.

"Yeah, I'm … wow, that was, umm, wow," she stammers as she stands up and turns to face me. We stare at one another, her cheeks are flushed. Her chest is heaving and it pushes her tits up, and all I want to do is bury my face in them.

"So do it," she says, and that's when I realize I said that out loud.

"We have a habit of thinking our thoughts out loud," I say with a laugh.

"Yes, yes we do," she agrees.

"I tend to lose all train of thought when I'm around you. You make me forget all reason, you make me…" I drift off, not sure if I should be so brutally honest with her.

"I make you what?" she questions.

Seeing the determined look on her face, I decide to just go with it, after all, they say honesty is the best policy. "You make me throw all the rules out. When I'm with you, I just want to go with the flow and live." *Fuck the consequences*, I silently add.

"That's what life is all about, Bradford. We only get to live once so I say, do what makes you happy and screw what everyone else thinks. As long as you're not breaking any laws and no one dies and you're safe, just do it."

"Just do it," I repeat, nodding.

"Yep, just do it and fuck the consequences." It's like she's in my head and with her giving me the courage I need, that's exactly what I do. I just do it. I grip her cheeks in my palms and press my lips to hers and kiss her deeply. My tongue pushes into her mouth, hers slides into mine. Our hands roam over one another's body. We hold on to each other so tightly you can't tell where I end and she starts. Sliding my hand down to her ass, I squeeze her globes and lift her up. She wraps her long legs around my waist. Pressing her pussy against my harder cock.

Spinning around with her in my arms, I press her against the wall and begin to grind her down on my cock. I realize it's only her dress and my pants separating us. The need to touch her intensifies so I just do it. I slide my hand between us and my finger effortlessly slides between her folds. She mewls into our kiss and the sound is music to my ears. I run my finger up and down her slit, her arousal coating my digit.

"I need to taste you," I mumble against her lips.

"Yes," she pants, "please."

Turning back around, I walk over to the island she

was just leaning against and I place her down on the edge. Lifting my hand, I rest it on her chest between her tits and press her back so she's lying flat on the counter. Her dark locks fan out beneath her like a chocolate halo. Moving my hands to her thighs, I slide them up her legs, lifting the hem of her dress as I go, bunching the material at her waist, I stare down at her pussy. She's waxed except for a heart-shaped landing strip. "A heart?" I question.

"I wanted to try something different," she nonchalantly says.

"You and me both," I reply with a wink.

Pressing my hand down on her stomach, I lick my lips and begin to lower my head. I can smell her arousal and it's the sweetest smell in the world. Closing my eyes, I breathe in deeply and nuzzle her clit with my nose. Darting my tongue out, I lick her from taint to clit. "You taste as good as you smell," I mumble before I cover her clit with my lips and suck the bundle of nerves into my mouth.

"Yes," she mewls, running her fingers through my hair, her nails grazing over my scalp. I remove my lips but she's not happy with that and she shoves my face into her pussy. "Don't stop," she demands, and who am I to deny her.

Returning my mouth to her mound, I continue to lick and suck her. When I slide a finger into her tight channel, her back arches off the counter and she screams as her orgasm detonates. Her juices soak my face and I lap up each and every drop of her release.

Her body falls lax and she lies there, breathlessly panting as she comes back to earth. She lifts her hands from my head and throws one arm over her face. Shuffling to my feet, I stare down at her splayed out on my kitchen counter. "Well, that was the best meal I have ever eaten in this kitchen."

She snorts and pushes herself up to her elbows. "Well, you have a favorite meal here, maybe it's time I have one too." Her gaze locks on to my dick, which is pointing to the heavens right now.

"By all means," I tell her, "I can't have my girl going hungry now, can I?"

CHAPTER 17

Fern

He called me his girl. *Swoon*. Why is that statement causing me to turn to mush? I don't fall for cheesy lines like that, but hearing that come from him and I'm done for.

He stares intently at me and even though I just came, from the carnal look he's giving me, I'm ready to go again but I'm not a selfish lover, it's his turn.

Sliding off the counter, I drop to my knees before him and flip open the button on his cargos and slide my hand in. Pushing his pants and briefs down, I free his cock. It's hard and that vein on the side is pulsating. The tip is glistening and I cannot wait to suck it. As far as dicks go, Bradford Manning's is beautiful, and let me tell you, in person, it's better than I ever imagined. The head is girthy but not so large that it'll hurt pushing into me. As for length, it's above average and I cannot wait to ride it, but for now, I'll have to settle for it sliding in and out of my mouth.

Reaching out, I wrap my hand around the base of his cock and gently stroke. Bradford hisses from above and when I lift my gaze, I see him hungrily staring back down at me. Pleasure is written all over his face and all I've done is squeeze his dick. Sticking my tongue out, I slide the tip through the slit at the end of his shaft, getting my first taste of him and I have to say, it's my new favorite flavor. Wanting to get more of a taste, I open my mouth and slide his shaft in. Wrapping my lips around him, I suck him to the back of my throat before repeating the process over and over.

His dick effortlessly glides in and out of my mouth. Bradford slides his hands into my hair, guiding my head back and forth along his dick. On the outward motion, I gently rake my teeth along his member, earning another hiss. Lifting my other hand, I cup his balls and press on that spot between his taint and anus.

"Fuuuuuck," he growls, "your mouth feels like heaven," he adds on.

With those encouraging words, I continue to suck his dick. Gripping on to his ass cheeks for support, I really go to town. Bobbing my head up and down, faster and faster. His dick slides in and out of my mouth, drool dribbles down my chin but I'm lost to the moment. Blow jobs aren't my favorite sexual action but I have to say, blowing Bradford could become a favorite past time of mine.

"Fern, babe, I'm gonna come," he grunts.

"Do it," I mumble around his dick and no sooner do I tell him to do it, he does.

The first spray of hot salty cum hits the back of my throat. I continue to suck and lick at him until every last drop is gone.

Pulling back, I sit on my knees and stare up at him, licking the last of his release from the corner of my mouth. He cups my cheek, running this thumb along my jawline. His touch is light but heated at the same time. Our simmering moment is interrupted when a deep voice sings out, "Honey, I'm home," followed by the sound of feet pounding up the stairs from the lower level.

My eyes widen when a familiar voice says, "Heeeey, guys."

Peering over the edge of the counter, my eyes widen when I see his brother standing there, I was hoping the voice didn't belong to him because there's no denying what just went down—pun intended, with us. Getting busted post release by your boss's brother, who also happens to be your other boss, is the last thing I wanted to happen this afternoon … or ever.

"Hey, bro," Bradford greets his brother as he puts his dick away. He then offers me his hand and hesitantly I put my palm in his and he pulls me up. My dress falls down my legs. I inwardly sigh in relief because I thankfully didn't rip my dress off and use my boobs to get him off, but I'm totally putting that in the 'we must try it' pile. Even if my tits are tiny, I think it could still work.

Bradford rests his palms on the countertop, right in front of where I came only moments ago. As if I'm not mortified enough, I can see a puddle of my release glistening in the kitchen light. Clearly Bradford doesn't because he strikes up a conversation with his brother. "What's up?"

"Ummm, we had plans to watch the game down at Squires tonight. It was going to be a double date, but Britney had other plans. Remember?"

"Shit, I totally forgot," Bradford replies.

"I see that you've made other plans." Carlton looks over to me. "Hey, Fern."

"Hi," I sheepishly reply with a finger wave. I glance to Bradford, but he looks upset he forgot about his plans with his brother. "Look, I'll ummm, I'll head home so you guys can watch the game together."

"Are you sure?" Bradford asks, just as Carlton says, "It's fine, we can do it another time."

My gaze flits between the two guys. Even though they're brothers, they look nothing alike. Where Bradford is tall and muscular with short, sandy-blond hair with a few silver specks, Carlton is tallish and stocky with more salt than pepper in his dark locks. The one thing they do have in common, their eyes. Both men have the most amazing hazel eyes and right now, they are having a silent conversation with said beautiful eyes.

"You two kids have fun now," Carlton finally says, breaking the silence that enveloped the room. Before I can protest that it's fine, he turns on his heel and heads toward the front door. "Don't forget dinner tomorrow night," he shouts before the door slams shut behind him.

Dropping my head onto Bradford's shoulder, I complain, "Oh. My. Fucking. God, that was mortifying."

"Umm, hello," Bradford protests, "I was the one who's dick was still out, but I'm glad it was me and not you who was exposed. No one gets to see your naked bits except me."

"Is that so, Mr. Caveman?"

"Yes, fucking so. You are mine, Fern. After one taste I'm addicted, and I'm never letting you go."

Holy swoon, Batman, I feel like I've said that several times now when it comes to this man, but I wholeheartedly agree with him.

"I feel the same way, Bradford. Is it crazy to feel something so visceral so quickly? I mean, we've kissed a couple of times and I've sucked your dick and you ate my pussy, that's nothing in the scheme of dating and love and life."

"When you know, you know," he nonchalantly replies with a shrug. He slides his arm around my waist and pulls me into him. He places a kiss on my temple and I melt into him. "Fern, I know this is fast and I'm older than you by a lot, but for the first time in a long time, I'm happy and content. I want to explore this with you, but I'm not going to push you. You need to decide if an us is what you want."

CHAPTER 18

Bradford

Waiting for her reply is agony.

It's only a few seconds before she starts speaking but for me, it feels like an eternity. "Bradford." She reaches up and cups my cheek. "I feel exactly the same way. It's crazy to feel so strongly about someone so quickly, but for me, I've been dancing around my feelings for you since I started at Manning Tech. It was lust at first sight for me, and I'm so glad you kissed me the other night. I never would have had the balls to make the first move."

"I'm glad I kissed you too, Fern. I don't normally kiss

women randomly in the office, but when I'm around you all rational thought goes out the window. I feel like a bumbling teenager again and not the well-rounded and educated forty-three-year-old I am."

Her eyes widen and she takes a step back. "Bradford, what about our age? What will people say?"

"Did you tell me not so long ago that age is just a number?" She nods in agreement and bites her lip. "And as for what other people say, fuck 'em. All that matters is you and I are happy and I am, Fern. You make me so fucking happy."

"You make me happy too," she whispers. "I've never felt happiness like this before."

Stepping to her, I slide my hand around her waist and pull her into me. She drapes her arms over my shoulders and I gaze adoringly at the woman who has captured my heart. "What do you say, Fern, will you be my girlfriend?"

"Yes, 'cause you'll be my boyfriend and that means, I can do this anytime I want." Before I can ask what she means, she slides her hands behind my head and pulls my lips down to hers. Her tongue licks along the seam of mine and then she slips it into my mouth. Like our first kiss the other night, everything around me fades into the background. It's just Fern and me and our growing affection for one another.

I'd given up hope of finding my other half but when I least expected it, she came into my life. In a short amount of time, I've fallen hard for this woman. I'm open to the possibility of a forever with her, but I can't come on too strong. It's only been a few days. I don't want to scare her off before we've even had a chance to begin.

She slides her hand down my spine to my ass and squeezes. I do the same but as my hand was on her waist, I don't have as far to slide. She moans into my mouth and my cock twitches. "Please," she begs against my lips.

"Please what?" I ask her.

She breaks our kiss and stares at me, her green eyes are ablaze with lust and hunger. "I want you to make love to me and then I want you to fuck me into next week. I want to still be able to feel you inside me tomorrow when I'm at home by myself and you're at dinner with your brother."

"How did I get so lucky to find a woman like you?"

"Your previous assistant died and the agency sent me, even though being an assistant was the last thing I wanted to do, but I'm so glad I did. Now, take me to bed and ravage me."

And that's exactly what I do, I throw Fern over my shoulder and I storm into my bedroom and we don't come up for air for the next few hours.

CHAPTER 19
Fern

One minute we're standing in his kitchen, and the next, he throws me over his shoulder and I'm upside-down staring at his pants-clad ass. He storms down the hallway to his bedroom, slapping my ass along the way and I can't help but moan. It reminds me of what we did earlier in his kitchen and arousal leaks out of me. He slaps me again and I return the favor. I slap him on the ass but through his cargos, it has little to no effect on him.

He steps into his room and lowers me to my feet. Gripping the hem of my dress, he lifts it up my body. His fingertips skim my skin, causing goosebumps to appear. He drops my dress to the floor and when he looks at me, I feel the heat in his gaze as it roams all over my body.

"You're naked," he states.

Nodding, I bite my lip nervously at the intensity of his eyes on me.

"Why are you not wearing any underwear?"

"You have my panties still and, umm, hello." I cup my boobs. "These itty-bitty titties don't need a bra."

He pushes my hands out of the way and covers my boobs with his hands. "These itty-bitty titties are perfect, Fern, and one of these days, I'm going to fuck them and come all over them."

"Yes," I breathlessly pant, "I thought of that scenario earlier."

"Great minds," he says. "Now, get on the bed and play with that pretty pussy of yours. By the time I'm undressed, I want you wet and ready for me."

"Yes, Sir," I purr.

Climbing onto the bed on all fours, I crawl up the mattress. He reaches out and grabs me by my hips, halting my movement. Looking over my shoulder, he smirks at me and quickly slaps me on the ass. Three times in quick succession.

"That's for being cheeky," he growls. "Now, get onto the task I set you."

"Yes, S—"

"You say Sir one more time and I'm withholding your orgasms."

My mouth drops open, and it's tempting to say, 'Yes,

Sir' again, but I want orgasms more than I want to taunt him, so I bite my tongue. Crawling up to the pillows, I turn around and lie back. Spreading my legs wide, I slide my hand down my body and begin to finger myself as he watches me.

"Less gawking, more stripping," I demand.

"Yes, ma'am." He salutes me and begins to unbutton his shirt.

"Call me ma'am again and…" I don't finish my threat because I've swallowed my tongue and died. I've gone to sexy man heaven. Bradford is standing before me in only his cargos and I'm staring at his beautiful body. His body is magnificent. I knew he'd have a rockin' hot body but move over Channing Tatum, there's a new eight-pack in town.

"And what?" he asks, staring intently at me as he slides his fingers into the waist of his pants and in one fell swoop, he removes his cargos and briefs. Leaving him buck-ass naked before me and my protest leaves my brain. I'm focused on his dick. His hard, throbbing dick. The end is an angry purple and the tip is leaking precum. Never have I ever seen a more perfect dick. As far as dicks go, this one if F I N E… fine and I cannot wait to have it inside me— mouth or pussy, I'm not fussy.

Licking my lips I move my gaze from his beautiful cock and up to his gorgeous face, "Bradford, you need to hurry up and get on this bed."

"I will climb on when I'm good and ready, Fern, and just so you know, I'm going to explore every inch of your body with my tongue … twice."

He makes no move to climb onto the bed, he just stands

there, staring at me with his hand wrapped around his dick. He strokes himself while his eyes are locked on my fingers between my thighs. Silently, we pleasure ourselves. I'm the first one to break when the sexual tension enveloping us becomes too much. "Please, Bradford, please."

"I love hearing you beg, Fern, but I need you now too so I will concede defeat, but this time only." He rests his knee on the end of the bed and like a panther stalking its prey, he ever so slowly slides himself up my body, peppering kisses and licking my skin along the way until he's cocooning me. His cock rests at my entrance and with one flick of my hips, he could slide home. This tortured foreplay right now is just as erotic as the act itself.

He swivels his hips and the head of his cock pushes my lips apart. He slides up my slit and brushes over my clit, causing me to hiss.

"Please," I beg and this time I lift my hips, hoping to guide him where I want him, but the asshole flicks his hips back an inch so he's no longer touching me. Pouting, I mourn the loss of contact. I'm just about to verbalize my protest when finally, he pushes inside of me. His dick effortlessly slides inside of me and never have I been so full before.

"Yesssssss," I hiss as we fall into a rhythm.

In. Out. Kiss.

Kiss. Out. In.

We repeat the process over and over.

My pleasure rising with each thrust. He does this amazing swivel thing with his hips, hitting that magic spot and then I'm soaring. I crash over the edge and I scream as the most intense orgasm in the history of orgasms detonates.

I see stars, literally, and I swear I black out for a few seconds. My release sets him off and he begins to come, but at the very last second, he pulls out, grips his cock, and spills his seed all over my stomach.

His warm cum splashes over my skin and that's when I realize why he did what he did. Thank fuck one of us was thinking clearly but when it comes to Bradford and his dick, all rational thought leaves my head. After one session, I'm addicted and I never want to let this man go.

CHAPTER 20

Bradford

That was amazing, absolutely amazing, and even that word doesn't encapsulate how good it was with Fern. I've had sex before—I'm not a monk—but never has it been like that. Fern and I clicked on every level. Our bodies worked in synchronization as if we've been doing this since the dawn of time. If I thought I was addicted after one kiss, after having sex with her, I'm now a full-blown addict. Hi, my name is Bradford and I'm addicted to everything that is Fern Halstead.

Somehow at the last second, I realized I wasn't wearing

a condom and pulled out. Marking her skin with my cum will be seared in my brain forever. I know there's still a risk that she could already be pregnant, but thinking of Fern's stomach swelling with my baby growing inside of her doesn't freak me out like it usually would.

"What's got you grinning like the cat who got the canary?" her sweet voice asks me.

"You," I honestly tell her, "I've got you."

"Dude, you've already got into my panties, you can stop with the sweet talking."

"Just stating a fact and, Fern, what we just did was amazing in every way." I'm still between her thighs and staring down at her gorgeous naked, cum-marked body. Her skin is flushed. Her lips are swollen. Her hair is a mess but she's never looked more beautiful. "You are amazing in every way, and I hope you don't have any plans for the rest of the weekend because we aren't leaving this bed. I need more of what we just did."

"I have no plans, and if it ends with you marking me with your cum like that, I'll never leave this bed again. That was so freakin' hot."

"Well, I realized at the last minute I wasn't wearing a condom, so I pulled out. I hope that's okay?"

"You're asking me if it's okay you pulled out to avoid a baby?"

"Yeah." I nod.

"Dude, seeing you grip your dick like that and mark me was H O double T… hot, but next time, we should use protection. Yes, I'm on the pill, but I'm too young to be a mom."

"And I'm too old to be a dad," I state, once again I'm reminded of our age difference and my face drops.

"You'd be a DILF," she tells me.

"What's a DILF?" I ask, confused at the term.

"Dad I'd Like to Fuck," she tells me. "And for the record, I don't care about your age. It's just a number. All that matters is what you and I feel. Anyone else's opinion is moot."

"You are something else, lovely lady."

"Why thank you." She reaches up and pulls me down on top of her, my cum squishing between us, but I forget all about that when she presses her lips to mine and pushes her tongue into my mouth. Her kisses are intoxicating.

The next thing I know, I'm on my back and she's straddling me. Grinding herself on my once again hard cock, this woman makes me, and my cock, feel young again. She's so aroused that my shaft easily slides inside of her. Pushing herself upright, she begins to ride me. Running her hands through her hair, she closes her eyes and drops her head back. Lifting my hands, I cup her tits and fondle them, earning myself a sexy moan from her delectable lips.

"I'm gonna come," I grunt and in the blink of an eye, she climbs off me and situates herself between my thighs. She wraps her lips around my dick and when the head hits the back of her throat and she sucks on my shaft, I come. She sucks me dry and then quickly straddles me again before my dick softens, but when I'm around Fern it's perpetually hard. She begins to ride me but she must be super worked up because she comes a few thrusts later.

She collapses on top of me, breathlessly panting.

Lifting her head, she gazes into my eyes. "We really need to remember protection, but I love blowing you so I really don't mind."

Cupping her cheek, I smile. "Where have you been all my life?"

"Living on the other side of the country," she tells me before rolling off and snuggling into my side. She runs her fingers across my pecs and I rub her back.

"Tell me about Silverdale."

"It's Silverbell and it's a small town on the Atlantic Coast. It's so picturesque, the beach is stunning and the main street is quaint. If I hadn't left, it was always my dream to live in an apartment on Main Street. I loved growing up there thanks to my two besties, Cali and Raven."

"The boy who I thought was your boyfriend?"

"The very one, he found it hilarious when I told him that, but he's happy in a throuple relationship."

"A whatle?"

"Throuple, three people in a relationship."

"How does that even work?" I ask her, genuinely intrigued.

She shrugs. "No clue, but it's all new and I have never heard him happier. His mom was diagnosed with cancer a few years back and it's been a rough patch for the Mitchells, so it's nice to see him happy again."

"And what about your family? You previously mentioned they passed, can I ask how?"

"Gas leak at home. I was away on an overnight school trip and the gas line began leaking. They went to sleep and never woke up again. If I hadn't had the field trip, I would have died too."

"Holy fuck, Fern, that's … I'm so sorry."

She shrugs. "It is what it is. What about you, tell me about your parents."

"Carlton's and my mom was the absolute best. Dad had his moments, he wasn't a shitty dad but he was focused on his work and the family came second to that. He did encourage us to follow our dreams and he, with Mom, was one of our biggest supporters in everything we did. Then one night, Mom went to sleep and never woke up, Dad died a few months later. I'm positive he died of a broken heart. As much as he was a workaholic, he loved her unconditionally."

"That's kinda sweet, I think if my parents would have grown old before they died, that would have happened too."

"What did you want to be when you grew up?"

"The first lady on the moon," she says.

"Well, to date, no lady has, so it's still a possibility."

"Yeah, that's not gonna happen. I'm not wearing a diaper, ever, and I'm not thrilled about using a contraption that straps me to the toilet, and I'm certainly not using a vacuum cleaner thingy to suck away my poop."

A laugh escapes me and she smacks me in the stomach. "Wow, you really looked into it"

"I did an assignment in middle school and it turned me off."

"What did you want to be then?"

"A supermodel but A. I'm not five ten. And B. My boobs are too small."

"I personally love your boobs." To reiterate my point, I slide my arms around her and cup one in my palm. "See, perfect fit."

"You have boob bias," she playfully throws back at me.

"When it comes to your tits, I will bias like no one has biased before."

"You are a doofus, Bradford Manning, but you're my doofus."

"I like being yours," I tell her, placing a kiss on her temple.

"I like being yours too." She places a kiss on my chest and snuggles back into my side.

A silence envelops us but it's not uncomfortable, Fern's breathing evens out and I can tell she's drifted off to sleep in my arms. Lying here, I watch her sleep. She's been through so much in her life, and I'm going to do everything in my power to make her smile each and every day.

CHAPTER 21

Fern

...three weeks later

Letting myself into Bradford's house, I'm immediately greeted by Mr. Woolley. Dropping my bag on the hall table, I see my stunning bouquet of sunflowers. A sense of happiness washes over me. I have never been happier and it's all to do with him. Since Bradford and I stared dating, on any given Thursday, I receive a gorgeous bouquet with the same note each month.

To brighten your day like you brighten mine.

After placing my things down, I kneel to greet Mr. Woolley with a scratch behind the ears. "Who's a good boy," I coo as the big goofy dog I've come to be quite fond of nuzzles his head into my stomach. Prior to Bradford, I was anti dog because when I was seventeen a stray rat-looking dog chased me down Main Street one afternoon, much to the delight of my besties Cali and Raven—assholes. Just like his owner, it's hard not to love Mr. Woolley. "Where's your daddy?" I ask the dog. As if he understands me, he looks at me and then turns on his heel and trots farther into the house. I pad after him and faintly hear music from upstairs, so I head up to the top level. I stop mid-step when I reach the family room and see Bradford. He's out on the terrace and he has his back to me. He's lost to the music playing on the record player, Frank is singing about flying to the moon, a far cry from the Metallica that's always blasting in the office. His taste in music rivals Raven's.

Leaning on the wall beside me, I watch as my sexy as hell silver fox sways to the music with a glass of red in hand, staring out at the ocean. He's wearing gray sweatpants that sit low on his hips and should be illegal. My body begins to sway to the music and like a moth to a flame, I start to move. I make my way over to him and when I'm behind him, I slide my hands around his waist. He covers my hand with his and holds on tightly. Gently, I place a kiss on his shoulder blades and his grip on my hand tightens. Something is up, but all I can offer him right now is this, so I squeeze him tighter.

He spins in my arms, looks down at me, and smiles. He's

breathtaking in the afternoon light, but there's a sadness in his eyes reflecting my way. "I didn't hear you come in."

"I noticed, you were lost to the music." Lifting my hand from his waist, I cup his cheek. He turns his head and kisses my palm. "Is everything okay?"

"It is now you're here." He slides his hand back around my waist and pulls me in closer, I hold on tightly, giving him all my love with my arms and body. He places a kiss on my head and whispers, "Never let me go," into my hair. Holy swoon, Batman, no one has ever made me feel like Bradford does and with four words he brings my inner romantic to the surface. I want to scream from the rooftops I'm hopelessly in love with this man but there's several things in the way, the biggest being our age. He's forty-three and I'm almost twenty-three. He's not ashamed of us. It's me with the problem, but after him being so swoony just now, it makes me want to throw caution to the wind.

"Never," I mumble into his chest. Lifting my head, I stare up at him. "What's wrong? And don't say nothing."

"It's just been a long day."

"I know, I was with you for eight hours of it. What's happened since I left?"

"Nothing for you to worry about." I hate that he won't open up to me, but I've learned Bradford Manning will talk when he wants to talk. "Dance with me," he commands.

Normally someone demanding me to do something would piss me off but when it comes to this man, I'll do anything he asks. My head begins to move up and down without me even thinking about it. He offers me his hand and I place mine in his. He puts his glass down on the railing before he pulls me into his arms. Sliding one arm around my waist, with the other he clasps my hand in his, holding it over his heart. Resting my head on his shoulder, I close my eyes and sway to the sounds of Frank singing about flying to the moon before it changes to "I Get a Kick Out of You." The words could not be truer, because I definitely get a kick out of being with him. I'm falling fast for this man and it's both exhilarating and frightening.

The record finishes and we stop swaying but we stay holding each other. Lifting my head, I stare up at Bradford and with the gorgeous sunset in the background it hits me. I love him. I love him with every fiber of my being and like my nod earlier, my mouth moves without conscious thought. "I love you."

He stares at me blankly. He doesn't utter a word and I'm pretty sure he's stopped breathing too. "What did you say?" he finally asks.

"I love you, Bradford. I'm head over heels in love with you," I honestly tell him. I've never uttered those words to another man before and meant them as deeply as I do right now.

"Say it again," he whispers, holding back a smile.

"I love you," I state once again.

Then my whole world is made. "Fern Halstead, I love you too. With every beat of my heart. With every breath I take. You are it for me and I'm never letting you go."

"Good, 'cause I'm never letting you go either. Now, shut up and kiss me." And kiss me he does. Each kiss with Bradford is better than the last and now that we've admitted how we really feel, it feels even better than before.

I was so not looking forward to this temp job at Manning Tech, but I'm so glad I took the assignment because it led me to this point. Life is grand and nothing, nothing can bring me down.

CHAPTER 22

Fern

Readjusting my skirt, I grab my notepad off Bradford's desk and head back to mine. There's a pep in my step and you cannot wipe the smile off my face. When he called me into his office just now, I was expecting a task to do but instead, my insatiable boyfriend and boss did me. He gave me an intense orgasm and I had hoped that the endorphin release would help with my current cyst issue. Alas, it did not and my stomach is still tight. I feel nauseous and I want to curl up and die. And that's no exaggeration, ovarian cysts suck donkey dick.

Dropping my notepad on my desk, I grab my coffee mug and head into the kitchen for a caffeine fix and a donut, thank you whoever brought them in today. With my mug of liquid gold and my doughy circle of sugar in hand, I make my way back to my desk and get back to work. Well, I try to work because I can't concentrate with the pain in my abdomen.

A few hours later, I stand up to use the bathroom but after a few steps, I fold in half and hiss. It feels like I'm being torn apart from the inside out. Pressing my hand into my stomach, I try to ease the pain but it doesn't work, if anything, the pressure intensifies the hurt. "Fucking cysts," I mumble as I take in a deep breath.

Stumbling back to my desk, I fall into my chair, reach into my bag, grab my pain meds, and throw two pills back. I really wish I had my heat pack right about now, but I'll have to wait 'til tonight for that luxury.

Leaning back in my seat, I close my eyes and groan. Needing to lie down, I fall forward and rest my head against my desk. I hold on to my belly and press harder. Taking deep breaths, I breathe through the pain, hissing like a snake.

"You okay?" a soft voice asks from above, startling me. When I flinch in fright, I let go of my stomach and the pain intensifies. My eyes widen from the sharp stabbing-like throb in my abdomen and when I look up, I see Britney. Concern is etched on her face and it totally confuses me. This woman has been nothing but a bitch to me since I started here, but now she's worried for me.

"I'm fine," I mumble through clenched teeth, and we both know from my tone, and the discomfort showing on my face, I'm not. "I'm prone to cysts," I tell her, surprising myself that I'm opening up to her. "I think this one has just decided it doesn't want to hang out on my ovary anymore."

"You poor thing, doesn't being a girl suck at times?"

"It sure does," I agree with her, leaning back into my chair. I wince as everything tightens and once again my insides feel like they're being pulled apart.

"Luckily for me, I don't have anything serious like that,"—*good for you, bitch*—"but a good friend of mine does, I've seen her when it's bad and it's not nice at all. Are you sure I can't get you anything?"

"I've just popped some meds, once they kick in, I'll be fine 'til I get home. Then I can snuggle on the sofa with my heat bag and some wine."

"Wine fixes everything," she jokes. "It's like a magic elixir that fixes things when it's shit and makes everything awesome even more awesome." I find myself laughing along with her, but instantly I regret it. The jiggling of my body from the chuckle radiates pain throughout my abdomen. "If you need to leave early, feel free to go."

"I'll be fine but thank you."

She nods, squeezes my shoulder, and walks away, leaving me totally confused. Who knew Britney could be so … so… nice.

My day continues and the pain progressively gets worse, and I begin to wonder if maybe it's something else. My meds usually dull the pain but not this time, they pretty much did nothing. I'm struggling to breathe and I can't focus for shit due to the pressure building in my abdomen. Closing my eyes, I breathe in deeply and decide I do need to go home. Standing up, I walk toward Bradford's office but after a few steps, my vision begins to dot. Reaching the door, I raise my hand to knock but he opens it before I get a chance. He startles me and I fall into him. He wraps his arms around me and I groan from the pressure of his hand on my hip.

"Fern, sweetheart, what's wrong?"

"I … I need to go to the hospital, something's wrong." And no sooner do I say that, everything turns black and I pass out.

When I come to, I'm lying on the floor in the doorway to Bradford's office. I can feel someone hovering and when I open my eyes, I see Bradford crouched next to me. Offering him a small smile, I whisper, "Hi!" I try to sit up but moving makes me feel woozy. I feel like I could vomit and as soon as that thought appears, I begin to heave. Pushing myself up into a sitting position, I cover my mouth just as a trash can appears before me. It arrives just in time because my donut comes up, actually everything in my stomach comes back up. Vomiting really hurts and the pain becomes unbearable and I begin to cry. Tears track down my cheeks as I continue to vomit and blubber on the floor in Bradford's office.

"Don't cry, baby, the paramedics are almost here," Bradford says from beside me. He's running his hand in circles on my back in a soothing way, and if I didn't feel like I was being torn apart from the inside, I'd be enjoying this moment.

Moving my eyes to the side, I continue to vomit and I see him staring intently at me. Worry is etched on his beautiful face and I hate that I'm the cause of that pain.

"I'm sorry," I murmur, wiping my mouth with the back of my hand. Handing him the trash can, I lie back down and curl into the fetal position, hugging my legs to my chest.

"Why are you sorry?" he asks me, brushing my hair off my face.

"Because I just vomited in your trash can."

"Don't be, besides, I don't have to clean it up, that's what I pay janitors for." This causes me to laugh and a searing pain shoots through my stomach and I scrunch my face up.

"Don't make me laugh," I cry through more tears.

"I'm sorry, but please don't cry, I hate seeing you cry."

"You've never seen me cry before," I tell him.

"I know, and I never want to see you cry again. When you hurt, I hurt, Fern."

If I wasn't on the verge of death, I'd be swooning all over that statement but right now, pain trumps swooning. "It hurts," I whine like a toddler, "it hurts so bad." Curling tighter into a ball on the carpet, I hold my stomach as the tears fall down my cheeks.

"I know, baby, but the paramedics will be here soon and you'll be getting the help you need."

The paramedics arrive and the cute young one asks me to roll to my back so he can assess me. "I just need to have a feel and we can go from there." Nodding, I take a deep breath and do as he asks. Once I'm on my back, I close my eyes and breathe deeply. I feel him lift my shirt up, he then grabs the side zipper on my skirt and gently tugs it down. He pushes my skirt over my hips, giving himself access to my stomach. I notice his eyes stare at the top of my panties before he refocuses and starts to assess me.

A growl from above has my eyes opening. When I look up, I see Bradford glaring daggers at the paramedic. The paramedic tries to school his smirk and I get the feeling this guy is going to push Bradford's buttons. Normally, I'd be all for it, but right now I wish he'd just get to work and maybe give me some hardcore drugs to dull the pain. He looks over my belly, poking and prodding me. He presses on THAT spot and I nearly jump out of my skin. I hiss through clenched teeth and I notice Bradford clenches his fists. *Please don't hit the good-looking paramedic, he has drugs and I need all the drugs.*

"Does it hurt when I do that?"

My immediate response is to growl *no fucking shit* but instead, I just nod, "Yeah, and the pain jumped up to a twenty when you pushed down low."

"I'm betting appendicitis, but we'll get you to the hospital and then after a CT and blood work, they'll confirm my suspicion."

"What happens then?" I ask, I don't know anyone who's had appendicitis before, so this is new territory for me.

"If it is appendicitis, it will be surgery for you to remove it before it ruptures."

Nodding my head, he finishes up his assessment, they then load me onto a gurney. I'm whisked away in an ambulance with Bradford by my side the whole way.

Just like the paramedic predicted, I do indeed have appendicitis. A few hours after arriving at the hospital, my doctor walks into the room "Fern, you have appendicitis and you're scheduled for emergency surgery later this afternoon." He looks to Bradford. "Your daughter will most likely be in overnight."

"She's not my daughter, she's my girlfriend," he growls and seeing him so alpha is such a turn-on. How can I be horny when I feel like my insides are being torn apart?

The doctor nods and then asks to look at my stomach again. He pulls the sheet down and lifts the gown the nurse had me change into. Like the paramedic, his eyes roam over my panties and my cheeks darken at the heated look in his eyes. What is it with guys and lacy panties?

"When did the pain start?" he asks as he pushes on my stomach.

"Last night it felt tight, but I thought it was just a cyst. I'm prone to them, but as the day wore on, it got worse. When I was at work, Alan the Asshole Appendix decided to have a rave and I passed out, and now I'm here."

The doctor continues to prod my stomach, his hand getting lower and lower to my panty line. When he pushes my panties down and out of the way, Bradford growls and comes closer to the bed. He takes my hand in his and presses a kiss to my temple, marking his territory. *Men.*

Sensing a shift in the air, the doctor quickly covers me back up and exits my room, saying something about following up on the test results but he just gave me the results. He pulls the curtain closed behind him, leaving Bradford and me alone.

"What was that?" I snap at Bradford.

"What was what?" He feigns innocence but I give him the eye. "I didn't like the way he was looking at you, and I really don't like how he had his hands all over you."

"He didn't have his hands all over me, he was assessing me."

"Assessing. Fondling. Same, same."

"Are you jealous, Mr. Manning?"

"No," he snaps too quickly.

"I think you are. You're jealous that the handsome doctor was touching me."

"He's not handsome, he's a handsy doctor, besides, no one touches what's mine."

My eyes widen at his words and if I wasn't in so much pain, I'd be swooning. *Damn you, Alan the Asshole Appendix, for ruining my sex life.* "I'm yours, am I?"

He nods and sits down on the side of my bed. He picks up my hand, brings it to his lips, and kisses my knuckles. My skin thrums where his lips just were. "Yes, Fern, you are mine. You've been mine since that first kiss and the day you told me you love me; it sealed the deal. You are mine forever."

"But—"

He presses his finger to my lips. "No buts, you are mine. End of story. Now, do you need me to call anyone for you?"

Shaking my head, I look at him. "No, I … I just need you. And for the record, you're mine too and I love you, even if you are a possessive caveman."

"Only for you, Sweetheart, only for you."

He leans down and presses his lips to mine.

The doctor returns and I'm officially admitted. Later that day, I'm whisked to surgery and they remove Alan the Asshole Appendix.

CHAPTER 23

Bradford

Seeing Fern collapse earlier nearly gave me a heart attack. I never want to see her in pain ever again. And I never want to see a handsy paramedic or doctor touching what's mine. If I wouldn't come across as a total asshole, I'd request only for females to assess Fern. However, when I return after her surgery, I don't want anyone touching her 'cause now the female nurse, Sarah, is flirting with her. Guess that's bound to happen when you're dating the sexiest woman alive, both sexes want to flirt with her. Even after an appendectomy, she's still sexy.

"You're here," she sings when she finally notices me standing in the doorway to her room with a bunch of sunflowers in my arms. She smiles and even though she's washed out and her eyes are glazed from the anesthesia, she's still beautiful.

"I'm here," I reply, walking over to her bed. I sit on the edge and brush a tendril of hair off her face before I take her hand and bring it to my lips. "How're you doing, Sweetheart?"

"I'm on the good drugs so I feel fan-fucking-tastic right now," she giggles.

"You gave me quite the scare earlier," I tell her.

"I'm sorry that Alan the Asshole Appendix decided he didn't want to live in my body anymore." A chuckle escapes me at the disdain she has for poor Alan, but then her eyes well with tears and she starts to cry. "Why didn't it want to be with me anymore? Why?" She's full-on sobbing now and I want nothing more than to pull her into my arms, but I know I can't jiggle her too much.

At the sound of her sobs her nurse, Ryan, comes into the room. "Ohh, honey," he says, "what's wrong?"

"My appendix didn't want me anymore," she tearfully tells him.

"Ohh, honey," he repeats again. "Trust me, you're better off without it. If it had burst, you'd be very sick and you'd possibly die. That would suck because then you wouldn't be able to gaze at this fine specimen of man who's been on tenterhooks waiting for you to return."

"You were worried about me?" she asks, looking sadly at me.

"Yep," I tell her. "As I said before, you scared the ever-loving shit out of me today."

"I'm sorry," she mumbles and she begins to cry again. "Will you stay with me?"

"Fern, I'm not leaving this place until you do. Remember, when you hurt, I hurt."

"Oh. My. God," Ryan coos, "you two are too cute but unfortunately, visiting hours are over and your man needs to go home. I know I'm not as good-looking as he is, but I am a good substitute … as long as you don't mind sharing me with three other patients."

"Are you sure he can't stay?" Fern tries again.

"Positive, but I'm sure if he brings coffees for the morning girls, they'll let him in early but I did not tell you that." Fern pretends to zip her lips. "Good," Ryan states. "Now say your goodbyes and then I'll get you up and into the shower."

"I'll do it," I growl at him.

"Such a caveman," Fern says, causing Ryan to groan and bite his lip.

"How about, I change her dressings and then you help her shower and change into her own clothes, but once she's back in bed, you have to skedaddle."

"Deal," I exclaim.

"Just no hanky-panky." His gaze flicks between the two of us. "You've just had major surgery."

"How long 'til we can hanky-panky again?" Fern asks Ryan.

"From memory, it's three to four weeks but your surgeon can clarify that tomorrow when he stops by."

"Ugh, Alan is fucking me over again," Fern complains, "and not in a good naked way. Asshole."

"You'll survive, Sweetheart," I tell her.

"I'm more worried about you. You're gonna leave me 'cause I can't put out."

"You really think I'm that shallow?"

"Well, no," she hisses.

"Then let's table the sex talk and let me get you into the shower."

"A sexy shower?" She waggles her eyebrows at me.

"Nice try, lady. Now, let the man do his job and then we can get you showered."

Ryan changes her bandages, telling us the incisions look good but I'm not sure how a stomach incision can look good. "Okay, now that's done, while you help Fern shower, I'll change her sheets, but once she's out, you need to leave."

Before we can reply, Ryan heads out of Fern's room. "Do you want me to help you up or can you do it?"

"Help would be nice, please."

"Anything for you, Sweetheart."

She shuffles into a sitting position, wincing in pain several times. Watching the woman you love struggle to get up hurts like hell. Once she's on her feet, we slowly shuffle into her attached bathroom and I help her strip off, being careful of the drip attached to her hand. Fern steps under the spray and I watch as the water cascades over her body. My dick likes it too and I'm at half-mast. Fern notices and then she starts crying again. "I can't play with that for three to four weeks," she whines.

"I'm sure we can find ways around it but, babe, you

need to stop thinking about my dick and sex. Right now, you need to focus on getting better."

"Well, you're going to need to wear a burlap sack for the next three to four weeks. I'm addicted to you, Bradford, and three to four weeks is forever."

"You will be fine, now, finish washing yourself so YOU can put a burlap sack on. Do you know how sexy you are all naked and wet with water cascading down your body? The water drips off your tits and sluices down between your thighs. I'm ready to bust a nut."

"And they say romance is dead," Ryan's voice comes through the partially open door. "I was just letting you know, the bed's made and there's a plate of sandwiches waiting for you."

"Thanks, Ryan," Fern sings out while trying to hold back a laugh.

"Thanks," I roughly growl, mortified he heard that.

"You're totes embarrassed right now, aren't you?"

"Totes," I playfully reply. "Now, are you ready to get out?"

"Yes." She nods and turns off the faucet and I wrap her towel around her. Running the scratchy thing over her body, I dry her. Dropping to my knees, I dry her legs and then I work on her stomach. Not being able to help myself, I place a gentle kiss on all three of her incision locations.

"I feel better already," she playfully tells me.

"Kisses make everything better," I tell her.

"Vagina kisses?" She waggles her eyebrows down at me.

"How about we test that theory in a few days' time

because I can't imagine that the tightening associated with an orgasm would be nice right now."

"You do have a point, but we will definitely test the vagina kiss theory in a few days' time."

And we do test that theory when she gets home—yes home, I refused to let her return to her apartment on her own—two days later. Fern tells me that it's the best medicine and she would like it three times a day. Who am I to deny a woman recovering from surgery?

CHAPTER 24

Fern

...two weeks later

I've been staying at Bradford's for the last two weeks and I know it's time I return to my crappy apartment, but waking up in his arms every day is bliss and living by the beach reminds me of Silverbell. I just love it here but I don't want to outstay my welcome, so I need to think about returning to my apartment. But today is my birthday, so I'm going to be selfish and focus on me. I mean, it's not every day a girl turns twenty-three.

I'm sitting up on the rooftop terrace, lazing on the outdoor lounger when a noise downstairs startles me, and I flinch in pain from the jolt. I'm at that healing stage where on the outside I feel pretty good but the insides are still healing. So the slightest movement can feel like I'm once again being torn apart like I was when Alan the Asshole Appendix had his vacating party, but it's in a different way now.

Pushing myself up into a standing position, I shuffle inside and make my way over to the stairs. They are the only part of this place I hate. Stairs and appendectomy recovery are not friends. I'm halfway down the stairs when a dark-haired man appears at the bottom of the stairs.

"Who are you?" I ask, just as he growls, "What the fuck are you doing here?"

"What's going on?" a voice says and when they come into view, I see Britney.

"Britney, what are you doing here?"

She looks panicked. "Dinner," she shouts. "We're all having dinner here tonight. My friend dropped me off and he needed the bathroom."

"Ohh," I reply. I don't buy it because it's my birthday and Bradford promised a night of just the two of us. I don't have the energy to deal with Britney and her Britneyness today, so I just go with it. "Well, you know where the bathroom is." Without another word, I shuffle the rest of the way down the stairs. The two of them just stand there and stare at me as I walk past them and head toward the kitchen.

Opening the fridge, I hear the two of them mumbling. Her 'friend' seems pissed and Britney looks shaken. Not my monkey, not my circus so I ignore them and grab the juice to pour myself a glass. Grabbing my favorite glass, I pour my drink and return the bottle to the fridge. Just as I close the door, I hear the front door slam shut and when I turn around, Britney is on the other side of the island, glaring at me.

"What's your game?" she spits at me.

"Excuse me?" I ask, completely confused.

"Your game," she hisses. "You're young enough to be Bradford's daughter and you're here slutting it up with him. You won't get his company or anything out of him, that's mine."

"Excuse me," I growl again. "I don't give a flying fuck about the company or his money, and what goes on between Bradford and I is none of your fucking business. Now, if you excuse me, I'm going to lie down."

Picking up my juice, I head toward the bedroom, leaving Bitchney—I inwardly chuckle at her new nickname—fuming. What's she playing at? What goes on between Bradford and I is none of her fucking business. By time I reach the bedroom, I'm pissed off. I shouldn't be surprised, that woman has that effect on everyone. Very few people at the office like her, they only tolerate her because she's married to Carlton and he's one of the big bosses.

Placing my glass on the bedside table, I kick off my slippers and climb onto the bed. The mattress hugs me as I lie back and I smile. I'm going to miss my afternoon naps when I return to the office. Before long, my eyes droop closed and I drift off to sleep.

I'm pleasantly woken with a kiss on the lips and, without opening my eyes, I know it's Bradford. Well, it better be, otherwise there's a burglar in the house who's kissing me. Blinking a few times, I finally keep my eyes open and I see Bradford hovering above me—thank God—and with the setting sun in the background behind him, he's like an angel. Shuffling over, I tap the mattress and he climbs onto the bed next to me. He rolls to his side and I turn my head so we're facing one another. Normally I'd mimic him, but lying on my side right now is not possible so this will have to do.

"Hi," I sleepily mumble, reaching up to run my fingers over his stubble.

"Hi, you looked so peaceful sleeping just now, but it's been eight hours since I kissed you and I couldn't help myself."

"Ohh no," I fake protest with my hand on my chest, "not eight hours. How did you ever cope?"

"Smart-ass,"

"I think my ass is more sexy than smart."

"Okay, let me rephrase, sexy smart-ass."

"Much better, how was your day?"

"Long. Yours?"

"Boring, I'm going stir-crazy here alone but I did receive a gorgeous bouquet of sunflowers for my birthday. Thank you by the way."

"You're welcome. If you were up to it, I'd give you twenty-three orgasms to celebrate but there's two things wrong with that plan."

"What issues?" I reach up and run my fingers through his hair, as he does a little contented sigh and that teeny tiny sound sets my insides on fire.

"Well, for starters, you're still recovering from surgery so there's no sex for a few more weeks and, in case you forgot, I'm old and would probably die before I came that many times."

"You might be old, Sir." I can't help adding that jibe in. "But you are one of the fittest men I know, and for the record, I don't think my vagina could handle twenty-three orgasms, but I will settle for twenty-three kisses."

"Now, that I can do."

He leans into me and presses a kiss to my shoulder. "One." He kisses the column of my neck. "Two." And on and on he goes. Kiss number twenty-four, for luck, is my most favorite. It's slow. It's sensual. It's perfect in every way that a kiss should be.

Pulling back, he cups my cheek and smiles adoringly at me. Then he lies back down beside me and we silently lie here staring at one another. I don't need a television show filled with hot men or books with alpha heroes because I have my very own, real life, hot alpha hero in Bradford.

My eyes drift closed and I fall asleep, again. When I wake, it's dark outside and Bradford is still lying next to me and staring at me. "I fell asleep. Sorry."

"No need to be sorry, it's your birthday, you can do what you want and you are also recovering from surgery." Nodding, I wipe the sleep from my eyes and roll to my back and then I remember, Britney. "Is Britney still here?"

"Britney was here?" he questions.

"Yeah." I nod. "She said something about dinner and with it being my birthday, I thought it was going to be a family affair," I tell him but he's looking at me blankly.

"That's news to me."

"Her friend was here too and it looked like they were arguing about something when they saw me. It's like they didn't expect me to be here or something."

"Hmmmpf, I have no clue. I'll call Carlton and check, maybe we had plans and I forgot since today is all about you."

Climbing off the bed, he pulls out his phone and dials Carlton. I watch as he chats with his brother, he looks tired and I don't like seeing him so run-down. I can only imagine the stresses of running a billion-dollar tech company and add in the nursing of me to the mix, it's no wonder he's run-down. As soon as I'm back on my feet, I'm going to do something to say thank you for looking after me, but how do you say 'thank you' to a billionaire who wants for nothing?

He hangs up and looks perplexed. "What's wrong?" I push myself up and wince when I move a little quicker than I should have. Bradford is immediately at my side, rearranging the pillows behind me.

"He said he didn't know about dinner and he has no clue who her friend is."

"That's weird."

"Yeah, it is. I think I know the person you're referring to though. He was at the office a few weeks back and they were arguing then too. When they saw me, they took off like there asses were on fire."

"What do you think's going on? You don't think she's cheating on Carlton, do you?"

"No," he immediately replies, "surely not. Is she?"

Not knowing what to say, I just shrug. Bradford's face

contorts with concern for his brother and I hate that I caused that. "I'm sorry," I mumble.

"Why are you sorry?"

"Because I just put that thought into your head. You already have so much on your plate, you don't need this too." And that's why I don't mention anything about the weird conversation with her earlier today. He doesn't need any more stress in his life.

"I'm fine," he says. I raise my eyebrows at him. "Really, I'm fine. Just a little tired."

"Well, come back to bed and we can have a nap before dinner. I've decided that you're taking me to Lonny's. And before you argue with me, I need to get out of this place and sitting in a restaurant isn't overdoing it."

"You've thought this through, haven't you?"

"Yep, now, come snuggle and then feed me."

"Yes, ma'am."

And that's what we do, we snuggle, nap, and then head to Lonny's. All thoughts of Britney and her man friend are forgotten and it's all about us, well me. Just like it should be on my birthday.

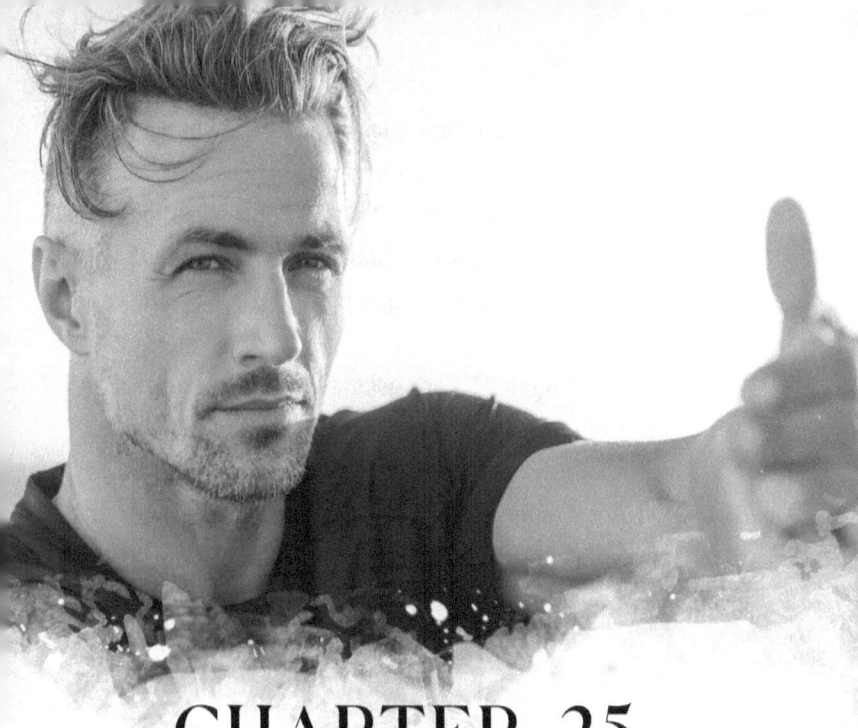

CHAPTER 25

Bradford

…a few weeks later

"Just stop," Carlton shouts at his wife and everyone in the office stops, well, everyone but the person he's yelling at. The sound of his office door slamming echoes around the room but you can still hear the heated argument, albeit muffled, through the closed door now.

The two of them are arguing more and more lately, and no doubt it's once again over Britney's desire to merge with Malum Industries. It turns out, the friend of hers from college is not in fact a collage friend and he's Malum Jax, the owner and CEO of Malum Industries. Britney and Malum have this grand plan to merge the two companies together and make us billions. Carlton and I are not on board with this plan, and it's causing issues between my brother and his wife.

"They at it again?" Fern asks as we walk back to my office after returning from grabbing coffee down the street.

"Yep," I reply, letting the 'p' pop as we step into my office. "I don't understand why she's so steadfast on this deal happening. It's a good deal for Malum, but not for us. No matter how Carlton and I put it, she won't budge. Luckily for us, we have a majority rules clause in the contract so unless Carlton and I both die and she inherits the company, we'll be safe."

"Don't even put that suggestion out into the universe, mister," she chastises me, poking me in the chest with her index finger.

"This is real life, Fern, it's not some episode of *Law & Order*."

"Clearly, you've never been to Silverbell 'cause that's exactly what would happen there."

"I call bullshit on that."

"I bullshit you not, maybe we should take a trip home and I can show you."

Staring at the woman across from me, I realize I'd travel anywhere with her and I would love nothing more than to visit her hometown. "Maybe we should plan a getaway to Silverbell. See if you can line it up for when you friends are there next."

"Really?" She squeals in delight and I nod. "Bradford, I'd love that so very much but just so you know, I'm one-hundred-percent positive they will give you the dad talk."

I've never been in a relationship that was serious enough for the proverbial 'dad talk.' And as much as I'm excited to meet her friends in person, I'm scared they won't approve due to our age difference. It's not an issue for Fern and me but I care about what her friends think, and I would hate to be the cause of any angst between them. I know Raven will be okay with it because he'd be pretty two-faced if he wasn't, he is in a throuple relationship after all. "I look forward to it, now, get back to work otherwise I'll have to spank you."

"You do realize that's not a threat, right?"

"I'm aware, but I can withhold your orgasms after turning your ass pink."

"That's fine, I have Clifford the Big Red Dick and if he's flat, I have these." She wiggles her fingers at me. She blows me a kiss and I plonk down into my chair and watch as she sashays out of my office, adding a swing to her step.

My lips lift in a smile as it hits me. Prior to Fern, I thought I was happy and content, but then this vivacious young woman swooped in and knocked me ass over tit. I've never been happier than I am right now. Then my smile drops when I think of my brother and his wife. They too were happy but now, they're at odds. Is their unhappiness due to my happiness? Is this the universe's way of leveling out the happiness in the world?

As I sit here and ponder this, Carlton knocks on my door and waltzes in. Without acknowledging me, he walks over to the bar in my office and pours himself a stiff drink, at eleven in the morning.

"You good?" I ask him but when he chugs it back and pours himself another, throwing it back immediately, I have my answer.

"Just fucking dandy," he snaps, before he pours himself another.

"Drinking won't fix it," I voice, earning myself a glare.

He lifts the tumbler to his lips but pauses. "Any suggestions on what will?"

Raising from my seat, I walk over to him and take the tumbler from his hand. "Nope," I honestly tell him, and I wish with everything I have I could fix this for him. "But you and I both know, this," I raise the tumbler, "won't fix it."

"I don't know what to do," he whispers and lowers his head. When he lifts it again, I see tears in his eyes. "Bradford, I love her with everything I have but I have a feeling, we won't recover from this. She's acting like a crazy woman."

"Dude, Brit has always been a wee bit crazy, she did marry you after all." He flips me the bird and it's nice to see him relaxed, even if only for a few seconds. "But this is next level crazy. Are you sure there isn't more to this? I mean, what do we really know about this Malum guy?"

"That he's an asshole, who every time we've met has flirted with my wife. He's a slimeball with a capital S."

"You noticed that too, huh?"

"Yep, I wish Brit had taken the line that Fern did."

That statement gets my attention, "What do you mean?"

"The first time he came here, he tried to flirt with Fern

but she told him to fuck off, he's old enough to be her father."

"Ummm, I'm older than that douchehole."

He shrugs. "Whatever the case, she crushed him. It was awesome to see. I wish Britney had done that, she's fallen for his charm, hook, line, and sinker. And now, she believes everything he says. Thank God we didn't give her a position that holds a vote when she came on board with us."

"Well, as long as you don't die, we'll be fine."

"Well, as long as you don't die, we'll be fine," he throws back at me.

"Okay, so no one's dying, we just need a way to kill this deal before it kills your relationship."

"Can I just stick my head in the sand and focus on the Frazer Inc. contract?"

"You can focus on that," I tell him, "but you and I are going to have to deal with this Malum thing once and for all. Let me think on it and I'll see what I can come up with."

"Thanks, bro, you really are the best brother a guy could ask for."

"Back at ya, Carlton, but stop with the day drinking."

He nods and walks out of my office.

Returning to my chair, I sit down and lean back, lacing my fingers behind my head and I start to think about ways to end this Malum thing once and for all. But that decision is made for me the following week when all hell breaks loose.

CHAPTER 26

Fern

This past week has been crazy at Manning Tech. On top of Britney's push to merge with Malum Industries, Bradford and Carlton are finalizing the pitch for Frazer Inc. and it's all-hands-on-deck. The three of us have worked into the wee hours of the morning every night this week and today, it's pitch day and everyone in the office is on edge.

Even, Britney is mellow today, surprising everyone. Maybe she's finally realized the Malum deal isn't the right call to make. Hell, even I know it isn't and I don't know shit about running a billion-dollar tech company or anything tech related to what the guys do.

My desk line rings and I answer, "Manning Tech, this is Fern."

"Fern, it's Margaret from the Neal Group, can I speak with Bradford, please? It's a dire emergency."

"He's about to head out for a meeting but let me see if I can grab him for you."

"Thanks," she says and you can hear the relief in her voice that I didn't blow her off. I know how much the Neal Group deal meant to Bradford.

Popping her on hold, I wheel my chair toward his door and lean back. "Bradford," I sing out, "I have Margaret from the Neal Group, she says it's urgent."

"Pop her through," he calls out.

"Will do, bossman."

Wheeling back to my desk, I put the call through to Bradford and get back to the email I was formulating. Five minutes later, I hear a roar from Bradford's office. Everyone freezes with wide eyes. It's so quiet you'd hear an ant fart. It's not often that Bradford loses his shit, actually in the almost six months I have been here, I have never seen nor heard him lose it. In the bedroom yes, but that's totally different. So for him to roar like that, something must be really wrong.

Standing up, I walk into his office and see him pacing like a wild lion. He's squeezing the back of his neck and mumbling to himself. He finally notices me and stops mid pace. "What's wrong?"

"There's an error with the Neal Group mainframe coding and they're down, meaning no business is coming in. It's costing them millions by the minute. Carlton is the only one who can fix the error, but we're due at Frazier Inc. in an hour."

"Can anyone else fix it?"

He shakes his head. "No, Carlton is the brains behind that one. It's the first of its kind and we were using the Neal Group as the test guinea pig, so to speak."

Staring at him, I tap my chin and think of what we can do and then it hits me. "What if I go with Carlton and help where I can, while you go present to Frazer Inc.? Two birds, one stone and when we're all done, we can head to Lonny's to celebrate fixing the Neal Group coding thingy-ma-giggy and you securing Frazer Inc."

"But we're a team."

"Yes," I agree. "You guys are a team and often teams need to split up. Divide and conquer and all that shit."

He stares at me and then gives me one of those smiles that melts my panties. "You are amazing," he tells me as he pulls me into his arms and plunges his tongue into my mouth. Kissing me deeply, so deeply I feel it in my clit. "And later tonight, I'm going to worship every inch of your body with my tongue and then I'm going to fuck you into a coma."

"Yes, please," I breathlessly pant, my already throbbing clit is now dancing as if she's at a rave. I wonder if we have time for a quickie but Carlton comes barreling into Bradford's office.

"We don't have time for fucking, we need to get to Frazer Inc. now. I just picked my car up from the mechanic. The tank is full and everything we need has been loaded."

"Change of plan," Bradford says, and he tells him what's going to happen now and you can see the relief on Carlton's face that we have this sorted. They are both Nervous Nellys at the moment and I'm glad I can help them out.

"Let's do this," I cheer after we've transferred everything from Carlton's car to Bradford's car. We split up and each do our thing. While Bradford conquers, Carlton and I crash … literally.

CHAPTER 27

Bradford

Sitting in Lonny's I wait for everyone else to arrive. Neither Fern nor Carlton are answering their phones, but cell service at the Neal Group is crap. If I know my brother, he will have demanded silence so he can focus on his work.

I'm on cloud nine right now. I nailed the presentation and Frazer Inc. signed on the dotted line, and as soon as Carlton and Fern manage to get the Neal Group back online, everything will be right in the world again and everyone will be happy.

Pouring myself a glass of wine, I'm just about to take

a sip when my phone rings and when I look at the screen, I don't recognize the number. It's an LA area code so I answer, hoping it's Fern or Carlton calling from a landline at the Neal Group, I answer. "This is Bradford."

"Mr. Manning, this is Officer Lutz with LAPD." I sit upright when I realize it's a police officer calling and that feeling of joy from moments ago plummets and my stomach is suddenly in knots. "There's been an accident. Your brother was involved in a serious car crash earlier this afternoon. He has been transported to the UCLA Santa Monica Medical Center in serious condition."

My heart begins to race as I process what he's telling me, this explains why they are late. A wave of nausea washes over me and I feel like I'm going to be sick. My brother was in an accident and here I am, drinking wine while he's possibly dying. "Shit," I hiss when I remember Fern was with him. "Fern," I mumble her name, " she was with him. Is she okay?"

"Fern Halstead?"

"Yes, she's my girlfriend."

"Yes, Ms. Halstead was also with your brother. She too has been transported to the hospital. However, I should let you know, she's in critical condition." He pauses and that uneasy feeling intensifies. "It's not looking good." This explains why they are late and why neither of them are answering their phones. I should have felt something was wrong, but I was on such a high after winning that bid this afternoon, I missed it.

"Shit," I say again, "what happened?"

"It looks like your brother ran a red light, a semi

coming through the intersection didn't have time to stop and slammed into them. Fern's side of the car bore the brunt of the collision, hence her critical state. How the two of them are still alive is beyond me." He pauses and then asks a question that has me raging. "Do you know if your brother has been drinking, Mr. Manning?"

"No," I shout into my phone. "He and Fern were working this afternoon and Carlton would never drink and drive. Never."

"We will wait for his blood analysis to confirm that." His tone pisses me off, he's already written Carlton off as a drunk driver but I know my brother. There is no way he would drive drunk. No way in hell.

"My brother was not drunk," I sneer into my phone. "Is the truck driver okay? Did you test him for drinking too?"

"He's fine but a little shaken up."

"Was anyone else injured?"

"No, just your brother and girlfriend. I'm about to head to the hospital to see if I can speak with your brother."

"I'll meet you there," I tell him and then I hang up.

Throwing some money down on the table, I grab my jacket and exit Lonny's and climb into my car. Pulling into traffic, I call Britney. I know she and Carlton are in a bad place right now, but deep down she still loves him. She'll want to be by her husband's side. Getting her voicemail, I leave a message asking her to call me. I can't leave a message like that on her phone.

I'm stuck in traffic due to an accident and I begin to wonder if this is where they crashed but as I pass by, I don't see a truck or Carlton's SUV so I sigh in relief. I'm not sure

I could handle seeing the wreckage.

Pulling into the hospital parking lot, I park my car and head inside. Walking up to the desk, I ask for my brother and Fern. I'm told to wait and someone will be out shortly. I want to yell and scream that I need answers but it won't do anyone any good.

After what feels like an eternity but would have been no more than ten minutes, a doctor calls my name out. I jump up and race over to him. "How are they? Can I see them? When can they go home? Please tell me something." I rapid fire the questions at him.

"Mr. Manning," he calmly says, "one question at a time. I'll start with your brother."

"Okay, sorry, yes, okay," I state.

"Your brother suffered multiple lacerations to his head. His right leg is broken in three places. He may need surgery but for now we are focusing on his other injuries. He also has three broken ribs, no doubt from when the air bags went off. One of them pierced his left lung and he's currently on his way to surgery. There's also damage to some of the vertebrae in his lower back."

"What does that mean?"

"There's a chance he may be paralyzed but until he wakes up, we won't know to what extent." He pauses. "You should also know that on the way to the hospital he crashed twice, his condition has been upgraded to critical condition. He is currently in a coma—"

"Fuck me," I say with a sigh.

"Mr. Manning, we are doing everything we can but until he wakes up, we will not know the extent of the injuries.

You need to prepare yourself for the possibility he will end up in a wheelchair."

Rubbing my forehead, I close my eyes and take a deep breath. Looking up at the doctor again, I ask, "What about Fern?"

"You are not family, so technically I can't tell you anything, but I can tell you she's in surgery and it's touch and go. We're trying to reach her next of kin, a Calliope Fischer—"

"That's her best friend but Fern is my fiancée." A white lie won't hurt right now.

"Really? I didn't notice an engagement ring?"

"It's only recent." *Like right now recent but I would say anything at this moment to get news on Fern but as soon as she is well, I'm making her my wife. I never want to go another day without her knowing just how much I love her.*

"I'm sorry, but I don't believe you, therefore, I cannot tell you anything until her next of kin advises me I can tell you."

"Fine" I hiss. "I'll try and reach Cali for you. Just tell me this, is she going to be okay?"

"I can't answer that, even if I could tell you anything. I cannot foretell the future, but I wish I could because it would make my job that much easier."

"Thank you, Doctor," I tell him. He leaves and I grab my phone to try and reach Cali. After googling for a few minutes, I manage to track down her number via Facebook and make a note to tell her to remove her number, that's not very safe but right at this moment, I'm glad.

Dialing her number, she answers on the second ring,

"Hello?"

"Calliope?"

"That's me, who is this?"

"I'm Bradford Manning, I'm—"

"Fern's boyfriend and boss, what can I do for you?"

"There's been an accident, the hospital is trying to reach you since you're Fern's next of kin."

"What happened? Is she okay? Where is she? Can I speak to her?"

She fires the questions at me like I did to the doctor only a few moments ago and I chuckle, but then I quickly school it because this is no laughing matter. "I don't know, they won't tell me anything since I'm not family."

"Just lie and tell them you're her fiancé."

"Tried that, he didn't believe me, but he will tell me once you give him permission to do so."

"Well, put him on the phone," she snaps. I can see why she and Fern are friends. They both have a similar tone when they speak and you can hear the emotion in their words.

"Sure, let me get him back here."

Walking over to the nurses' station, I tell her I have Fern's next of kin on the line and she tells me she'll page the doctor. I walk over to the door and wait for him to return. Calliope and I don't say anything to each other, but I can tell she's crying from the quiet sobs coming through the line. The doctor appears and I switch the call to speaker. After Calliope confirms she's Calliope, he gives us an update on Fern.

"Fern was unconscious when she was brought in. She has a broken arm and four broken fingers. She dislocated her collarbone. She broke her femur and ankle on her right leg and her femur and tibia on her left. Her left lung collapsed and she has multiple lacerations to her face and arms. She's covered in bruises from the impact."

Cali breaks down and I stand here, staring at the doctor, processing what he just said.

"Do you have any questions?" he asks after giving us a few moments to process everything he just told us.

"Is she going to be okay?" Cali timidly asks, her voice is soft and broken.

"Like I said to Mr. Manning earlier, I can't answer that but she is in the best possible hands here, Ms. Fischer."

"I'm jumping on a plane and I'll be there as soon as I can. Please keep Bradford updated while I'm in the air."

"I'll make a note, Ms. Fischer. Have a safe flight and I'll see you soon."

He walks away and I take the call off speaker. "Are you okay?"

"No," she cries. "I can't lose Fern, she's my sister from another mister."

"She's strong, she'll pull through this. I'll arrange for a private charter for you, it'll be quicker than commercial."

"You don't have to do that."

"I know I don't, but Fern will want you here when she wakes up."

"What if she doesn't?" Calliope sadly asks me.

"She will. She has too," I state, but even I'm not one-hundred-percent sure she'll recover from this. The doctor was less than enthusiastic but I'm hoping with everything I have that he's just being cautious.

Hanging up with Calliope, I book a jet for her and send her the details. Then I take a seat and wait for an update on Carlton and Fern. I plead with the universe to watch over them. I even barter saying I'll give everything away.

I can't lose either of them.

I just can't.

CHAPTER 28

Fern

"**D**ude," I say to Carlton as we pull into traffic after leaving the Neal Group, "you are a machine when you get in the zone. It was amazing to see you do your thing firsthand."

"I do kinda zone out, don't I?"

I nod but he's focusing on the road so I turn to face him, leaning my back against the door. "You work in such a different way than your brother. It's fascinating to watch."

"I think it's why we make such a good team. We have different approaches and it's why everything comes together how it does."

"I agree. I tried to text him while you were in the restroom and let him know we're on our way to Lonny's, but service here sucks. I'll try again when I get service."

"Sounds good, I left Brit a voicemail to let her know we were leaving but I haven't heard back from her yet."

Grabbing my phone from my purse, I ignore his Britney comment. That woman rubs me the wrong way, but she's Carlton's wife and Bradford's sister-in-law so I have to smile and pretend I can stand her. *The things we do for love*, I inwardly giggle as I bring up Bradford's name to text him but before I can start the message, Carlton starts chanting, "Shit. Shit. Shit!"

When I look up, I see an amber light ahead but the car isn't slowing down. He's pushing his foot down on the brake but nothing is happening. He's pressing on the horn, hoping to get the attention of those around us but it feels like everyone is oblivious to what's happening. The light changes to red and we enter the intersection. We've just about made it safely across when I turn my head and my eyes widen when I see a semi-trailer right there. Before I have a chance to do anything, the rig slams into the side of the car. The force jolts us.

Metal on metal screeches.

Glass shatters raining down around us.

My head is thrown around, as is the car. It rolls and rolls. A scream tears from my lips as we tumble and tumble. Finally, the car stops spinning but we're still sliding. Just when I think we're okay, I look up and see a brick wall coming toward us. We slam into the wall and a few moments later, the truck that hit us slams into us again. What's left of the car crumples around us. I scream as my body contorts into a position that's not normal.

Darkness envelops me and I give myself over to it.

※

I feel like I'm floating.

Everything is numb, but at the same time there's a pressure pressing down on me.

My eyes are glued shut, I'm trying to open them but I can't. It's like they are weighed down. I try to move but like my eyes, my body won't cooperate.

There's a loud beeping echoing in my head. In amongst the beeps there are voices but they're muffled and I can't hear properly. It's like I'm underwater and my ears are full of water.

Exhaustion slams into me and even though my eyes are closed, I drift back into the dark abyss of nothingness.

※

Like before when I woke, I feel like I'm floating again, but this time I feel everything. My body feels heavy. There's something in my throat and I don't like it. I try to lift my hands to scratch at it but I can't move. I'm paralyzed, is it from fear? Or has something horrible happened?

Why can't I move?

Why won't my eyes open.

I'm trapped and I don't like it.

Panic begins to flow through my system.

My heart feels like it's going to beat out of my chest.

There's a commotion but with the fog I'm trapped in, I have no idea what's going on.

A coldness filters through my veins and that floating feeling intensifies. The urge to sleep overtakes me and I once again drift off.

※

My eyes flutter and this time when I try and open them, they do but I quickly slam them shut. It's bright, ohh so bright. The light in the room is brighter than the sun. Edging one open, I squint into the glare and when it all comes into focus, I open my other eye and glance around the room. The walls are a pale green color, there's medical equipment everywhere, and I realize I'm in a hospital room. Then I find him, Bradford. My Sir.

He's sitting in a chair under the window, his head is bent in an awkward position and he's sound asleep. I take the time to look at him, he looks like shit. There are dark circles under his eyes. There's a stubble on his normally clean-shaven face and his clothes are rumpled. His normally glowing skin is not so glowy, and even though he looks a mess, he's still the most handsome man I have ever seen.

Shifting, I try to sit up but I can't and that's when I take note of my injuries and the casts. Plural. Both my legs are in casts and one is up in traction. There's another cast on my left arm. I smile when I realize it's my left and not my right, but the fingers on my right are in a splint and bandaged, indicating I broke them too. *What the hell happened?* It feels like I've been hit by a Mack truck. My body hurts like never before.

"You're awake," a soft feminine voice says, and that's when I notice Cali in the corner of the room. I didn't even see her there.

"What are you doing here?" I ask her, genuinely confused.

"Well, as your next of kin and sister from another mister, I needed to be here. You gave me the scare of my life, Fern Winifred Halstead, and you better not do that ever ever again. You hear me? When I got that call, I thought it was a joke at first, but it wasn't. You really were in an accident. I nearly lost you and I don't ever want to lose you. You're the peanut butter to my jelly."

"Can I be the jelly? I'm allergic to peanuts, remember?"

"Nope, it's your punishment for nearly dying."

"You want me to die from the peanuts too?"

"Fine, you're the eggs to my bacon."

"Better and for what it's worth, I'm sorry," I blubber. My eyes well with tears and all the emotions of waking up pour out of me.

"Don't cry, babe, you don't want puffy eyes as well as all this." She spins her finger around and I laugh. Well, I try to laugh 'cause the motion hurts and I groan through my tears.

"Fern," a deep voice I'd recognize anywhere says and when I look over, Bradford is awake. We silently stare at one another, my gaze roams over him. He looks exhausted but he's still the sexy Sir I love with every fiber of my being.

"You're awake," we both say at the same time, causing us all to laugh, but I stop when the pain becomes too much and then I start to cry harder.

"Babe," Cali says, walking over to me. She takes my hand and gently squeezes. The meds I'm on must be good 'cause I don't feel any pain, just comfort from my sister from another mister. While I'm staring at my bestie, the bed on my other side dips and when I turn my head, Bradford is sitting on the edge staring down at me. I look up and smile at him. He reaches out and cups my cheek in his palm.

Leaning into it, the tears fall faster down my cheeks and he brushes them away. After letting me cry, he pushes a stray hair off my face and tucks it behind my ear. "Hey, pretty lady."

"I don't feel so pretty, I feel like I've been hit by a Mack truck."

"It was a Peterbilt," he says, causing me to laugh but then I stop, my eyes widening as the events of the crash all come back to me.

Coasting down the street.

Carlton pushing on the brake and nothing happening.

The yellow light.

The intersection getting closer and closer.

The yellow changing to red.

Carlton is pushing the horn while I wave my arms, hoping people will see that we're in trouble.

We're almost through, we're going to make it.

Then the sound of metal crunching and glass shattering filters through the air.

Then I'm flying.

Then nothing.

"Oh. My. God," I voice, covering my mouth with my hand and FYI, covering your mouth when your fingers are in a splint isn't easy. "There was an accident." He nods his head. "Something hit us."

"A truck," he informs me.

Nodding, I try to remember the accident but it's all still kind of fuzzy and then my eyes widen when I realize Carlton isn't here. "Carlton," I whisper. "Is he okay?" No one says anything and when I look up at Bradford, I don't like the expression on his face. "Bradford," I demand, "where's Carlton?"

Silence.

"Bradford, where's Carlton? Is he okay? Please tell me he made it." The machine beside my bed begins to beep erratically as my heart rate accelerates. Fear is coursing through my veins over Carlton. My gaze flicks between Cali and Bradford but neither of them speak. "Tell me," I demand.

"Sweetheart—"

"Don't you sweetheart me, Bradford. Is Carlton okay?"

CHAPTER 29

Bradford

S he's awake. Her beautiful eyes are open but they lack the brightness that's normally in them, but she's awake.

She's staring at me and talking. She's talking with sass—confirming she is indeed back—and right now, she wants to know about Carlton. I know Fern, as soon as she hears about Carlton, she's going to blame herself because she has the biggest heart. That's one of the many many things I love about her.

"… is Carlton okay?" she demands and I know I can't ignore her question any longer.

"He's … he's in a coma," I finally tell her.

She nods her head, silently processing my words and shocking me, she doesn't demand to see him. She doesn't demand a rundown of his injuries. She doesn't ask for anything. I think she's in shock and even five days later, I'm still in shock too. I feel like I'm living in a movie right now because this cannot be my life. My brother is in a coma and my girlfriend was unconscious for four days. For the past twenty-four hours, she has been in and out of lucidity. The doctors assured me she'd wake when she was ready and thank fuck, she was finally ready. I was going out of my mind not seeing her gorgeous eyes.

"Can I see him?" she finally asks, but I shake my head and look toward her leg up in traction. Returning my gaze to her face, her flicks between me and her leg and her face falls when it registers that she won't be seeing him. "Ohh, will … will he be okay?"

That's the million-dollar question right now. I wish I had a fairy godmother to wave her wand and bippity-boppity-boo, he's awake and healthy. Then I'd get her to bippity-boppity-boo one more time and get her to make Fern whole again too. "We don't know," I tell her. "We'll have to wait for him to wake up and knowing how much he loves to sleep, we could be waiting a while." She nods and when she looks up again, her eyes are full of tears. She swipes at a stray one that falls, but as quickly as she wipes one away, another falls. She's sobbing now and, carefully, I pull her into my arms and hug her as she lets it all out.

"Thank you," she tearfully mumbles.

"What are you thanking me for?"

"I don't know," she chuckles, "it felt like the right thing to say."

Nodding, I'm about to ask her what she remembers of the accident but the nurse walks in and she kicks Cali and me out so she can assess Fern now that she's awake.

"Is she going to be okay?" I ask Cali as we both look through the window into Fern's room.

"Eventually, yes, she's strong that one, but it will take her a while. She hates relying on others and right now, she needs us more than she knows."

Nodding, I stare at the woman I love more than anything in this world and know Cali is right. This road to recovery is going to be tough for her. Pulling out my phone, I order her a bunch of sunflowers. I love seeing the joy on her face when she receives them and I want to see her happy again, even if it's only for a brief moment.

The nurse leaves and tells us we can head back in. Sitting back in my chair, I shuffle it closer to the bed and gently clasp her hand in mine, being mindful of her broken fingers. Running my thumb back and forth over her wrist, her eyes droop and she drifts back to sleep.

Sitting here, I watch her sleep, thanking the heavens she's okay. Cali just left to grab some coffee but not long after she left, Fern startles awake with a fright.

"Bad dream," she mumbles.

"Do you want to talk about your dream?" She shakes her head. "Can you, can you tell me what happened the day of the accident?"

She nods and takes a deep breath. "We'd left the Neal Group and were heading to meet you for dinner. The light changed up ahead but the brakes wouldn't work. There was nothing we could do. We coasted along and … and then we entered the intersection. We were almost through and I thought we'd be okay, but then BAM, something hit us. The sound is something I will never forget. I was knocked out immediately, I think. I … I don't remember anything after that."

"You were both lucky to escape alive. When I got that phone call, I thought I was going to die. It wasn't until I laid my eyes on you and saw you breathing for myself that I stopped freaking out. But then, when you didn't immediately wake up after surgery, that worry returned. Please don't ever scare me like that again."

"Not planning on being hit by a truck again, so I can promise I will be safe."

"Good, I can't lose you, Fern."

Leaving Cali and Fern to go get a few things for Fern, I swing by Carlton's room. Britney is here standing by his bed, her back is to me and she's mumbling to herself. "Hey, are you okay?" I ask, walking into his room. She jumps in fright and her eyes widen when she sees me. She slides her hands into her pockets and she shrugs at me. Stopping beside her, I pull her into my side and press a kiss to her temple. "He'll get through this, he's a tough bastard. Not even a semi could take him out."

She doesn't say anything, she just stares at her husband. She hasn't shed a tear since the accident, I think she's in shock. Worried that she's going to lose her husband and every day that Carlton doesn't wake up is another day closer to the end for him.

"No matter what happens, Brit, you're family and I will always be here for you."

She blankly stares at me but the moment is interrupted when the machines he's hooked up to begin to rapidly beep and an alarm sounds. Doctors and nurses descend on the room. Brit and I are ushered out and all we can do is watch on while they attend to my brother.

A few hours later, they confirm Carlton had a stroke but until he regains consciousness, we will not know the extent of the damage.

Britney leaves, mumbling something about 'can't watch him fade away' and she races out of the room. Dropping into the seat by my brother's bed, I take his hand and beg, "Please, bro, you gotta wake up. We need you … I need you."

CHAPTER 30

Fern

...two weeks later

Cali returned to New York a week ago but we FaceTime every day, sometimes twice a day. It was day a billion, well it felt like it had been a billion days, and she was curled up in the shit-green chair by my hospital bed and we were watching *Clueless* for the billionth time. Cher had just had her ah-ha moment about being in love with Josh and I just spat it out. "You need to go back to New York," I told her. "There's no point in you sitting by my hospital bed day in, day out."

"What?" she asked, pausing the movie but there was no need to because I'd made up my mind and we wouldn't miss any of the movie since we knew it words-for-word.

"You heard me, go back to New York."

"You're kicking me out?"

"Yep," I replied matter-of-factly. "I love you, Cali, but you need to go. I would rather you come back when we can do stuff together. It's pointless you being here."

"I'm offering you support," she defended her case.

"And you can do that from New York, I don't want you to fall behind on your studies 'cause I was in a little accident."

"It was more than a little accident, Fern. You. Nearly. Died." She pauses between each of the last three words for emphasis and to add salt to the wound, gives me that doe-eyed look that reiterates how scared she was.

"I did not nearly die, it's just a few broken bones."

"A few is three, you have a billion—"

"There aren't even a billion bones in the human body, Cali. What are they teaching you at FU?"

"Marketing, not anatomy."

"Thank fuck for that, 'cause you suck when it comes to the human skeleton and FYI, Cali, there's two hundred and six bones—"

"There's two hundred and seven in mine when you're naked," Bradford states, walking into my room and winking at me before he bends down and gives me a hello kiss that leaves me breathless.

"I'm gonna go get coffee," Cali says, slinking out of my

room while I make out with Bradford.

"That was quite the hello," I tell him when he pulls back.

"I missed you," he says with a shrug.

"It's been like two hours but missing me aside, what did the doctors say about Carlton?"

His face deflates and I just know what he's about to say. "There's been no change, he's still in a coma. The good piece of news is there's still brain activity. He's still in there."

"It takes more than a semi-truck to take he and I out. He's a fighter, Bradford, he'll get through this." And I mean it, I'm not just blowing wind up his ass to make him feel better. Carlton is one of the nicest people I know and that's why this is so hard. Why couldn't this happen to an asshole? The world works in mysterious ways at times, I just wish it wasn't so dire. I lost my parents to a gas leak and I could have lost my life due to car brakes failing. I think that's enough shit for my life, maybe after this it will be smooth sailing?

"Come here," I tell him and I pat the bed next to me, Carefully, he climbs on and hugs me, resting his head on my shoulder. Pressing my lips to his head, I whisper, "I love you."

"I love you too," he murmurs back, "I don't know what I would have done if I'd lost you."

"Well, I'm not planning on dying for a very long time, therefore, you are stuck with me, Sir."

"You just had to go there with the Sir stuff. You know what that does to me."

"Hey, if I have to be a horny, wanton mess, you can too, but do you think the next time you come, you can bring Clifford the Big Red Dick? I hear orgasms are great for recovery."

"For fuck's sake," Cali complains from the doorway. "I sure walked in at the wrong time, again."

"Ohh hush now, girl, you're a stripper. Hearing about my dildo is nothing."

Bradford's eyes widen and I shake my head at him and mouth, "later." He nods and takes the coffee Cali just handed him. She hands me mine and takes a seat. "While I was waiting for the coffees, I booked a flight home for Friday."

"Good," I tell her, "and as soon as I'm on my feet again, I'm coming to the Big Apple to visit you."

"Good, but promise me one thing?"

"What?"

"You don't ever scare me like that again or I will kill you myself."

"Deal."

Friday rolled around quickly and Cali left to head back to the Big Apple. It was another two weeks before they released me and today is the day. Today, I'm being discharged, but my leg will be in traction for another four weeks. So Bradford, being the amazing man he is, has converted one of the bedrooms at his place into a makeshift hospital room for me. He's hired a team of nurses to look after me since I apparently can't care for myself properly at the moment, and he advised me he will continue to bathe me once home too. Pretty sure, each wash session ends with an orgasm, for me. I've offered to blow him but the stubborn asshole says he's fine … and I have to admit, the thought of watching him pleasure himself is a turn-on, even if it's left me breathlessly panting for his cock.

Bradford has had to duck into the office just now and he's left me in the capable hands of my day nurse, Katie, and Mr. Woolley. She has just gotten me settled when there's a knock at the front door. She leaves me to answer it and a few minutes later, she returns with a bunch of sunflowers. "It must be Thursday," I mumble with a smile.

"What's so special about Thursdays?" she asks me as she places my flowers on the chest of drawers at the end of my bed.

"Bradford sends me a bunch once a month, on any given Thursday."

"That's so sweet, you have yourself a good man there."

"Yeah, I do," I agree with her, grinning widely. I wouldn't have survived this accident if it hadn't been for him. I hate that I'm confined to this bed and I wish I could do more, especially with Carlton being out of action. If only he'd wake up, that would be a huge relief to Bradford. To all of us actually. Britney is well, Britney, snapping at anyone at the drop of a hat. At least she's stopped pushing the Malum merger, but I would rather her be harping on about that than have Carlton be in a coma.

They let me visit with him today before we left. It was hard seeing him like that because that could have quite easily been me.

Staring at my flowers, I lie back in the bed Bradford

ordered and I drift off to sleep.

I'm pleasantly woken a couple of hours later when my man kisses me on the lips when he gets home from work. Blinking my eyes open, I look up at him and smile. "I could quite happily wake up with you kissing me like that forever."

"And I will happily oblige in doing that. How are you feeling?"

"For once, I don't feel like I've been hit by a semi, it's more like a Mini Cooper now." He chuckles and when he laughs like that, it does things to my insides. He eases himself down onto the edge of my bed and takes my hand in his. He kisses my broken fingers and then cradles my hand on his thigh. He's so caring and it's not in the overbearing kind of way.

"Well, that's a good sign. I can't wait 'til you just feel sexy again."

"You and me both but I really think being home, well, at your place, is going to be good for my recovery."

"Home, I like the sound of that." He reaches up and cups my cheek. "We should make it permanent."

"Excuse me?" Did he just ask me to move in with him? This is just a temporary thing while I recover and as soon as I'm back on my feet, I'll move back in with the girls. Besides, it's too soon to move in together. We haven't even been dating for a year yet.

"I want you to stay, Fern. Once you're better, move in here permanently. You pretty much stay here most nights anyway, and I love waking up with you in my arms and being able to kiss you whenever I want. So what do you say, wanna make this living thing permanent?"

My mouth opens and closes, I was not expecting this but now that he's planted the seed, I think I want it. Without thinking about it, my head starts to nod and I smile. "Yes, Bradford, yes, I'll move in here permanently with you, BUT I will contribute to the bills. I don't care that you're Richie Rich rich, I will contribute my share."

"You can do whatever you want, babe, I just want you here with me twenty-four seven."

"You know, if I wasn't confined to this bed, I'd blow you right now."

"You know, with you confined to that bed, I can be in control." My insides quiver and my eyes darken at his words. "I think we should seal the deal with a kiss."

"Then pucker up and kiss me … Sir."

"Brat," he teases.

He shuffles around on the bed and slides his hand down my throat. He gently trails his finger over my healing collarbone and down to my breasts. He circles my nipple and cups my boob, causing me to moan like a wanton hussy.

"My lips are up here." I circle my finger around my mouth and to tease him, I slide my index finger into my mouth and suck.

"I never said I was going to kiss your lips." He waggles his eyebrows at me and before I can question what he means, the duvet is pulled back, my panties are torn from my body, and he has his head between my thighs. He licks me from taint to clit and then circles his tongue around that little bundle of nerves. His fingers thrust in and out of my vagina while he kisses my pussy, sealing the deal of us moving in together. After an intense orgasm, he finally kisses my lips, on my face, and together we drift off to sleep.

Too bad for me, my happiness of living by the sea with the man of my dreams is only fleeting because in the coming weeks, my world is once again shattered.

CHAPTER 31

Bradford

It's been a month since the accident and Fern and I have officially been living together for a week, and I can say I have never been happier. I have moments where I feel guilty for being happy and living because Carlton is still in a coma. There's been no change since his stroke, and I don't know if that's a good thing or not. I don't know what I'll do if I lose him but thank-fucking-God, I have Fern. She's finally on the road to recovery, so that's one less worry I have.

It's almost nine and I'm just about ready to leave the office for the day and head home to my girl.

Home, I love saying that.

Home used to just be a place by the sea but now, now it's where I want to be all the time. Home is where Fern is and if I lost everything tomorrow, all I would need is to have Fern by my side and I'd be okay.

After nearly losing her, I will no longer take things for granted. In an instant she nearly lost her life and my brother is still fighting for his. Sure, Fern has a long road ahead of her but my girl is strong, she'll be back on her feet in no time … as will Carlton. I just know my brother will be okay. And I will be beside both of them, every step of the way.

I've just finished up some paperwork and am about to head out when my phone rings. I quickly answer when I see it's our family friend, Paula Talcott, who also happens to be investigating the accident.

"Paula, what can I do for you?"

"It looks like the brakes were tampered with," she says, getting right to it. There are no pleasantries when it comes to this woman, and normally, I love her directness, but right now, a heads-up would have been nice. It hurts to hear her talk without any emotion but then again, I need her to be taking this seriously.

"What do you mean?"

"The brake pads on Carlton's car were shaved down to a dangerous level. The brakes failing was no accident, Bradford, it was sabotage."

"But he'd just had his car serviced, he picked it up that morning and I remember him bitching about the loaner car they gave him while they did the service."

"I know, I spoke with the repair shop but they can't tell

me anything. They did confirm that the night before they were broken into. Suspiciously, nothing was taken and I'm positive that during the break-in, his breaks were tampered with. This was intentionally done."

"Are you saying someone tried to kill Carlton and Fern?"

"That's exactly what I'm saying."

"Who would do that?"

"Beats me. Does he have any enemies?"

"No," I tell her. "Everyone loves Carlton. You've met him, he's like the nicest person you will ever meet."

"A business rival wanting revenge?"

A laugh escapes me as I think of Malum Jax. He's an unscrupulous businessman but a murderer? No way, besides, what could he possibly gain from killing Carlton? "We have a few, but none I could see doing this."

"Think on it and if anything comes to mind, let us know immediately. This is now being treated as an attempted murder. I can no longer keep you abreast like I have because I won't jeopardize this case. Carlton and Fern don't deserve that, but whoever did this will pay. I won't be the cause of this case getting thrown out. I've already crossed the line updating you like I have, but you and Carlton mean the world to me." I smile when I think about our friendship. There was a point in time when I thought she and Carlton would get together, but he met Britney and, I guess, fate has another plan for Paula.

"I appreciate that, Paula, more than you will ever know."

"Bradford, I will not rest until I find who did this, and I will make that asshole pay for what they've done."

"Thanks, Paula," I pause, I don't want to voice this next question but I need to know. "Do you think he and Fern are safe now?"

"No, I don't. Until the assailant is apprehended, both of them are still in danger."

"Shit," I hiss.

"You might want to arrange security for both of them."

"Can't you do it?"

"We're short-staffed and to be honest, I wouldn't trust anyone here to do what they need to keep them safe."

"That's comforting to hear about the LAPD."

She laughs. "Just sharing a truth. Look, I'll send you the details for a firm I highly recommend, but I'd also suggest looking into another facility for Carlton. Somewhere with better security and doctors. I was already suspicious about this case and now, my Spidey senses are tingling."

"You think they will try again?"

"Considering they didn't succeed, yes, I think they will."

Shit. Fuck. Hell. "Thanks, appreciate it, Paula, and for the heads-up."

"Anytime. You know I'd do anything for you guys," I know she means that wholeheartedly. "Look after yourself and stay safe."

"Will do."

We say our goodbyes and I toss my phone down onto my desk, making a mental note to look for a new center for Carlton. Closing my eyes, I rub my forehead in frustration. "Fuck," I hiss, slamming my fist onto the desk.

"You all right?" Britney asks from the doorway.

Lifting my head, I stare over at her. She looks wiped and I realize that I'm about to add to her plate. "Take a seat, Brit," I tell her. "I have something to tell you."

"Why? What's going on, Bradford? Is Carlton okay?"

Nodding, I stand up and walk over to her. Taking her hand in mine, I pull her over to the sofa in my office and I push her down before I take a seat next to her. "I just got off the phone with Paula." She scrunches her face at the mention of Paula. The two of them have a love/hate relationship, more hate than love. Britney has always been jealous of the bond between Paula, Carlton, and me. At one point she even accused Carlton and Paula of having an affair, but Carlton loves Brit unconditionally, he would never cheat. When his wife is around, he sees no one but her. Prior to having Fern in my life, I thought he was just a pussy but now that I've found my penguin, I get it. "The accident wasn't an accident," I tell her.

"What?" Her eyes widen and her back stiffens.

"Someone tampered with the brakes."

"What?" she questions again. "Who would do that?"

Shrugging at her, I sigh. "I don't know who or why. Everyone loves Carlton."

"Maybe Fern was the target?"

"Why tamper with Carlton's car?"

"Right." She nods and stares off into space.

"I think Carlton and I were the intended targets but at the last minute, Fern went in my place."

She nods and a look crosses her face. "What do we do now?"

"Hire security to make sure whoever did it doesn't

come back and try again. I'm also going to look into a private facility for Carlton. Security at a place like that will be easier to arrange."

"Who would do this?" she mutters again, staring into the distance. Her voice and face are void of any emotion. Since the accident, this is what she does. She's turned into a robot, going through the motions without any emotion.

"I won't rest until I find the fucker who did this and when I do, they will regret the day they messed with a Manning."

Britney leaves and I go back to my desk and look for a place to send Carlton … and Fern.

She's going to refuse to go away but I will not jeopardize her safety. She was injured because of me and I could not live with myself if whoever is out for us tries again and succeeds in hurting her. For her safety, I need to send her away.

CHAPTER 32

Fern

...two weeks later

Bradford has been distant and aloof the last week or so. Whenever I ask him what's wrong, he brushes me off and says everything is 'fine' but we all know when someone says they are fine, they are anything but.

We're down on the lower-level deck, which is kinda dark and gloomy 'cause the weather is shit today. Maybe he's just in a mood 'cause of that but it feels like it's more. When he suggested we head out here with a bottle of wine, I thought we were going to have an enjoyable afternoon. The wine is enjoyable, the company? Not so much. Bringing my glass to my lips, I watch him over the rim and my mind begins to wonder if my recovery is finally getting to him? Or is it something else?

I wish he would just talk to me but men are stupid sometimes and right now, he's the stupidest of them all.

"This is a nice wine," I tell him after taking a sip.

"Yep," he replies and continues to stare into space.

"Crappy weather?"

"Mmmhmpf," he replies, not even looking at me.

Once again, a silence envelops us and when I can't take the silence any more, I slam my glass down on the table between us and growl, "What's wrong?"

"Nothing's wrong, why do you ask?"

"'Cause you're all in your head and you're giving me one-word answers. Has something happened with Carlton?"

"He was moved to another facility today."

"Why?"

"Because he can get better care and security there," he snaps.

"Why didn't you tell me?"

"Because I didn't," he snaps again. Then he turns to face me, finally he looks at me but I don't like what I see on his face. "I've arranged for you to stay at Limitless Therapeutic Rehabilitation and Wellness Center in Brookvale, Nevada."

"Why?"

"You'll get better treatment there than what I can offer you here."

"But I want to stay here."

"Too bad, I need you better and Limitless can provide

what I can't."

"How long will I be there for?"

He shrugs at me. "Until you're on your feet again."

"Will you come and visit me?"

Once again he shrugs.

"Why are you really sending me away?"

"So you can get better."

"Bullshit," I hiss, "I have a perfectly fine physical therapist here, why are you doing this?"

"I … I …"

"Be a man and spit it out, Bradford. You don't want me here anymore, is that it?"

He refuses to look at me.

"Answer me."

"I … I'm sorry, Fern. I thought I could do this but I can't." He stands up and slides his hands into his pockets. "Katie will help with the transfer tomorrow."

Tomorrow, he's sending me away tomorrow? What has happened in the last week? He asked me to move in with him for fuck's sake. There has to be more to this.

"Why are you doing this?" I cry, tears track down my cheeks as the man I love breaks my heart without an explanation.

"It's what's for the best."

"The best for who? You? Or for me?"

He turns toward me and I see heartbreak written all over his face. "I'll always love you, Fern." He bends down and presses a kiss to my temple. My heart shatters and I sit here in tears, watching the man I love walk back inside. I want to call out and stop him from doing this, but I refuse to beg him to not send me away. I still have my dignity.

The door to the garage closes and I hear his car turn over and then the rumble of the engine as he pulls out. Sitting here, I stare out at the beach with tears pouring down my cheeks. Bradford just obliterated my heart and I want to give up. Never will I love another man again.

CHAPTER 33

Bradford

It's been four months since I sent Fern away and the last four months without her have been miserable. Carlton is still in a coma and the authorities are no closer to figuring out who tried to kill him and Fern. Paula is doing everything she can but with no leads, the case has come to a standstill. Britney is still acting strange and I have a feeling she's hiding something from me.

This morning I flew out to Brookvale to see Fern. When I got to the center, I checked in with the manager, Linda, and spoke with her therapist, Nancy. They informed me Fern is doing well but when I saw how happy Fern was, I knew I had to stay away because I can't offer her what she wants, me. So for her happiness and safety, I left without saying anything to her.

Seeing her laughing and carefree was brilliant but at the same time, it hurt because she wasn't laughing and carefree with me. That's what I loved about our relationship, it was easy. The silences weren't awkward, the conversation was riveting, and the sex, holy hell was the sex perfect in every way. Hearing her call me Sir and seeing her ass turn pink when I'd slap it was erotic beyond belief. But until I find out who tried to kill them, for her safety, I need to stay away.

The flight home was uneventful, thankfully, and now Mr. Woolley and I are up on the rooftop terrace, enjoying the last of the afternoon California sun. My phone rings and I think about sending it to voicemail, but when I see it's the facility I sent Carlton to calling, I know I have to answer. Picking up my phone, I answer and when I hear the words, "Mr. Manning, he's awake," I begin to cry happy tears. Those tears turn to anger when she tells me that he's paralyzed from the waist down and at this point in time, he cannot speak either. The damage to his spinal cord was significant but as she pointed out, he's alive and awake. They will be running more tests in the coming days but so far, all is looking good that there's no brain damage.

I tell her I'll be there the next day and after hanging up, I call Britney. "He's awake," I tell her in place of saying hello when she picks up.

"What?"

"Carlton is awake," I tell her again. "The doctor just

called me. I'm heading up there first thing tomorrow to see him."

"I … I, he's awake?"

"He's awake, Britney. This is what we've been hoping for."

She keeps repeating he's awake, she's clearly in shock but I arrange to pick her up first thing tomorrow and we'll travel up to visit him together.

Picking Britney up the next morning, she's a nervous ball of energy the whole trip. "You okay?" I ask her when I can't take the leg jittering anymore.

"Yeah, I'm just nervous. What if he's not the man I fell in love with? You've seen those movies where someone wakes up from a coma and they aren't who they used to be, or they don't remember anyone. I'm just scared that even though he's awake, he won't be the Carlton we know and love."

"You can't think like that. He's awake, that's what we need to focus on. And if he's a raging asshole, it'll match your raging bitchiness."

She rolls her eyes. "I never thought the 'in sickness' part of our vows would ever happen."

"Life has a funny way of dealing sometimes. Just know, I'm here if you need me."

"Mmmhmpf," she replies and then she turns her head and looks out the window.

Ever since the accident, she's been on edge and not herself. Sometimes I get the feeling she's angry that he's still alive. It's almost like she wishes he'd died but that can't be right, she loves my brother. Deep down I know she does and now that he's awake, hopefully she will fall in love with him all over again.

Pulling into the parking lot of the facility, I turn off the engine. "Do you mind if I go in first?" she asks me.

"Not at all, he's your husband."

Without another word, she climbs out. I sit here and watch her walk inside. While I wait, I call Paula to let her know Carlton is awake. She wants me to call her back later after I've seen him and spoken to the doctors, she wants to know if he'd be able to chat.

When I hang up from her, I torture myself and flick through my photos of Fern. I should delete them all because every time I look at them I miss her dearly but until this threat is taken care of, I can't be around her.

After my torture session, I climb out of my car and head inside. The coolness of the air-conditioning hits my skin and I shiver. After checking in with reception, I head toward Carlton's room. I stop mid-step when I reach his room because it sounds like Britney is crying. That causes goosebumps to break out but then I hear her say, "Why didn't you die?" That statement piques my interest. Why is she saying that? She should be happy he's still alive, I know I am.

Peeking into the room, she's standing over Carlton, but any anger I had toward her 'why didn't you die' comment evaporates when I see my brother's eyes open, he's staring up at her. He's mumbling incoherently and he's rapidly blinking, something I never thought I'd see again.

"Carlton," I sing out and walk into the room. He moves

his eyes toward me and they well with tears. I throw myself at my brother and hug him. And the waterworks really flow when he lifts one of his arms and hugs me back. Pulling back, I stare down at my brother and smile. "Enjoy your four month snooze?"

His speech is slurred and I don't understand what he's saying. He begins to get agitated but from all that I've read about coma patients, this is to be expected. It will take time for him to get back to normal, for him to get back to the Carlton we know and love. And it will be a big adjustment learning to live in a wheelchair.

Britney and I don't stay long because Carlton is really restless. I promise to visit him again soon and then Britney and I head back to LA.

Dropping Britney off, I tell her I'll see her in the office tomorrow and then I stop in at Lonny's for dinner. They were excited to hear Carlton is awake and like usual, Isabella slaps me up the side of the head for pushing Fern away.

Speaking of Fern, I realize she'd want to know about Carlton so I pull up her number and press call. It only rings once and she declines the call, sending me straight to voicemail. Hearing her voice for the first time in months is a punch to the stomach and makes me realize how much I miss her. For a few brief seconds, I wonder if I did make a mistake sending her away, but then the memory of her in that hospital bed appears in my mind and I know I did the right thing.

Not wanting to leave this news in a voicemail, I hang up and text her the good news, without the mention of his paralysis or his frustrations.

BRADFORD: *Carlton is awake.*

Her reply comes in immediately.

FERN: *That's fantastic, thanks for the update*

Not wanting to let her go, I send another message.

BRADFORD: *Hope you're well. I miss you.*

FERN: *You can't say shit like that when you sent me away. I haven't heard from you in four months. You don't get to miss me. Lose my number. Forget you ever met me … 'cause I'm trying to forget I ever met you*

I guess I deserved that but her safety is more important than my happiness, I just hate that I hurt her in the process. Finishing up my meal, I head home and decide to watch Netflix. Mr. Woolley climbs up onto the sofa and joins me.

Scratching him on the head, he looks up at me and rests his head on my thigh. The three of us used to do this, lie on the sofa and watch reality television together and it's just not the same watching *Below Deck: Down Under* without her.

"What am I going to do about Fern?" I ask my furry friend and at the mention of her name, he barks. He misses her too. "I think I fucked it all up, buddy. Let me get Carlton settled and home and then I can see what I can do about her because I never should have let her go."

CHAPTER 34

Fern

For the first time in months, I was happy, well, for a few brief moments I was. When I got that text about Carlton last night, I smiled a genuine smile but then he had to go and ruin it by telling me he misses me. Fuck him, he doesn't get to miss me. He's the asshole who sent me away … and today he's the asshole who had me dreaming sexy things again. I woke up twice last night with my hands inside my panties. And twice he had me wishing I had Clifford the Big Red Dick to help get me off. My fingers just aren't cutting it anymore. *Damn you, Bradford Manning, and your sex god qualities.*

"What's got you on fire today?" my therapist, Nancy, asks me. "You're like the Energizer Bunny on crack."

"Nothing," I snap and as soon as I do, I immediately feel bad about it. "Sorry, I shouldn't be taking it out on you."

"I thought you'd be in a stellar mood after that silver fox stopped by to see you last week."

"Huh?" I scrunch my face up in confusion, "I didn't have any visitors last week."

"Yeah, you did. He asked to speak with me about your recovery and since the boss was with him, I gave an update on your progress. Then he and Linda went looking for you."

Bradford was here? No way, he wouldn't have flown

here to visit me, would he? And if he did, why didn't he speak to me?

"I've had no visitors since I arrived and even if he was here, I wouldn't want to see him, he's a dickhead asshole buttface and—"

"Dickhead asshole buttface, wow, he really did a number on you. What did he do?"

"I don't want to talk about it. Now, let's finish this set so I can be done for the day."

And because Nancy is amazing, she zips her lips—she literally mimes the motion and adds on a chucking the key away flick of the wrist—and she helps me with this last repetition. I'm so close to not needing my cane to get around anymore, and it's all because of this amazing woman. She and her aqua therapy are miracles.

Twenty grueling minutes later, we are done with my exercises for the day and she tells me to relax in the hot tub for twenty minutes, and who am I to deny my trainer. Sitting in the bubbling warm water is bliss. I just wish I had a cocktail in my hand and I was on a beach somewhere and not Bumfuck, Nevada.

Returning to my room, I shower and head to the dining room for an early dinner. The chef here is amazing, it's like fine dining each and every meal. I'm just finishing up my decadent dessert when "Love Is Here To Stay" by Frank comes on. My eyes well up with tears as I'm assaulted with memories of dancing with *him* to this song…

…The sun is setting and we're up on the rooftop terrace. This has become our spot when we are at home, and what's

not to love about it. The view is phenomenal. The couches up here are comfy, and even though the beach is bustling below, it feels like it's just Bradford and me left in the world.

We've just opened a bottle of red and Frank is singing in the background when out of the blue, Bradford looks over at me and offers me his hand. "Dance with me," he demands and like a moth to a flame, I place my hand in his and he pulls me up.

We walk over to the space between the furniture and the built-in barbecue. He spins me out and when he pulls me back in, he slides his arm around my waist and brings our clasped hands between us. I drape my arm over his shoulder and rest my head on his chest. The thrum of his heartbeat echoes in one ear, and in the other, Frank sings to us about love being here to stay.

Everything around me fades away as I focus on the words and Bradford. When I'm with him all my worries disappear. He makes everything better. Lifting my head, I look up at him. "I'm so glad to have you in my life," I whisper.

"The feeling is mutual, Fern." He smiles down at me and I feel that lip lift deep in my soul, it warms me from the inside out. I've never been happier and as if he's in my head, he says exactly that. "I have never been happier than I am right now and it's all because of you. I'm so glad I threw caution to the wind and kissed you that night. Even if for the next few days I fretted that you were going to sue me for taking advantage of you in the office."

An unladylike snort escapes me when I think about that weekend because suing him never even entered my mind.

"Did you just snort?"

"No, I, umm, breathed deeply."

"Also known as a snort but snorts aside, I'm glad we are where we are and now that I have you, you're stuck with me."

"Good, 'cause you're stuck with me too."

HA, I think to myself. When life got hard he pushed me away. He cast me aside and left me alone with no explanation whatsoever. Then I think about what Nancy said earlier, that he was here last week. Why was he here? And if it really was him, why didn't he come and see me?

Needing to get away before I break down in the middle of the dining room, I head back to the privacy of my room. I need Cali and Raven and I need them now. Without the support of my peeps, I would not have survived this. The emotional turmoil over losing Bradford has been harder to deal with than my physical injuries. Thankfully, I can always rely on the two of them, even if I'm sure Cali is hiding something at the moment.

By the time I reach my room, the tears are flowing. Swiping away the wetness on my cheeks, I climb onto my bed, curl into a ball and I continue to cry. My time here is almost up and when I leave, I don't know what I'm going to do. I don't want to go back to LA, not that I have a job or Bradford or a place to live. I'd be starting over, again. I also don't really want to go back to Silverbell, but I think maybe that's where I should go. I can get an apartment on Main Street, just like I've always wanted to. The world is my oyster and after Limitless, I can do whatever I want …

but what do I want?

CHAPTER 35

Bradford

I f I thought life with Carlton being out of his coma would begin to return to normal, I was mistaken. Sorely mistaken because the man who woke up is not my brother. My Carlton is laid-back and easygoing, but the Carlton who woke up is the complete opposite of that. He's constantly agitated and is angry all the time. Along with his lower half being paralyzed, it seems his voice box is too. He can't speak. He can't articulate what he wants and he grows frustrated at the drop of a hat. Somedays it feels like he's begging me with his eyes, and I wish I could speak eye because it would make life that much easier. I know his brain is still healing from the trauma but I just want my brother back. I lost the love of my life from this accident, I cannot lose my brother too. Hasn't he, me, us, been through enough already?

Britney didn't want to come up with me today and, to be honest, I'm fine with that. She's just as frustrating to be around as Carlton is at the moment. I'm starting to think she's up to something. She's always on the phone with secret calls and, like Carlton, she's agitated all the time too. Maybe it's her agitations reflecting in Carlton, or vice versa, therefore I think that some one-on-one time with him today without her is just what he needs.

I'm signing in at the front desk when his doctor approaches me. "Dr. Edwards, how are you today?"

"I'm good, Mr. Manning," he says. He's good but his mannerisms and facial expression tell me an entirely different story. "I was hoping I could speak with you before you visit with your brother."

"Of course." I follow him into his office, where he takes a seat behind his desk, and I drop into one of the chairs across from him.

"I ran some more blood work on your brother, due to his constant temperature spikes and the seizure that he had earlier this week. I, umm, I found something…" He drifts off and I hate the look on his face. If he tells me Carlton has cancer or is dying, I'm just going to give up. I can't take any more shit news.

"Spit it out, Dr. Edwards, is Carlton dying?"

"Not anymore."

"What?" I hiss in confusion, "What do you mean, 'not

anymore'?"

"Someone has been poisoning your brother, Mr. Manning."

Sitting across from the doctor, I rapidly blink and process what he just told me. Is this why Carlton is the way he is, because someone has been poisoning him? Is this the person behind the accident coming back to finish what they started?

"What?" I growl, sitting upright. "What do you mean, poisoning him?"

"Your brother's scans show little damage to his brain but his symptoms don't reflect that. My gut was telling me we were missing something so I ran his blood work again, but this time, I did a full analysis. Something we wouldn't normally do when a person wakes from a coma. I'm glad I trusted my gut because that's when I discovered it. Someone has been injecting strychnine and small amounts of arsenic into his system. The levels in his system are low so it's only been a recent occurrence, but we have started treatment to counteract the poisons."

"What does that involve?"

"We started chelation therapy?"

"Chela-what-tion?"

"It's the medical treatment for people experiencing heavy metal poisoning. The therapy involves the administration of chelating agents to remove the metals from Carlton's body. These substances bind to heavy metals and transport them out of the body. It can remove useful minerals as well but we can boost his system with supplements. This is the best treatment for the arsenic poisoning."

Nodding, I process the words. "You mentioned another poison. How are you treating that?"

"We are flushing his system with fluids and are administering medication for the seizures."

"Is he going to be okay?"

"You know I cannot guarantee that, but now that we know what we're playing with, we can treat him accordingly. Mr. Manning, your brother is strong, don't give up on him."

"What do we do now?"

"Medically, we are doing all that we can. As for the rest, we have to wait for Carlton's body to catch up to the treatment. I would also like to let you know that just before you arrived, I notified the authorities. A Detective Talcott called me back and she should be here shortly."

"Thank you, Doctor, I really appreciate it. I knew moving him here was the right move, but how did this happen? Only Britney and I visit him."

"And your sister-in-law's brother?"

"Britney doesn't have a brother," I tell him, immediately on edge.

"He has arrived several times with Mrs. Manning."

"No one but myself is to visit with him anymore, you hear me?"

"Yes, I will inform the front desk. I'm sorry we let this happen, Mr. Manning, but I assure you, we will treat your brother and get him back on his feet as quickly and safely as we can." Both our eyes widen. "I … shit, I'm sorry, it was insensitive of me to say that."

"Is it possible that he could walk again if we treat this poisoning?"

"I'm afraid not, the damage to his spinal cord was done in the accident, the poisoning bears no reference to that."

His desk phone rings and he excuses himself to answer. "Please send them in," he says and then hangs up. "Detective Talcott is here," he tells me and a few moments later, there's a knock at the door.

Paula and her partner arrive, but since Paula is here in an official manner, there are no pleasantries between us. Dr. Edwards brings her up to speed and I can tell Paula is just as pissed off as I am. She cares for Carlton deeply, deeper than I think she ever realized. It's only with him nearly dying that it's brought those feelings to the surface. Unfortunately for her, he's married and she cares too much to ruin his marriage. However, as we discuss everything, it becomes clear to me. There's only one person who could be doing this, Britney, but why?

Paula and her partner come up with a sting operation to catch Britney, or whoever it is red-handed. I'm told to act normal around her. It's going to be hard to do that when all I want to do is strangle the bitch and/or the person who has single-handedly ruined my life.

CHAPTER 36

Bradford

The sting operation went just as we predicted it would, and the culprit was caught in the act three days later. Like we suspected, Britney was caught red-handed trying to inject the poison into his drip. She was arrested for poisoning Carlton and is currently behind bars awaiting trial for attempted murder.

"You look like shit," my brother says when I walk into his room.

"I think I preferred it when you were in a coma," I tell him as I drop into the chair next to his bed and look at him.

It's amazing the difference a week makes. This time last week, my brother was being poisoned and was agitated because he knew what was happening, and he had no way to tell us it was his wife doing it. "How you doing?"

"Each day is better than the one before."

"That's good." A silence falls over us. "I'm sorry, Carlton."

"What are you sorry for?"

"For not realizing your wife was a scheming vindictive bitch who was poisoning you."

"She had us all fooled, Bradford. Me more than anyone. Should have known a knockout like her would have screwed me over like that."

"At least she's behind bars now and you're on the road to recovery. I say we forget all about her and Malum and we focus on getting you out of here."

"Yeah, but I'll never walk again."

"Walking's overrated and just think, now you'll get premium parking everywhere you go."

"Bradford," Paula berates me as she walks into the room and slaps me up the back of the head. "That's a horrible thing to say."

"It's true," Carlton says, nodding in agreement with my statement. "Another positive, I'll have a chauffeur for the rest of my life now too. Never again will I be DD 'cause I'm BS."

"BS?" Paula questions.

"Broken spine."

A chuckle escapes me and Paula just shakes her head at the two of us. Then her face changes and I know that friend

Paula is gone and Detective Paula is here with us now. "I have good news."

Carlton and I wait for her to continue but she just stands at the end of his bed, "And that news is?" I encourage her.

"Britney has been arrested an—"

"That's old news, Paula."

"If you let me finish, I know who was behind the accident."

"No fucking way," I growl.

"Yes, fucking way. Now, stop interrupting me so I can tell you all that I know. Turns out, you're lovely wife—"

"Ex," Carlton growls, "papers were filed today."

"Okay, turns out, you're lovely soon-to-be ex-wife was working with Malum Jax to get control of Manning Tech. The accident that wasn't an accident was orchestrated by the two of them."

"Fuck me," Carlton and I mumble at the same time.

"The accident was meant to take out both of you, leaving her the sole beneficiary of Carlton's estate and with you also gone, she would have gotten everything since you left everything to him."

"Fuck me," I mumble again. "How did you figure that out?"

"She made a deal with the DA to give them all the information she has regarding Malum and his involvement for a reduced sentence."

"Did she say why she did it?"

"Blackmail. She had an affair with Malum and he was holding it and a sex tape over her head."

"Did she ever love me?" Carlton dejectedly asks.

"I wish I could answer that for you, Carlton, but let's focus on the positives. You're alive and the threats, plural, are behind bars."

"And you now get sweet parking," I add, causing everyone to laugh. Then it turns serious again when I ask my next question. "So what happens now?"

"I've handed everything I have over to the DA and now they'll do their thing, but she and Malum will be going away for a long, long time."

After dropping all of that on us, Paula leaves. She had to get back to work, and it left Carlton and me alone to process all that was revealed.

"How you doing?"

"It's a lot to process but I think I'm relieved. Both threats have been taken care of and now I can focus on the future."

"And what does your future entail, little brother?"

"A new house, new car … and sweet parking spots."

Laughter bubbles up and I can't help but chuckle. I missed moments like this with my brother and now that I have him back I will cherish them, and life in general, that much more now.

CHAPTER 37

Fern

I've been back in Silverbell for a few months now and I'm happy … ish.

After I finished my rehab at Limitless, I went to New York to visit my bestie and my trip to the Big Apple was an eye-opening experience, that's for sure. I discovered many secrets that my bestie had been hiding from me and it made me look at her in a whole different light—in a good way, not a bad way. Who knew that sweet and innocent Calliope Fischer was not as sweet and innocent as we all thought? But truth be told, I'm so fucking proud of her. She took a shit situation and made it her bitch.

I settled back into small-town life again quite quickly and for the first time in a long time, somewhere felt like home. Upon my return, I followed my childhood dream and got an apartment on Main Street. It's exactly what I hoped it would be and more. I just love living by myself, which surprised me. I had always lived with someone and was worried my own company would bore me, but I'm fabulous and life is never boring.

Needing a job and not knowing what I wanted to do, I jumped from job to job for a while when I eventually scored a temporary gig at The Clifton. As of a few weeks ago, you are now looking at the new, permanent head concierge of The Clifton. Sure, it's not what I dreamed I would be doing with my life, but I actually enjoy it. My coworkers are so much fun to work with and Kane is an amazing boss, not as amazing as Bradford was, but he's still amazing, nonetheless. He cares for his staff and I can see why this place is always so busy, especially in the summer.

I've just gotten home from work and my phone pings with a text. Glancing at the screen, I see it's from Cali so I kick off my shoes, pour myself a glass of Pinot Grigio, and settle in for a texting session with my bestie.

CALI: *Guess who's coming to Silverbell for a visit?*
FERN*: Ryan Gosling?*
CALI: *No, guess again*
FERN: *Nick Bateman*
CALI: *Wrong sex*
FERN: *SMG*
CALI: *Why the hell would Buffy visit Silverbell?*
FERN: *I don't know, maybe to be my new BFF cause I*

killed my current one for holding out on who's coming for a visit

I know that'll piss her off and I knew three guesses ago it would be her.

CALI: *I am, you doofus. Mom and Dad are having an anniversary party for the big 25 this year*

FERN: *WOW, 25 years. That's crazy*

FERN: *You should stay with me*

CALI: *I totally should ... I'm sure it'll piss Dad off*

FERN: *Leave Daddy Fischer to me, he loves me*

CALI: *Sometimes I think he loves you more than he loves me*

FERN: *Well, he does have good taste in 2nd daughters*

CALI: *Third, I have a sister, remember?*

FERN: *Sister schmister, either way, he loves me and he will love for you to stay with me. That way he and your mom can bump uglies all night long after the party*

CALI: *LALALLALALALLALALALALA ... why would you put that image in my head? I hate you*

FERN: *No you don't, you love me*

CALI: *I'm debating that*

Cali and I text back and forth until my bottle of wine is empty and before you get all judgey judgey, it was an already open bottle when we started our text-a-thon. With a slight buzz, I climb into bed and dream sexy things about the man who I cannot forget. No matter how many different men I date, in the future, I cannot and will not ever forget about Bradford-fucking-Manning.

CHAPTER 38

Bradford

...four months later

D o you ever have those moments where you feel like you're living in a dream? Or in my case, a nightmare. Well, that's exactly how I feel most days and I've been living in this insipid cycle ever since Fern and Carlton were in the car accident. Well, the accident that wasn't an accident. That crash started the cataclysmic domino effect on events that followed, and it culminated with me sending the woman I love away, breaking both our hearts in the process.

When my brother woke up, I thought the craziness was behind us and life would return to normal but then we discovered the unthinkable. Something so outrageous you'd think we were in an episode of *Law and Order*, ending with my brother divorcing the woman who caused all the drama. Leaving me to stand by and watch the woman I love be with another man. I knew I shouldn't have Face-stalked her, but I needed to see her. I just didn't count on seeing her with another man.

"You look like your puppy died," Carlton says, wheeling into my office.

When I look up and see him, I smile. I never thought I'd see him in my office again. Yes, he's in a wheelchair but, thankfully, all the other issues from when he woke up are only around because his soon-to-be ex-wife was poisoning him.

"Do not even say that," I growl. Looking to the heavens, I smile upward, "Fate, please, if you're listening, ignore my brother. Mr. Woolley and I are happy together, please don't take him away from me too."

Carlton wheels over to me and stares at me. Then he glances at my computer screen and smirks, asshole. "You know, you can go to Silverbell and win her back."

"She's got a boyfriend," I dejectedly tell him.

"And you are the love of her life. You just need to pull your head out of your stubborn ass and go win the girl back."

"Just 'cause you're loved up and happy, doesn't mean the rest of us need to follow suit." The one good thing to come from this mess, Carlton and Paula. Seems while Carlton was in his coma, Paula visited him all the time and when he was going through the betrayal of his wife trying to kill him, she was once again there for him. It's so great to see him happy, like happy happy. He was never this happy with Britney, so it's fantastic to see.

"Yeah, it does, and because you're a stubborn fuck, I took matters into my own hands. You fly out of LAX in two hours. Go to Silverbell and get the girl."

Staring at him, my mouth opens and closes. Is it that simple? Can I just fly to Silverbell and swoop Fern off her feet? "Do you think it's that simple?" I ask him, fear lacing my words. I'm not sure I could handle her rejecting me.

"Nothing is simple when it comes to love, Bradford. But you have to ask yourself, is she worth it?"

"Yes," I state without even thinking.

"Then get on that private plane, be your charming self, and go declare your undying love and get the love of your life to love you back." Sitting here, I stare at him and silently process his words. "But you better get going now, otherwise you'll miss your flight."

Jumping up, I grab my things and race out of my office without so much as a goodbye to Carlton. Turning on my heel, I pop my head back into my office. "Thanks, man, wish me luck."

"You've got this, Brother."

Nodding at him, I race through the office and luck is on my side because the elevator arrives and then traffic is smooth all the way to LAX. I'm strapped into my seat, waiting for departure, and I think of Fern and wonder if this is going to be as easy as Carlton thinks.

Fingers crossed he's right because Fern is the love of

my life and I will do anything to win her back.

After checking into The Clifton hotel, I make my way up to my room, drop off my things, and after unpacking, I decide a drink is in order. I head down to the bar and pull up a seat. When the barman greets me, I order a glass of scotch and peruse the food menu.

"Scotch at three on a Thursday, rough day?"

Looking toward the voice, I see a gentleman around my age sitting a few spots down from me. He has a laptop open, files scattered on the bar top and a half-eaten burger on a plate, looks like he's settled in. "Rough few months, no years," I tell him.

He nods and asks the barman for another mineral water. "Kane Heatherington," he offers me his hand.

"Bradford Manning," I reply, shaking his hand.

"What brings you to our little seaside town?"

My mouth opens and closes, I can't tell him I'm here to win back the woman I sent away and I promised never to do that to, so I just shrug and take a sip of my scotch. He chuckles. "Enough said." Then he gets this look on his face, almost as if he knows what I'm going through and how I'm feeling. "Look, life's too short to not take risks. If she's worth it, take a leap."

Nodding, I bring my glass to my lips and finish the rest of my drink. "You know what, Kane, you're right. Thanks for the pep talk."

"Anytime."

Settling my tab, I decide to explore this little seaside town before I come up with a game plan to see Fern and win her back because Kane is right. She's worth the leap and the possible crash if this doesn't go my way.

It really is a picturesque place, it's just like a postcard. After walking around for a bit, I find myself on the beach. Dropping to the sand, I sit and stare out at the ocean. There's something so serene about the sound of waves crashing into the shore. I am so lost in the view and my head that I don't see the storm rolling in until it's too late. Jumping up, I race off the beach as it begins to lightly rain. I'm walking back to The Clifton when I see The Irish Giant. It's calling to me, so I head over to the quaint little tavern for a pint and to hide out from the impending storm.

Pushing open the door, I shake off the water droplets from my head and when I look up, I see her standing in the middle of The Irish Giant looking just as gorgeous as I remember. Our eyes connect and like that first day she walked into Manning Tech, my heart begins to beat rapidly within my chest, but the moment is broken when a man slides his arms around her waist from behind and nuzzles her neck.

Her eyes are still locked on mine when he whispers something to her and gets her attention. She smiles up at him over her shoulder. They get their drinks and I still stand here staring at her. I watch her walk away with him and that's when it hits me, I've lost her. Fern Halstead will never be mine again.

CHAPTER 39

Fern

Holy shit, he's here.

He's really fucking here.

Bradford Manning is standing in The Irish Giant staring at me and he's just as delicious as I remember. *Is he hotter?*

"Babe, pool table is ours," Tucker says, sliding his hands around my waist. I cover his hands with mine and lean into his embrace, but I continue to stare at Bradford.

What is he doing here?

Why is he here?

"Coming," I manage to squeak out.

"Yeah, you will be," he says, and if *he* wasn't across the room staring intently at me, my pussy would be soaked and I'd be dragging Tucker into the restrooms for him to use that magical tongue of his and get me off.

"You are such an animal," I tell him, half joking and half serious.

"Only for you, baby, but first, I want to ogle your ass bent over the pool table."

Pulling my gaze away from Bradford's, I look back over my shoulder at my boyfriend, and for the first time since Tucker and I hooked up, I don't feel that pull. That connection. I do however feel that pull and connection with the man on the other side of the room. I shouldn't want him like I do, but I've always been attracted to Bradford. Seems even with him smashing my heart and pushing me away, I still want him, but no, I can't go there. I won't let him hurt me again.

Walking over to the bar, I order our drinks and when Rosie places them on the counter with a smile, I smile back, the first genuine one since I laid eyes on *him*. Grabbing our drinks, I give Tucker his before grabbing mine. With my beer in my grasp, he offers me his hand. Looking between his hand and his face, I smile before placing mine in his. Lacing our fingers together, I follow him over to the pool tables.

Grabbing a high-top, we place our drinks down and Tucker begins to rack up the balls. I grab two cues and chalk the ends, trying to keep myself busy. I try and focus on Tucker and his sexy butt, but I can't. All I can focus on is the man I never thought I would ever see again. He's currently sitting in a booth staring at me. Even in the packed pub, my eyes keep finding his and without looking at him, I can feel his gaze on me.

Tucker steps up behind me when I bend over to take my shot, he rubs himself against my ass and I feel nothing for him. I'm a shitty girlfriend because I know without a doubt if Bradford were to step behind me and rub himself on me, I'd combust and come within two point five seconds.

Needing a moment, I take my shot and miss spectacularly. "Be right back." Before Tucker can say anything, I make my way to the restrooms.

Locking myself in a stall, I bring up the group chat with Cal and Raven.

FERN: *SOS ... I'm so fucked and not in the good way*

RAVEN: *Did you kill someone?*

RAVEN: *Kiss someone you shouldn't have?"*

CALI: *Screw you, Mitchell but this isn't about me, it's about Fern. Now, what's got you fucked and not in the good way*

FERN: *He's here*

CALI: *Who's here?*

RAVEN: *?????*

FERN: *Bradford is here*

FERN: *Bradford fucking Manning is currently in The Irish Giant and he's staring at me like he wants to eat me*

RAVEN: *So let him eat you alive. If I remember correctly, he's the best pussy muncher around—your words not mine*

FERN: *I'm with Tucker ... literally ... he and I are here on date night, but all I can focus on is the silver fox on the* *other side of the room*

RAVEN: *Babe, we know all Tucker the Fucker is good for is his tongue, again, your words not mine. Maybe this is the sign you need to move on*

FERN: *Why do you both live so fucking far away? I need you both right now*

CALI: *No, you need to go and speak to the man who still owns your heart*

FERN: *But...*

RAVEN: *Nope, no butts - even though you should totally try butt stuff. Butt stuff is ah-may-zing*

RAVEN: *Babe, you need to chat with him and you'll either get the closure you need or you'll ride off into the sunset together and get your HEA*

CALI: *Butt stuff aside, he's right, Fern*

FERN: *Is it wrong that I'd rather the butt stuff than to face Bradford???*

FERN: *But thank you for talking me off the ledge. You guys are the best besties a girl could ask for*

CALI: *Anytime, babe, anytime. Love you*

RAVEN: *You know we've got your back, girl*

Pocketing my phone, I take a deep cleansing breath 'cause I know they're right. I need to face Bradford and get closure. I cannot move on and be happy until I face him.

Unlocking the stall door, I walk out with my head held high. I'm Fern Winifred Halstead, I don't shy away from anything, and when I open the restroom door, I come face-to-face with *him*. No time like the present to face your past.

CHAPTER 40

Bradford

L eaning against the wall across from the ladies' room, I wait for Fern to step out. Waiting outside of restrooms is the creepiest thing I have ever done, but I need to speak with her. I can't go another minute without talking to her, but she's been in there for an awfully long time. I start to wonder if maybe she snuck out the window, but no sooner do I think that and the door swings open. After what feels like an eternity, I come face-to-face with her.

My Fern.

She is just as stunning as I remember. Her eyes are still

that gorgeous shade of green and her hair is the longest I have ever seen it. It flows in waves, coming to a stop just below her tits. Her gorgeous tits that I've missed caressing, sucking, and fondling.

"Bradford," she says my name breathlessly. "Wwww … what are you doing here?"

"I need to talk to you."

"You want to talk. To me. Outside the ladies' restroom."

Nodding, I swallow. "I want to talk with you and clear the air, please."

"You want to talk," she repeats and steps closer to me. My hopes soar but then she shoves me in the chest and glares at me. "You don't get to come to my hometown and want to talk. The time to talk has passed. You let me go rather than talking and I can't forgive you for that. I loved you, Bradford, I loved you unconditionally and when things got tough, rather than stick around you sent me to Bumfuck, Nowhere to recover. I hated you for that and I still hate you now." She pauses and takes a breath, her eyes well with unshed tears. "Bradford, what you did broke me more than the accident did. I never want to see you again."

And with one last shove, she storms away from me. She swipes frantically at her face and I can tell that she's wiping away tears. Once again I made her cry and that was the last thing I wanted to do, but I needed to talk to her and I still need to. I'll let her calm down, but Fern and I will talk. I need a chance to explain.

A few moments later, her boyfriend enters the hallway, I brace for the punch that's coming for upsetting his girlfriend but surprising me, he knocks on the ladies' restroom door.

"Fern, babe, you in there?"

Silence.

"Fern?" he shouts again and this time without waiting for a reply, he pushes the door open and steps in. Returning alone a few moments later, he finally notices me standing here. "You see a chick come out?" Shaking my head, he growls, "For fuck's sake, where the hell are you, Fern?"

He turns on his heels and storms off, back to the main part of the pub. Pushing off the wall, I follow after him and my eyes dart around the room looking for her, but I too come up empty. Fern is nowhere to be seen.

Walking back to my table, I finish my drink and throw ten bucks on the table and head back to the hotel. Stepping out into the evening air, I notice it's still drizzling but it leaves the town majesticalesque. Lowering my head, I put one foot in front of the other and head back to my hotel … at the top of the fucking hill.

Entering my room, I close the door and lean against the cool wood. Tonight with Fern didn't quite go how I expected it to. I need to come up with a new plan, but first I need a shower to warm up. Stripping off my wet clothes, I head into the bathroom. Reaching into the stall, I turn the faucet on and wait for the water to heat up. Once it's hotter than hot, I climb in. The scorching droplets pierce my skin like a thousand daggers, much like how my heart feels right now. I thought as soon as Fern saw me, it'd be like the movies and we'd run toward one another. She'd throw herself at me and after a passionate kiss, we'd make love and live happily ever after. Instead, I got a verbal lashing and a push on the chest.

Closing my eyes, I think about how beautiful she is. Even with anger coursing through her veins and her eyes throwing daggers at me, she's still stunning. No one compares to Fern Halstead, no one. My cock agrees because at the memories of Fern, it hardens. Sliding my hand down my chest, I grip my shaft and begin to stroke. I imagine Fern is on her knees, staring up at me as her dainty hand wraps around my shaft. She flicks her wrist and pumps my cock, up and down, squeezing tighter on the upward stroke. My balls begin to tingle and quicker than is appropriate for a man my age, or any man really, I whisper her name into the shower cubicle as I spray my release all over the tiled wall.

Leaning my head on the cold tiles, a wave of shame washes over to me. I just jerked myself off to images of the woman I hurt. I really am an asshole.

Climbing out, I dry myself off and pull on a pair of sweats. Calling down to room service, I order a bottle of scotch. It arrives fairly quickly. Pulling the cork out, I pour myself a glass, and climb onto the bed.

Leaning against the headboard, I sit here and sip at my scotch, wondering what I can do to win back Fern.

It's just after midnight and my phone pings with a text, picking it up I smile when I see it's from Fern.

FERN: *You're right, we do need to talk. We need to clear the air.*

BRADFORD: *When and where?*

FERN: *I'm working tomorrow 'til 2, can you meet me at The Clifton?*

BRADFORD: *I'm staying at The Clifton so that's perfect. I can't wait to chat.*

BRADFORD: *I've missed you.*

FERN: *Bradford, you can't say that*

BRADFORD: *Why not? It's the truth.*

FERN: *You sent me away and I've moved on. I shouldn't even be texting you. You're my ex. This is wrong*

BRADFORD: *It's just two friends catching up.*

As soon as I send that message I regret it, she's more than a friend. She always will be.

FERN: *Friends don't push friends away without a reason.*

BRADFORD: *I'm sorry, Fern, but I'll explain everything tomorrow.*

FERN: *Fine. See you then.*

BRADFORD: *Good night, Fern.*

FERN: *Nite Bradford*

The next day, I swear time ticks by slower than usual. I've been pacing in my room for the last hour. My nerves are frayed and my heart feels like it's going to beat out of my chest.

The alarm on my phone finally goes off, indicating I have ten minutes until my chat with Fern. And yes, I set an alarm so I wouldn't be late. I'm ashamed of myself for how I acted when I got back here last night, but Fern causes such a reaction that even now, my cock is twitching just at the thought of seeing her again.

Grabbing my phone, wallet, and room key, I head downstairs. I realize we didn't say where we would meet so I make my way to the concierge desk. Stepping into the lobby area, I smile when I see her. She's behind the desk and when she steps out and bends down to pick up a box, my cock is once again at half-mast seeing her sexy ass. I feel like a damn teenage boy right now. Sure, I haven't had sex with anyone since I sent her away but I do have a hand. I shouldn't be this worked up but then again, it's Fern I'm talking about. Her hair is pulled up in a messy bun and she's wearing a white blouse that's tucked into a navy pencil skirt and on her feet are the sexiest heels I have ever seen. Now I'm imagining her in nothing but those heels. Rearranging my hardening junk, I make my way over to her.

She looks up when she hears me and her eyes widen when she realizes it's me. I'm wearing dark chinos and a white-button down with the sleeves rolled up.

"Hi," she timidly says when I reach her.

"Hi," I reply back, nervous as all hell.

"I just need to finish unpacking this, head into the bar, and I'll be there in a jiffy." She doesn't wait for my reply, she just picks up the box and walks away from me. My eyes drop to her ass and I can't help but stare at it.

Turning around, I head to the bar, take the same seat as yesterday, and order myself a scotch while I nervously wait.

"Back again," a deep voice says from behind me and when I turn around I see the man from yesterday standing there, laptop once again in hand.

"Seems like you are too."

"Touché, but I own the joint so I have to be here."

Of course he owns the place, and then I wonder if he and Fern have hooked up. I know she's with that emo guy now, but this man must be around my age. He's good-looking. Owns this place. He's the Silverbell version of me. and then he says my girl's name and I growl lowly.

"Kane, what are you doing here?" Her voice is high and it almost feels as if she's ashamed to be seen with me, but then again, this is her boss and she probably doesn't want her colleagues knowing her personal business.

"I'm just heading to my office to have a meeting with Hannah. What are you doing here? Didn't your shift finish at two?"

"Yeah, I'm um …"

"She's meeting me," I voice when she trails off. His gaze then flicks between us. He smiles and without another word, walks away, leaving us alone.

"Hi," she whispers and I get a déjà vu moment from when I saw her earlier. "Do you want to head out to the terrace?"

"It's still raining," I tell her.

"Ohh, yeah, right." She seems nervous but then again, so am I. I'm just hiding it better.

"Your drink, sir," the barman says. "Can I help you, Fern?"

"A glass of Pinot Grigio for the lady," I tell him, not taking my eyes off of her.

"Thank you," she murmurs.

Silently we stare at one another until the barman places her drink down next to mine.

Picking up her glass, I hand it to her and when our fingers brush, the spark that's always been there between us ignites. Both of us gasp and go back to mutely staring at one another.

"Let's sit over here," she says, breaking the silence.

Following her to a table in the corner, I pull her chair

out for her. "Thanks," she murmurs and without thought, I place a kiss on her head like I used to when I'd do this for her. She gasps and lifts her gaze to mine.

"Sorry. Habit," I tell her as I take my seat across from her. She nods but doesn't say anything as we silently stare at one another. The silence is deafening so I ask, "How are you?"

"You really want to know?"

"Yes, Fern. I do, I never stopped thinking about you."

"No, Bradford, no." She shakes her head. "You can't say that to me. You sent me away when I needed you the most. My body may have been broken but my mind wasn't, until you sent me away without any explanation and that hurt. It cut me deep, Bradford. It cut me real deep." She swipes at a stray tear and seeing her so upset hurts more than I ever thought it could. "Tell me why, why did you let me go?"

"The car accident you were in with Carlton, it wasn't an accident."

"What?" she hisses, shock written all over her face.

"Britney and Malum conspired to take myself and Carlton out when he and I refused to merge the two companies. They orchestrated the accident, but it didn't quite go as planned."

"Oh My God, the joke from that day came true."

"Yes, but unfortunately for them, it didn't work because that fateful day I wasn't in the car."

"I remember, I stepped in at the last minute so you could present at Frazier Inc. and I went with Carlton in your place."

"Yeah." I nod. "You went in my place. You were hurt because of me. That accident was meant to take us both out, but instead you were injured and Carlton ended up in a coma."

"Holy shit," she whispers.

"It gets worse, she tried to kill Carlton again once he woke up.

"What? How? What?" She's totally confused right now.

"Carlton's doctor became suspicious after he woke up because he wasn't improving."

"How so?"

"Carlton wasn't getting better, even though his brain scan was clear. He was anxious and on edge and angry all the time. At first, we put it down to frustration at being paralyzed but now that he was awake, he was aware of what Britney was doing. She'd taunt him as she'd administer the poison. Gloating that one day he'd succumb to the poison and then it was only a matter of getting rid of me and then she could do what she wanted. She didn't count on the fact my brother is a tough bastard or the doctors at the facility care about their patients."

"Holy shit, I always knew she was a bitch but this is next level. How is Carlton now?"

"Alive. Healthy. Back at the office. Yes, he's in a wheelchair but he's alive and that's all that matters."

"Ohh my God, that's so amazing to hear. Please let him know I'm so happy to hear he's on the mend." She bites her bottom lip. "I have a question."

"Shoot," I tell her.

"Why did you push me away? You promised you'd

never let me go and then one day, that's exactly what you did. With no explanation."

"I panicked," I honestly tell her. "I was worried that whoever made the first attempt would try again. That they'd come after you to get at me, so I pushed you away. I … I never stopped loving you, Fern."

"Hence, my flowers on any given Thursday once a month."

"Hence, your flowers. I'm sorry I hurt you, but I didn't know what else to do to keep you safe."

"And am I safe now?"

Nodding, I reach over and take her hand. "You are. Britney and Malum are both behind bars now, and neither of them will be out for a very long time."

"How are they behind bars? I doubt they would just confess."

"When the doctor at the facility confirmed Carlton's poisoning, he called the authorities. Paula and her partner set up cameras in Carlton's room to catch the culprit and we caught Britney red-handed. She was arrested and it didn't take much for her to confess and throw Malum under the bus."

"Why did she do it?"

"She cheated on Carlton with Malum and he was blackmailing her."

"Holy shit, if only she was honest, you and I would still be together and Carlton wouldn't be in a wheelchair."

"We could still be together, if you'll have me back?"

She looks to me, her mouth opening and closing. I've left her speechless, something I never thought would ever happen.

"I … I, I can't, Bradford. You, you hurt me without any explanation. Yes, you've told me everything now but that hurt is still there and … and I'm with someone now." She sadly looks across the table at me. "I'm sorry, Bradford. I wish I could be who you want me to be, but I can't risk my heart again." With that, she stands up to leave. She walks around the table, leans down, and kisses me on the cheek. "I'm really glad Carlton is getting better and is safe. I hope you're both happy." She sadly smiles at me and walks out, leaving me alone with a broken heart.

Turning around in my seat, I watch her walk away, realizing this is what it felt like for her when I pushed her away. When the waitress clears away her untouched wine, it hits me. I've lost her and it's all my fault.

CHAPTER 41

Fern

...a few weeks later

Cali is flying in later today for her parents' anniversary party this weekend, and I cannot wait to see her. It's been too long since we had girl time in person and after Bradford's bomb the other week, I need a weekend with my bestie to decompress. I haven't told her or Raven what happened when I saw Bradford, and I don't know why I haven't. I've told them everything about us previously but not this time. Is it because they'll tell me I made a mistake telling him to go away? Or will they agree, effectively removing him from my life forever.

After cleaning my apartment and making sure the spare room is ready for her, I climb into my car and head to the airport to pick her up. Metallica comes on and I immediately think of Bradford and his love for the rock band. And as if the universe is fucking with me, just as I arrive at the airport, Frank-fucking-Sinatra comes on, reminding me of the nights Bradford and I would listen to him and dance under the stars.

Shaking off thoughts of him, I straighten my shoulders, head into the terminal, and make my way toward baggage claim. As soon as I see my bestie, I smile. "Cali," I shout out and then I race toward her. She walks toward me too and I open my arms wide. "You're here," I singsong into her ear, as I hold on to her tightly.

"I'm here," she replies, hugging me back harder than ever before.

When I look up, I notice Kane is also here and he's staring at her. He has a lustful look in his eyes, and I have everything crossed that these two have finally sorted their shit out. "Is he here for you?" She shakes her head and that's when I see Kane's son, Konrad, is here too. "Ohh, I see Konrad's here." The two of them walk toward us. "Fern Halstead," Konrad purrs, yes, he purrs. "Looking good."

If I wasn't with Tucker, I'd totally take him for a ride. My cheeks darken when I think of the dirty things he and I could get up to together. Then I picture he and Tucker taking me at the same time. Realizing I need to say something, I shake off the pornesque thoughts and say his name in greeting, doing the same to my boss. "You must be happy to have your son home early for the weekend?"

"You knew?" he questions me.

"Maaaaybe," I draw out the word but the tension between Cali and Kane is stifling and I need the gossip and I need it now. "It was great seeing you both, but we have to get going. Cali and I have big plans before the big party tomorrow night." Taking her bag from Kane, I grab her hand and turn away from them. Remembering my manners, I call over my shoulder, "Later, fellas." Then I pull Cali toward the exit.

"What? Why? Fern, have you lost your mind?"

"Maaaaybe," I reply with a shrug before I giggle. "But I had to get you out of there before you two started banging."

"Please, Mr. H and I will never bang. If he was turned off by a kiss, I can only imagine what he'd think if we, you know."

"Fucked like rabbits?" I offer as we reach my car.

"Your inner Raven is showing," she tells me and before she climbs into my car, she looks over the roof at me. "And I freakin missed it."

"I've missed you too," I say with a smile.

"So, what's new with you?" she asks as I pull out of the airport parking lot.

"As you know, I'm seeing Tucker."

"What happened to the other guy?"

"Francis?"

"No, Bobby?"

"It didn't work out. Seems I was missing a penis."

"No way?"

"Yes, way. I caught him getting a BJ from his roommate, Steve."

"You really know how to pick them." *Yeah, tell me about it*, I think to myself. I never went into detail over what happened with Bradford but then again, I didn't have all the details at the time. Now I do and well, I still am hurt over it. All she knows is that one day we were together and happy and I'd officially moved in, and the next, he was shipping me off to Bumfuck Nowhere, Nevada to recover. Realizing I never answered, I quickly throw out, "Says the woman lusting after her dad's best friend."

"Touché, lady. Touché. So, what's new around here?"

"It's Silverbell, there's always something going on but I haven't heard of anything so scandalous since you became Miss Sunshine." Not only has my bestie kissed her dad's bestie, but my bestie is a stripper in an exclusive club in New York. She started dancing to help pay her way through FU. She dances under the name, Miss Sunshine and my girl has the moves. When I went to visit her before I returned to Silverbell, I discovered her secret and one night I got to see her in action. She's since finished at FU, but instead of being a marketing guru using her degree, she's swinging around a pole using her tits and ass to bring in the big bucks.

"I find that hard to believe, to quote you, 'It's Silverbell.'"

"Speaking of your alter ego, when are you going to give up being Miss Sunshine?"

We have a heated discussion about it. I even beg her to move back here but she's stubborn and refuses to come back home because of Kane. *Damn men* messing with my life.

If I thought I was moping when I returned to Silverbell, Cal takes the cake with that one. She's miserable and so is Kane. There's a connection there, I felt it at the airport and at dinner earlier this evening, and right now, Cali is puttering about in my kitchen. Clearly something is on her mind, and I bet that something is Kane. I hate seeing my bestie so down and even if it's stupid a.m., I will do whatever it takes to make her smile again. "I can hear you thinking from my room. What's got you braining so loudly at stupid o'clock in the morning?"

Climbing onto the bed next to her, I take the teacup from her and take a sip, I'm disappointed when it's actually tea and not tea-quila. "You should be drinking tequila."

"Had two shots while I was making this." She taps the cup and then continues, "Two things. One, the tequila didn't magically make everything better. And two, that was some nasty cheap shit tequila."

"Tucker bought it, but I'll be sure to let him know he has shit tequila taste."

"You do that. The next time I have a midnight meltdown, I want the good stuff to commiserate with."

"Why are you breaking down alone, with tequila, in the middle of the night anyway?" She averts her gaze and I know she's hiding something from me. "Calliope Victoria Fischer, what are you hiding from me?"

"Ohh, you full full named me," she teases and I know it's her way of prolonging what she has to tell me. We haven't been best friends for years to not know each other's ticks. And yes, I'm aware I'm a hypocrite since I haven't told her the specific details of my accident and return to Silverbell.

However, this is about her, not me and the silver fox who broke my heart when he promised me he never would.

"And I will vagina punch you if you don't spill the beans. I know something happened when you went to the bathroom at the pub, now tell me."

"Fine," she hisses. "Mr. H pulled me into the handicapped restroom and we…"

"You fucked him in the handicapped restroom?" I screech, digging my nails into her arm and nearly causing her to spill hot tea all over herself. *Oops.*

"No," she scoffs, and I'm slightly disappointed she didn't do that. "And remove your freakin' talons from my arm."

"Sorry," I reply and remove my talons as she referred to my hand as from her arm. "So, did you?" I ask again, as I cross my legs and lean my elbows on my knees for story time.

"Have I ever been known to fuck in a restroom?" she throws back at me and I can't help but laugh, that's totally more of a me thing, but then again, my bestie has been doing a lot of things I never thought she would ever do.

"No, but I also never pegged you to be a stripper and…"

She sticks her tongue out at me and I'm tempted to squeeze it but I don't. I want the deets of what went down tonight. "We spoke, for the first time since the kiss and all the memories of that kiss came flooding back. We were, ummm, about to kiss again but someone knocked and we jumped apart."

"Kissblocked by some fucker." Shaking my head, I'm devastated for her.

"Yep, and then I agreed to meet him at The Clifton tomorrow to chat."

"Where you will finally fuck him," I state matter-of-factly. I maintain these two just need to fuck and get it over with. I'd bet my left tit that when they do, all the issues will float away and the two of them will run The Clifton and live happily ever after … as long as Mr. Fischer doesn't murder his BFF for fucking his daughter.

"I'm not fucking him at his workplace. Nor will there be any fucking. Nothing good can come from he and I being together."

"Says who?" She opens her mouth to protest but I raise my hand and give her the 'shut your piehole, I'm not finished yet' look. She rolls her eyes at me so I pinch her arm and continue, "The va-jay-jay wants what the va-jay-jay wants, Cali, and yours has wanted Kane Heatherington for as long as I can remember. Sure, there's a bit of an age gap. And, sure, he's your dad's BFF, and your sister is best friends with his youngest daughter, and you're currently a stripper living in NYC while he's a hotel owner here in Silverbell but, babe, what about what you want? What you both want? Personally, I think everyone else can shove a pineapple up their ass, pointy end first. Follow your va-jay-jay … and heart."

"They both want Mr. H," she honestly tells me and I'm glad to hear that.

"Then that's all you need to focus on. I know your dad, after the initial shock, he'll come around."

"I don't know about that, he still hates Raven after he caught the two of us practicing to kiss when we were eleven."

"Most people hate Raven 'cause, well, he's Raven."
She nods and we both smile. Raven is an acquired taste but
when you get to know him, he's the bestest. "You're now
twenty-three and a responsible stripper. Maybe you should
tell him you're stripping, that might soften the blow before
telling him you're in love with his BFF."

"He can NEVER find out about that. He'd be more
pissed at that than me and Mr. H being together."

"With Garrick Fischer, anything is possible, but in all
honesty, chat with Kane tomorrow and go from there."

"Mr. H and I have sooo much to chat about."

"Just try keeping your tongue out of his mouth, that
might help you iron things out." I pause. "You do realize,
if you two start dating, you will have to start calling him
Kane?"

"That's future Calliope's problem. Current Calliope is
going to finish her tea and then Calliope is going to go back
to sleep. Also, Calliope likes referring to herself in third
person. Calliope thinks Fern should try it."

"Fern thinks Calliope is losing it and is going to go back
to bed to have some middle of the night nookie, so Calliope
might want to turn some music on or get to sleep quickly."

"Calliope thanks Fern for the warning. Calliope also
reminds Fern that if it's not on …"

In unison we repeat, "It's not on."

Then I think about *him* and all the times we did it
without protection. Clearly fate knew not to tie me to him
with a baby 'cause I don't think I could handle that.

"Thanks for the midnight pep talk, Fern, I appreciate

it," Cali says.

Smiling at her, I pull her in for a hug and wrap my arms around her shoulders and squeeze her tightly. "Anytime, lady, anytime."

Kissing her forehead, I exit her room and head back to my room. Slipping back into bed, Tucker reaches over for me and cups my boob and then he begins to play with my nipple. For the first time in a while with him, my body sparks to life. A moan slips free and then he nuzzles my neck. "Babe," he whispers, "can I play with your ass?"

His words shock me 'cause we haven't ventured into ass play yet.

"What did you have in mind?" I inquire. I'm not one to shy away from anything sexual and my partner before Tucker, Bobby, really liked anal. Totally should have seen the signs there since I found him getting a BJ from his roommate, Steve, just before we broke up.

"Well, I know you love when I tongue that tight little cunt of yours." I groan at that word, I hate the 'c' word. "So I thought I might tongue your ass and when it's good and wet, I'll finger your ass and cunt, and once you've come all over my fingers, I'll fuck your ass."

"Where is this dirty talk coming from?" I ask him, genuinely confused because apart from his talented tongue, there's nothing much else going for him.

"I picked up that book you were reading where the chick has multiple partners and there was this scene, and well, I haven't been able to stop thinking about it."

"Are you saying you like my smut?"

"Maybe, now what do you say? Shall we get our smut

on?"

Nodding, I roll into him and press my lips to his.

Tucker gets going and before long, I'm crying out in ecstasy, "Tongue my ass, Tucker, tongue it good and then fuck it. Fuck it harder than you ever have before."

After Tucker does as he says he would, he rolls over and drifts immediately off to sleep. Climbing out of bed, I freshen up and then slide back in, but sleep eludes me. When I do finally fall asleep, I dream of sexy times with *him*. Thankfully, when I wake the next day, Tucker has already left because I feel guilty about dreaming of *him* with Tucker next to me, especially after he did that thing with his tongue and my ass.

I'm still worked up from my dream so I reach into my bedside drawer and fix the ache between my thighs with Clifford the Big Red Dick. Even though I come, I'm wracked with guilt. Tucker gave me an amazing orgasm in the middle of the night and I still dreamed of *him*. I am a horrible human being. Why can't I move on and forget? He promised to never let me go and he did let me go, but he still holds my heart, and I think he always will.

CHAPTER 42

Fern

Today has been crazy, and it all started when I woke up and Cali was missing, and I really hope right now she's getting down and dirty with Kane. Tucker just left and not wanting to cook, I decide to head to the bakery for a croissant and coffee.

Opening the front door, I run into the person who I was hoping would be naked right now with her crush. "Morning, hussy, where did you ru—" I stop when I see the man in question behind my bestie. "Ohh, good morning, Kane."

"Good morning, Fern. Lovely morning, isn't it?" He

seems chipper.

"Yep," I reply, letting the 'p' pop. My eyes dart between Kane and Cali. As soon as he leaves, I'm totally grilling her, the Spanish Inquisition will have nothing on me.

"I will see you later this morning, Calliope," he says to a beaming Cali.

"Sure thing, Kane."

My eyes widen when she says his name, his first name. My bestie immediately knows she made a mistake and I can't wait to see her squirm.

Kane says goodbye and I guarantee he's not even out of earshot when I start in on her. "Oh. My. Fucking. God, girl, you and I need to debrief now. Is it too early for wine?"

"Wine, yes … but maybe a mimosa—"

"It is a brunch drink," we finish that sentence in unison.

And over brunch, she fills me in on her adventures this morning, but one text message dampens her happiness and I'm once again left with a sad Cali. Thankfully, we have her parents' anniversary party to help set up. Hopefully she will have something to keep her mind off of Kane.

Later that day, we are all done and this place looks amazing. Cali, Jayne, and I are having a celebratory drink when out of nowhere, her mom asks, "So, Cali, honey, are you seeing anyone?" I'd just taken a sip and said sip sprays everywhere and I start to cough and splutter. Cali, the bitch, laughs at me while her mom, goes into mom mode. "Fern, sweetheart, are you okay?"

"I'm fine, Momma J, just went down the wrong way."

"That's what she said," Cali mumbles under her breath, causing me to now choke on a laugh.

"You'll pay for that, Fischer," I warn, but my bitch of a best friend just shrugs.

"Bring it on, Halstead."

Jayne shakes her head and smiles at us. "Please never change, girls."

"Not a chance," Cali and I say in unison as I drape my arm around Cali, pulling her in for a side hug.

"She's my Cal, Momma J, and she's stuck with me forever."

"More like you're stuck with me, babe." We smile at each other and then Cali looks to her mom. "Well, we all better get home and make ourselves beautiful."

"I'm already gorgeous," her mom sasses, just as her husband arrives, sliding his arms around her waist. "Hell yeah, you are." He kisses her cheek and Jayne's smile widens.

"My parents are too cute," Cali says, just as we hear her mom and dad agreeing to a 'quickie' before the evening's festivities. "And on that note, Fern and I are going to go. We'll see you both back here later."

"After their quickie," I mumble under my breath, earning myself a jab in the ribs. "Oof," I hiss, rubbing my ribs.

"Bye, girls," her mom sings out, and thankfully she didn't hear what I just said. Jayne would be mortified to know we heard her. "Thank you again for all your help, I couldn't have done it without you."

We say our goodbyes and then Cali and I quickly get out of here before we need to bleach our ears and eyes. But me being me, as we walk away, I start singing, "bom-chiccca-wow-wow," as we exit the country club, earning myself a smack on the arm and another rib poke.

"I hate you," she sneers.

"No, you love me. Now let's get home and make ourselves beautiful."

A few hours later, I'm almost ready when there's a knock at the door. "Can you get that??" I shout out because when I say almost ready, I mean my hair is done and I'm in my underwear about to slip my dress for the evening on.

"Sure," she calls out and then I hear her stomping down the stairs and then I hear, "Delivery for Fern Halstead."

"When will he stop?" I mumble to myself.

Walking into the kitchen, my eyes widen when I see them. He really went out with this month's bouquet.

"These are for you," Cali says.

Smiling at her, I walk over and pluck out the card, knowing it will say the same thing. Every month it's the same eight words. But this month, there's more than eight words and it's not a Thursday.

To brighten your day like you brighten mine.
It was so good seeing you.
I miss you and always will.
Bradford Xo

After reading the card, I throw it, and the flowers, into the trash. As much as I love sunflowers, I wish he wouldn't. How am I meant to move on when he keeps being all sweet like this?

"Everything okay?" Cali hesitantly asks me.

"Fine," I snap like a bitch and before she can probe me, I turn around and walk back into my bedroom, slamming the door behind me. Collapsing face-first onto the bed, I scream into my pillow. You'd think after all these months I'd be over it, but no. I still miss and love him as much as I did the day he sent me away. And to this day, I still think he sent me away because deep down, he blames me for the accident and for the fact that Carlton's now in a wheelchair. I know it's irrational to think like this and I know he did it for my 'safety' at the time but it still hurt that he wasn't honest. And why was I lucky to walk—not literally—away with only two broken legs and a broken arm? Fate is a fickle bitch at times and some days I wish it was me in the coma and not Carlton. It would have made life so much easier if the roles were reversed in the accident.

My phone pings with a text and a wave of guilt hits me when I see Tucker's name on the screen.

TUCKER: *Rain check on tonight, something's come up*

Even Tucker is starting to push me away. Am I that unlovable? Not wanting to dwell on the fact that no one wants me, I decide to let my hair down tonight and have a blast, and it's all going to start with an outfit change.

Pulling my dress off, I walk to my closet and change into a simple, little black dress that stops just above the knee. It has a deep V in the front—thank God for itty-bitty titties and tit tape—and then I slip on a killer pair of sparkly heels.

Spinning around, I take in my reflection and smile. I look and feel amazing, grabbing my clutch, I head back out to the living room.

"Fuck me, babe, you look hot," Cali sings as I come to a stop in front of her.

While I was changing, so did she and wow, she looks H O double T… hot. "Ummm, says the hot one." She's wearing a blush-pink dress that hugs her curves and looks sexy as hell, but is also classy at the same time. It's perfect for Cali and Kane is going to be hard all night when he sees my girl. "Girl, Kane is totally going to be sporting a woody all night long when he sees you in this."

"Doubt it," she snaps, clearly she's still pissed he ditched her earlier.

"Who pissed in your Cheerios?"

"No one," she screeches, but we both know someone did. "Fine," she harrumphs, "he canceled our date, catchup, what-ever-the-fuck it was earlier, and it hurt. This morning at the beach it was perfect and then he cancels. Is he having second thoughts? Is he just another douche leading a girl on?"

"Why did he cancel?"

"He said something came up."

"Yeah, his dick," I tease, earning myself a roll of her eyes but then I look at her. "Seriously, talk to him. Something probably did come up."

"But—"

"Nope, no buts. Give him a chance to explain. From what I know, he has never done anything to lead you on. Maybe he got scared and that's okay. I mean, he wants to bang his bestie's daughter, that's big—pun intended—and it definitely entitles him to a freak-out."

She smiles and I know my words have sunk in. "Thank you for pulling me off the ledge. I just …"

"I know what you just want." *'Cause I once had it with an older man of my own.* "Now let's get to this party so you can put your mind at ease and see your man."

"It's not like we can shout to the world that we are, whatever we are. We agreed to keep it quiet."

"You know that's not going to end well, right? Secrets are always exposed."

"I know, but what if we don't work out? Why implode Daddy's and his friendship if he and I go boom?" From experience, I can see that but she and Kane are different than Bradford and me. Those two have had years around one another. They've always had a bond and, really, it's no surprise this is happening.

"You two will definitely go boom boom." I waggle my eyebrows at her. "Your dad too, possibly, but when he sees how Kane treats you, he'll come around. Cal, babe, that man has it bad for you. Anyone with eyes can see you two have a connection. Follow your heart."

"But what—" I press my finger to my lips and shake my head, "Nope, no buts, unless you're into that. Just see what happens and stop trying to make everyone happy. As long as you're happy, that's all that matters. Now, let's go celebrate the love of your parents WHO I might remind you, got together against your nanna's wishes, and now look at them."

She nods and we leave for the anniversary party.

Pulling up at the country club, I park in the lot and Lady Luck is on my side and we get a spot close to the building.

Arm in arm, Cali and I walk inside and head out to the gazebo. In the dark it looks even more stunning. The fairy lights really add to the ambiance and I find myself smiling.

"This looks amazing," I say, "We did a fucking fantabulous job."

Cali heads off to find her parents and I head to the bar, wondering if I will ever hit a milestone anniversary with Mr. Fern, but since my current beau ditched me tonight and I think I'll be single again soon, I can't see that ever happening.

CHAPTER 43

Bradford

...Eleven months later

Thank God that week is over. It felt like anything that could go wrong did go wrong. Needing a moment to collect my thoughts, I grab a glass of red and head upstairs to the rooftop terrace. This used to be my favorite place to enjoy a glass of wine, but now I'm riddled with dozens and dozens of memories of Fern being up here with Mr. Woolley and me, or Fern and I exploring each other's bodies from head to toe before making love to her under the sun or stars.

Dropping down onto the lounger, I stare out at the setting sun and sigh. The sky is stunning tonight, filled with pinks, purples, and oranges but it means nothing to me. Life has little to no meaning anymore. I miss Fern more and more each and every day, but I need to respect her wishes. She wants nothing to do with me and it's my own fault. Well, no, I blame Britney and Malum. They fucked my life up and now the woman I love with every fiber of my being is living on the other side of the country, but it may as well be another planet.

Thankfully her and that Tucker the Fucker, are no longer together. How do I know that? I Face-stalked her, again. She made a beautiful post about being single and owning it, and followed it up with a selfie that caused my cock to harden immediately. If I hadn't been in the office, I would have whacked one out right there. I really should tell her to make her account secure because any perverted asshole—hello, waves hand—could look at her page and all her beautiful selfies, but she can never know I'm stalking.

Tonight I'm going to dinner with Paula and Carlton, apparently they have something important to tell me. Don't know why he couldn't just tell me at the office earlier, but when I voiced that I was told, "You need to get out and this isn't news to be shared in the office."

Looking at my watch, I realize I need to get my butt into gear, otherwise I'll be late and Paula is a stickler for time management, so I finish my wine and head inside to get ready. Once dressed, I order an Uber since I've already had a drink, and if tonight goes how I think it will, we will be celebrating with a few more drinks too.

The car drops me off out front of Lonny's and a longing hits me. This is where Fern and I came for our first date. I now love and loath this place. Shaking off my sad memories, I head inside. Paula and Carlton are already here, they are chatting with Lonny and Isabella and as I watch my brother, pride filters through me. I have never seen him happier. Who knew that for him to be deliriously happy, he just needed his ex-wife to orchestrate a car accident that left him in a coma and then start poisoning him when he woke up, so he and our longtime friend—who was investigating said accident and poisoning—would fall hopelessly in love.

"So, when's the wedding?" I jokingly say in greeting as I walk over to the four of them.

"You told him?" Paula screeches at Carlton.

"No," he defends himself, "and going by the shocked look on his face right now, he was just messing with me."

Paula turns to face me and when she realizes I was only joking, her anger dissipates, but she quickly holds out her hand and shows off her new bling.

"I'm so happy for you guys," I tell them, pulling them both in for a celebratory hug.

"Then you'll be even happier to know that you're going to be an uncle in six months' time too."

"No way," I say, shaking my head and grinning.

"Yes way."

"But how? I thought you know…" I nod at his crotch. "…you wouldn't be able to get it up."

"Viagra," he tells me and then he goes on to explain that around ten percent of men can conceive naturally with a little erection medication. That's more than I needed to know but I'm so happy for them both. If anyone deserves to be happy, it's my brother.

"Ohh," Paula adds, "and after dinner, we're flying to Vegas and I'm going to make an honest man of your brother."

My eyes widen again and I shake my head. "I was not expecting this when I came to dinner tonight, and I could not be happier for you both." Looking over to Lonny, I shout, "Lonny, a bottle of your finest sparkling … mineral water, please. We need to celebrate."

"You can drink, you know," Paula says, taking her seat.

"I know, that's for you," I tell her. "And Lonny, a bottle of your finest red for Carlton and me, please."

He nods and goes about getting our drinks. Isabella delivers our drinks and a few moments later, Lonny returns with our appetizers. After he leaves, we dig in.

For the first time since returning alone from Silverbell, I feel happy. I'm excited for my brother's future. A new wife and a baby. Life after the accident could have been dire for him, but he didn't let a little paralysis stop him from moving on. I just wish I could be as happy as him, but Fern made herself clear eleven months ago that it was over between us. Maybe it's time for me to move on too.

That thought was confirmed the following night. Carlton and Paula are now hitched and we hit up a club on the strip in Vegas to celebrate, and Fern just so happened to be at the same club. She was dancing with her friends and she looked stunning in her figure-hugging emerald-green dress. A guy sidled up to her and then the two of them started grinding all over one another. My fist clenched around the glass of scotch in my hand, I'm surprised it didn't break from the pressure. I'm also surprised I didn't throw the glass at his head when he lowered his lips to hers. Right there, in the middle of the dance floor, he kissed my Fern and that's when it hit me.

We are over.

I lost the best thing to ever happen to be because of Britney and her stupid vagina.

Not wanting to hang around and watch some guy maul the love of my life, I said my goodbyes to the newlyweds and made my way back to the hotel where I drank the mini bar dry to commiserate losing Fern.

I was done with women.

I will forever be a bachelor, living it up with my dog by the beach.

CHAPTER 44

Fern

...one month later

"**F**ern, babe, you need to fly to LA and win back your man," my best friend says out of nowhere.

We're sitting on the patio in her and Kane's backyard. She and Kane returned from their honeymoon a few days ago, and this is the first family barbecue since they got married. The rest of the family will be here later for dinner, but I needed my girl. Kane's famous brisket is brisketting away and Cali and I have just finished prepping the salads and side dishes and have taken our drinks outside to soak up the afternoon sun.

"But—"

"No, stop making excuses. I've watched you mourn Bradford for far too long." My mouth opens and closes because I'm speechless. I thought I was hiding my Bradfordbreak—like heartbreak but instead of my heart it's Bradford—from everyone, but clearly, I'm not a very good actress. "Babe, you weren't even this upset when you and Tucker the Fucker broke up. Hell, not even kissing that hottie in Vegas at my bachelorette party the other week turned your frown upside down."

"He really was hot, wasn't he?" I ask her, remembering the feeling of his tongue slipping into my mouth, but it wasn't *his* tongue. And his hands felt wrong on my hips and ass.

She nods and murmurs, "So hot."

That comment earns her a growl from Kane, who is clearly listening in to our conversation from his position near the grill, and I can't help but chuckle. She blows her husband a kiss, reaffirming that he too his hot—and I agree, not Bradford hot, but Kane Heatherington is still mighty fine on the eyes. After eye-fucking her husband, she focuses back on me. She takes a deep breath and I know I'm about to get a lecture. "Fern, look at me." Ignoring her, I stare into my wine glass, wishing it would magically give me all the answers. "Fern," she says my name in that mom tone that has you jumping to action immediately, and that's exactly what I do. Slowly turning to face my bestie, I stare at her. Married life suits her. Sure, she's only been Mrs. Heatherington for a couple of weeks, but she got her happily ever after with the man of her dreams and she's never been happier. She literally married the man of her dreams, Cal has dreamed of marrying Kane for as long as I can remember and it finally happened. I thought that might have been in the cards for Bradford and me, but I let my hurt pride push him away when he came here almost a year ago. There's not a day that goes by where I don't regret pushing him away when he came to Silverbell. My stupid pride got in the way and now I'm destined to be a lonely old cat lady, sans cats 'cause I hate cats.

"You know I love you, Fern—"

"And I love you too, Cal. You're my person, always will be."

"Stop with the sweet talking," I laugh at her. "Look, I want nothing but the best for you and the best for you is Bradford." My eyes widen at her. "You were never happier than when you were with him. Yes, he broke your heart when he let you go, BUT he did it out of love for you AAAND he came back. For you. Take a leap like I did and go after him."

"But what if he's moved on?"

"That's a risk you need to take, but what if he's still pining for you too?" My eyes widen at that, what if he is? It's been nearly a year since he came and told me everything and not a day has gone by that I haven't thought about him. He's probably the reason Tucker broke up with me. "Look, you'll either get closure or an orgasm."

"When did you get so wise?"

"I've always been wise, Fern, so what are you going to do?"

Staring at her, I think about it for a few seconds. "I'm going to eat me some brisket." Her face deflates but then I add, "And then, tomorrow, I'm going to go to LA and get my man." She smiles, it's larger than Ronald freaking McDonald right now, and it increases when I tack on, "Once he's mine, I'm never going to let him go."

She squeals like a kid and hugs me tightly. "That's my girl."

For the first time in a longtime, I'm excited about something. I just hope I don't get my heart broken, again, when I get to LA.

*

The plane touches down the next day after an uneventful flight and as soon as I step out of the terminal and breathe in the smoggy LA air, I know I'm where I'm meant to be. Closing my eyes, I sigh in contentment. A breeze picks up and my yellow sundress flaps in the cool breeze, causing goosebumps to appear on my skin.

Shaking off the chill, I walk to the curb just as a cab pulls up. A couple climb out and I jump into the recently vacated car. Giving the driver Bradford's address, he pulls away and we head straight to Bradford's place in Venice Beach. Traffic is light today and twenty minutes later, I'm standing in front of his house. Walking around to the beachside of his place, I walk up the side stairs. My heart races with each step I take toward the door.

Raising my hand, I knock.

Mr. Woolley barks and I smile, I missed that big furball. Knocking again, I'm met with silence and I frown, but when I look at my wrist and see that it's three in the afternoon, I realize he'll be at the office.

Dropping to my butt, I lean back against the door and wait for Bradford to return. While I wait, I text Cali.

FERN: Made it to LA

Her reply comes in immediately.

CALI: *Why are you texting me and not having hot and steamy reunion sex?*

FERN: *He's not home. He's still at work*

CALI: *So go to the office, win back your man*

FERN: *I can't do it there. I don't want any witnesses if he rejects me*

CALI: *If he rejects you, I'll fly there myself and kick his ass*

FERN: *As much as I would love to see you kick Bradford's ass, you're too pretty for jail. Just stay in Silverbell with your husband*

CALI: *Husband, I love hearing that word.*

CALI: *Holy shit, Fern, I have a husband!*

FERN: *Tends to happen when you get married to the man you've been dreaming about since you were two*

CALI: *I wasn't two when I fell for Kane, that would have been just wrong*

FERN: *And marrying your dad's best friend isn't?*

CALI: *No, it's not. We are mature responsible adults who are in love*

CALI: *...well, maybe just adults now **WINK WINK***

CALI: *But keep me posted, you've got this Fern*

FERN: *Thanks, Cal, you are the best friend a girl could ask for*

CALI: *I know ... and I'm totally telling Rave you said*

I'm the best

FERN: *Not what I meant and you know it*

CALI: *Whatevs **screenshot saved***

CALI: *Good luck. Love you*

FERN: *Love you too, Mrs. H*

Putting my phone down, I lean back against the door and wonder how this is all going to play out. Picking it up, I play that dumb brick and balls game that Bradford got me addicted too and after doing this level for the fifth time, I pop my phone on my lap and close my eyes. After a long day of traveling and waiting, I drift off and fall asleep waiting for Bradford to return.

I'm woken sometime later when the door I was leaning against opens and I fall backward. A very girly squeal slips out of my lips and when I open my eyes, I'm staring up at Bradford. Even looking at him backward and upside down, he's just as beautiful as I remember. His hair is a little longer but his eyes are still that hypnotic shade of green and his lips, his kissable lips are plump and perfect in every way that a lip can be perfect.

Suddenly, there's a fluffy head above me and then a massive tongue coming at my face. Mr. Woolley greets me with a face lick. "Mr. Woolley," I coo, "hello to you too." Reaching up, I scratch him behind his ears and he flops down next to me, resting his head on my shoulder.

"Fern," Bradford's deep voice says and I turn my attention back to him.

"Hi," I murmur.

A silence falls between us and I just lie here and stare up at the man who owns my heart.

"What are you doing here?" he finally asks.

"I, umm." Needing to bide my time, I push myself up and climb to my feet. Spinning around, I turn to face him and my eyes widen when I see a woman behind him in the kitchen. She's not much older than me and she's stunning. Blonde hair. Blue eyes. A killer rack and a smile that would light up a small village. My heart stops beating when I realize he's moved on. I've lost him to this other woman. He notices me staring and turns his head to see what I'm looking at. She smiles over at him, and it's like a punch to the guts when I see him smile back at her. "I, umm, shit," Before I can make this situation worse, I start backing out the door and across the landing. My gaze keeps flicking between Bradford and his girlfriend. My eyes well with tears and I continue to back away, but I'm unable to take my eyes off of them. I take another step backward but this time, my foot doesn't find the landing. I'm at the edge of the steps and I have nowhere to go. My arms flail about and I begin to fall backward.

One minute I'm about to fall down the stairs and to my death, and the next, a set of arms is sliding around my waist and I'm being pulled into a muscular chest. My heart is now rapidly racing for a completely different reason.

"Shit, Fern," he says, "are you okay?"

Staring up at him, a feeling of being home washes over me but before I can answer, he looks over his shoulder. "Sarah, can you get a glass of water for Fern, please?"

"Yes, Mr. Manning," she says, her voice sweet and soft.

"Sweetheart, are you okay?" he asks me again.

"I … I'm fine. I should go," I manage to spit out.

"Please don't," he says, his tone begging for me to stay and I don't know what to think right now. His new girlfriend is getting me a glass of water and here I am, lusting over someone I cannot have. Over someone who has moved on.

His arms are still around me when Sarah returns and I quickly push myself out of his embrace, immediately missing his touch.

"Here," Sarah says, handing me the glass. She looks concerned for me and I hate that. In any other situation, I could see Sarah and I being friends. She has that aura about her, no wonder Bradford fell for her. She looks to Bradford. "I'll head out and see you tomorrow."

"Thank you, Sarah," he says and then turns his attention back to me. "Please, Fern, come inside."

Without any conscious thought, I follow him inside and it's just as I remember. He escorts me into the sunken living room and I take a seat on his sofa and a little moan slips out. This sofa is like a cloud, it's so soft.

"You need to stop moaning like that, Fern, or I won't be held accountable for what I do to you." He stares down at me sitting here.

"What would you girlfriend think about that?" I throw back at him. My tone gives way to the disappointment I have in regard to him wanting to cheat on Sarah with me. I will never be *that* girl, no matter how much I want him.

"I don't know, what would you think about me cheating on you with you?"

Scrunching my eyebrows, I look up at him. "Huh?"

"Sarah isn't my girlfriend, Fern. She's my assistant."

"Ohh," I reply, relief flooding my system

"Yeah, Ohh. Now, girlfriends aside, unless you want to be mine that is?" Once again, I sit here and mutely stare up at him. He chuckles and drops down onto the sofa next to me. "Why are you here, Fern?"

"I, umm, shit, I thought I knew what I wanted to say but then I saw Sarah and I was …"

"Jealous?"

"Yeah, that." He smirks at my admission. "Don't go getting all cocky, mister."

"Hey." He raises his hands in surrender. "It's not cocky when it's the truth but for the record, I was jealous when I saw you with that guy."

Once again, I'm confused. "Huh?"

"I was in Vegas a few weeks ago." My eyes widen at that revelation. "I saw you on the dance floor with that guy and I wanted nothing more than to pummel him and tell him to back off, but I lost that right when I sent you away."

"I, um, you were in Vegas?" He nods. "Why?"

A smile graces his face. "Carlton and Paula got married."

"Oh My God, that's so amazing. Please pass on my congratulations."

"And they're having a baby."

"Holy shit, I didn't think that was possible when you were paralyzed."

"Neither did I, but turns out, it's just his legs that don't work. His swimmers are Olympic champions. They're due in six months' time."

"Well, you'll have to pass on double congratulations then."

"Carlton's happiness aside, what are you doing here,

Fern?"

Shuffling around to look at him, I lower my face and take a deep inhale. Lifting my head, I stare into the eyes of the man I have always loved. "I made a mistake," I whisper. "When you came to Silverbell, I should have said yes and if it's not too late, will you have me back?"

CHAPTER 45

Bradford

I've dreamt of this moment many times in the last year, and having it finally happen in real life is so much better than in my dreams. "Nothing would make me happier," I tell her. "I still love you today just as deeply as I ever did."

She shuffles closer to me and reaches up to cup my cheek. Leaning into her palm, I nuzzle in and smile at the love of my life. "I love you, Bradford, now and forever."

Reaching over, I cup her cheek like she's doing with mine. Running the pad of my thumb over her lip, I rest my forehead against hers. Our hurried breaths mingle together and I pour it all out. I pour out everything I have for this woman. "Fern, I fell in love with you the moment you walked into Manning Tech. The more I got to know you, the harder I fell. The day we fell in the boardroom, and we kissed for the first time, was when I started living. Being with you was the happiest time of my life. When I pushed you away, it was the hardest thing I have had to do, but your safety was more important to me. When we were apart, Fern, I never stopped loving you and now that I have you back, I'm going to love you and kiss you with everything I have for the rest of my life. You are it for me, Fern Halstead. You. Are. It."

"Bradford," she cries, "promise me one thing?"

"Anything," I declare and I mean it. I would do anything for this woman.

"Never let me go."

"Fern, Sweetheart, now that I've got you back, I'm never letting you go. You and me, we're a forever kind of thing. Now come here and kiss me."

And that's exactly what we do.

As soon as her lips touch mine, everything is right in the world again. Her tongue pushes into my mouth and kissing her is just as I remember, if not better. Our tongues battle it out. Our teeth clash and it's the best fucking kiss of my life. It gets better when our hands begin to explore each other's bodies. My skin comes alive under her touch and my cock is the hardest it's been since I left her in Silverbell all those months ago.

Fern climbs into my lap, straddling me. Not once do her lips leave mine. Sliding my hands up her back and into her hair, I gently pull on the strands and she moans into my mouth. The noise is music to my ears and has my cock thickening further between us.

She starts to rock against my shaft and I'm ready to combust. I need her to slow down or this will be over before we've even begun. Sex was always phenomenal with her and I want our first time again to be perfect. For it to be slow and sensual.

"I need you," she pants against my lips. Breaking apart, she stares intently at me. "I need you to fuck me now, Sir."

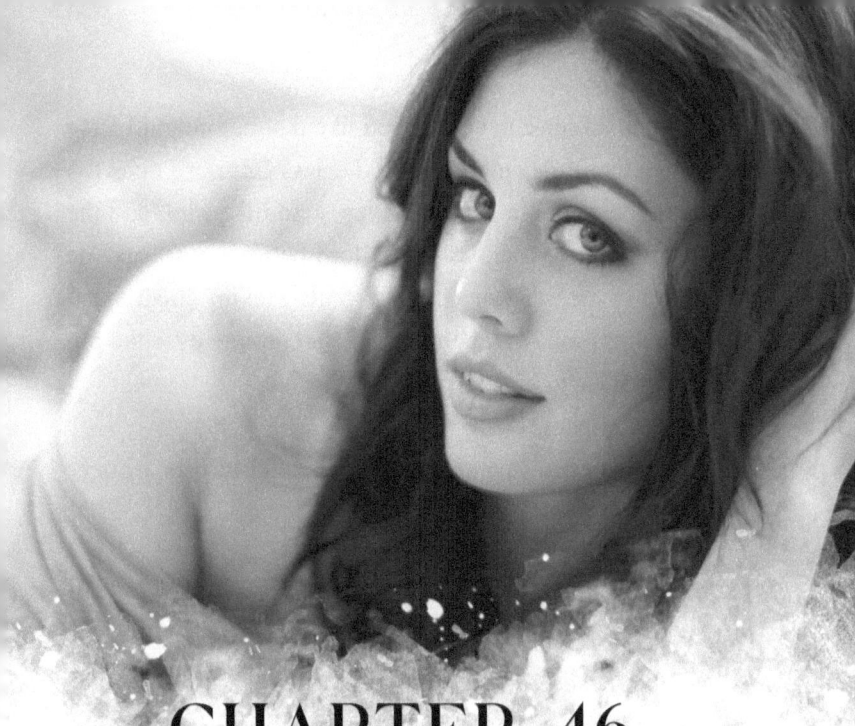

CHAPTER 46

Fern

"I need you to fuck me now, Sir," I demand. I've never been this worked up in my life and after a few little amazing kisses, I'm ready to combust. I need him to fuck me and I need him to fuck me now, hence my demand.

"Sweetheart, I want us to go slow. I want our reunion to be perfect."

"It will be perfect," I tell him, "but we have the rest of our lives to take it slow. Right now, I want you to pull your dick out of your pants and slide it into my vagina until we both fall apart. I need you to fuck me into the middle of next week." I have never spoken like that before but I have to say, I like dirty talking Fern. I guess Bradford does too because one minute I'm in his lap straddling him, and the next, I'm on my back with Bradford between my legs. He pushes my dress up my thighs—halla-fucking-lujah that I wore a dress today—and then he's licking me over the top of my panties.

"Yes," I pant.

He pushes my panties to the side and thrusts a finger inside.

"More," I plead.

He lifts his head up, continuing to finger fuck me. "Tell me what you want, Sweetheart."

"You, Bradford. I need you to fuck me."

With his eyes locked on mine, he pulls his fingers from me and I mourn the loss. That is until he hooks his fingers into the top of my panties and gives me the sexiest look I have ever seen. With his eyes locked on mine, he begins to slide my panties down my legs. He pulls them off, brings them to his nose and sniffs. "Fuck, I missed that smell." He throws my panties to the side and flips open the button on his pants, lowers the fly, and pushes them and his briefs down. Lifting my hands, I massage my breasts through my dress and watch as his cock springs free, I lick my lips at the sight before me and my vagina weeps with want.

His dick is rock-hard, the tip glistening in the afternoon light. He grips his shaft, giving it a few strokes while watching me play with my tits. "Can I help you?"

"Yes, you can guide that beautiful dick of yours into my vagina and fuck me."

"As you wish."

He shuffles between my thighs, lines his dick up with my slit, and with a flick of his hips, he thrusts balls deep inside me. My eyes roll back in my head and I see stars. Pleasure fills me from head to toe as our bodies rock back and forth. He reaches down, grips my ankle and lifts my leg up, resting it on his shoulder. From this angle, he hits that magic spot deep inside and a guttural sound comes out of me.

"I'm close," I mewl.

"Play with your clit, Sweetheart. Rub it for me."

Sliding my hand between us, I press on it and before I know it, I'm crashing over the edge, screaming his name as an intense orgasm ripples through me. My walls clench his dick tightly as I ride out my release. Bradford pumps a few more times and then his body stiffens and he comes deep inside of me.

He pulls my leg off his shoulder and collapses onto me, both of us panting. "You happy now, Sweetheart?"

"Deliriously so, Bradford, and I'm never leaving."

His head shoots up. "Does that mean you're moving back here?"

"I … ummm … I … I don't know. I didn't really think past us getting back together."

A silence falls over us and I hate it, one slip of the tongue and I may have ruined our reunion before dinner, but I should have expected it. I should have thought about this more, been more prepared. So I do the mature thing and change the topic and turn it back to sex. "Let's not ruin the moment, I think I have another round in me."

"Only one?" he teases. "You've lost your touch ORRRR those losers you were with just didn't know how to please a woman."

"Well, right now, there's no pleasing. You better put your money where your mouth is."

"I'd much rather put my mouth between your thighs."

"Have at it ... Sir."

And have at it he does ... several more times.

The next few days with Bradford are pure bliss and just like the first night I was here all those years ago, we fell asleep up on the rooftop terrace together. We've reconnected in every way possible, my poor va-jay-jay has had a thorough workout. Sexual compatibility has never been an issue with us.

Bradford is in his office catching up on some work so I decide to call Cali and Raven, I need my besties to help me gain clarity so I send an urgent SOS group text.

FERN: *SOS. Face chat in 5*

CALI: *Give me 10 ... I'm busy*

RAVEN: *I need 15 ... I'm doubly busy*

FERN: *You are both hos, chat soon Xo*

With a cup of coffee in hand, I head up to the terrace and get comfy. Ten minutes later, I dial Cali and Raven.

"Hey hey ho," Cali says in greeting when she joins the FaceTime call. "I'm surprised you're calling, I thought you'd be in Orgasmville right now."

"Ohh, I have been, population two, but my va-jay-jay needs a rest and I have a dilemma."

"Already?"

"Yeah," I dejectedly say just as Raven joins the chat.

"Hey, my besties, what's up?"

"Bradford broke Fern's hoo-ha."

"Dats my girl," he cheers. "So why are you really calling? A broken hoo-ha doesn't really seem like an SOS."

"Where am I going to live?"

"What do you mean?" Raven asks, sipping on his own coffee.

"Well, I live in Silverbell. Bradford lives in LA. What do I do?"

"Move," Cali and Raven say in unison.

"Is it that simple?"

"Yes," they shout at the same time.

"Fern, babe," Cali voices in her 'I mean business' tone and gives me her 'look at me' look. "Ask yourself, can you live without that man?"

"No," I reply, shaking my head. "I can't live without him. He's my endgame."

"Then you know what to do."

"But you moved back to Silverbell."

"And now I'll have somewhere to vacation in LA," she affirms.

"And Chicago," Raven adds.

"That too," she agrees.

"Thanks, guys, I knew you would give me the clarity I needed."

"And what clarity is that?" a deep voice says from behind me. When I turn around, Bradford is standing in the doorway, his hands shoved into his chino pockets, and he's staring straight at me.

"Gotta go," I squeak out.

Before I disconnect, Raven singsongs, "bom-chiccca-wow-wow" and Cali shouts, "Hiiiiii, Bradford," and then she makes exaggerated kissing noises.

Clicking the red disconnect button, I throw my phone down and then look up at my man. "Come here." I tap the lounger next to me. "We need to talk."

"Ohh no, that's never a good sign," he says as he strides over and sits down next to me. He pulls me onto his lap and he kisses me deeply. Pulling back, he's left me breathless but he looks cool as a cucumber. "So, what do you have clarity over?"

"Us," I tell him.

"And what clarity over us do you have?"

"I … I wanna move here permanently."

"You wanna live here permanently?" he repeats and I nod. "Where will you live?"

"I was hoping here with you."

"You wanna move here permanently and live with me?" Again, I nod. My heart is racing and my hands are sweaty, why is this so nerve-wracking? "Can we reinstate naked Sundays if you move in?"

"Duh," I mock. "That's a given, and to sweeten the deal, I'll throw in a blow job on the days you send me flowers."

"Looks like you'll be getting flowers every day then because, Fern, you are the blow job queen."

"Why thank you, Sir."

"Fuck, the things you do to me when you call me Sir."

"The things I'm going to do to you as your new roommate."

"Roommate, I love that." Leaning forward I press my lips to his and kiss him deeply. Pulling back, I rest my forehead against his. "So, should we seal the deal with a blow job?"

"Sweetheart, you can blow me anytime you want."

And blow him, I do.

We seal our new living arrangements with a blow job, followed by the best sex of my life. Later that night, I drift off to sleep, naked in Bradford's arms, happier than I ever have been before.

CHAPTER 47

Bradford

...the following weekend

"So, Mr. Manning," Cali says, eyeing me across the table at the country club. She steeples her fingers and leans forward, for a wee thing, she exudes power and if I'm honest, I'm a little scared of her right now. "What are your intentions with my sister from another mister?"

Looking to the love of my life, I smile brightly at her and take her hand in mine. I never thought I'd get another chance with Fern, not after my last time here in Silverbell, but now we're here, packing up her apartment and she's moving in with me, again, but this time, it's going to be forever. Now that I have her back in my arms, I will do everything in my power to keep her happy, safe, and loved. "Well, Ms. Fischer—"

"It's Heatherington," she interrupts and with a smile as she reconfirms her married name, "Mrs. Heatherington."

"My apologies, Mrs. Heatherington, as I was about to tell you, I love Fern with my heart and soul. I know I hurt her pushing her away, but I did it for her safety. Now that she's back, I'm never letting her go again."

"I still can't believe that all happened." She shakes her head and takes a sip of her wine. "Like seriously, it was like an episode of *Law and Order* or some other cop show."

"I assure you, it was worse than what you see on television but thankfully, the baddies are behind bars. My brother is now happy, married, and about to have a baby, and me, well, I'm the luckiest son of a bitch alive 'cause I finally got the girl."

"So it all worked out for the best." Nodding, I smile at her and when I see her lift her knife and point it at me, my eyes widen and I slightly begin to fear for my life. "You break her heart again, Bradford, and I will kill you."

"Settle down, dear wife of mine," Kane placates his wife and takes the knife from her. "Orange doesn't look good on you, remember?"

"Fine," she huffs, crossing her arms. "I just don't want to see Fern get hurt again."

"I will never do that again, Cali. Your best friend is the

love of my life, and I will spend the rest of my days making up for lost time."

Looking over at Fern, I smile. She's at the bar getting a round of drinks for everyone. She's laughing with the lady behind the counter and I realize I am a lucky lucky man. "Excuse me," I tell Cali and Kane.

Standing up, I walk over to my girl and when I reach her, I slide my arms around her waist. She covers my hands and leans back into me. "Everything is right in the world once again," I whisper into her ear before I kiss her temple. She turns her head and looks at me over her shoulder.

"Everything is perfect, Bradford, and I have never been happier."

"Good, and I'm going to make sure you stay that way. My life's mission will be to make you smile each and every day, Fern Halstead."

"Well, you are off to a great start, Bradford Manning, and I cannot wait to grow old with you."

EPILOGUE

Fern

...*five years later*

Today is my thirtieth birthday and I'm happier than I have ever been. Life since moving to LA to be with Bradford after our time apart has been everything I wanted it to be and more. My dream of becoming a Hollywood makeup artist finally became a reality and now, you're looking at the lead makeup artist for Beyond Studios. Next week, I get to do the makeup for Chris-freaking-Hemsworth on his next blockbuster movie, but most of all, I got my Prince

Charming.

Bradford and I got married eighteen months after I returned and our little boy, Alex—named after my dad—arrived nine months later. Yep, my husband knocked me up on our honeymoon in the Maldives, but considering we were naked and his penis lived in my vagina while we were in paradise, it's not surprising at all.

Leaning back on my arm under the beach umbrella, I sip on my iced tea and watch Bradford play with our little man. Meanwhile, our soon-to-be born little girl uses my bladder as her first squeeze toy. Sophie, named after my mom, is due in three weeks and I'm the size of a house right now.

My phone rings and I smile when I look down. "Hey hey, Momma Cal."

"Ugh, why did I tell you that story," she complains, and I can't help but chuckle.

"'Cause you tell me everything and your stepkids calling you that was priceless."

"I hate you," she teases.

"No you don't, you love me."

"You're lucky I do but it's not about me, today is all about you getting old, happy birthday, lady."

"Thanks, Cal, I wish you guys could have gotten out here for it."

"Well, you could have come back to Silverbell for your birthday. I mean it's not like you don't have a stunning beach house here or anything."

"I have a stunning beach house here too and in case you've forgotten, I'm the size of Raven's ego right now, and I cannot fly."

"Semantics, but I'm excited to meet your little girl … and you can meet my little one in six months' time too."

"You're pregnant again?" I shout into the phone, garnering the attention of Bradford and Alex. "But Vi is like three months old."

"Well, seems I'm super fertile 'cause, I shit you not, we've had sex once since Vi was born. Once, Fern, once. That's all it took for Kane to knock me up again."

"He's got super sperm."

"That he does it seems but whatever the case, you will be an aunty again soon."

"I'm so happy for you guys, Cal. Please pass on my congrats."

"Will do, so, what are the plans for your birthday today?"

"We are down on the beach right now. Bradford is trying to wear Alex out so while he's down for a nap, he and I can have some fun. Might be our last chance before Sophie arrives."

"Birthday sex is always fun, so I will let you go get your sexy on. Try not to get pregnant again."

"I don't think you can get pregnant while you're eight months pregnant."

"Never say never, look at me."

A laugh slips free. "I'm not the fertile queen like you, therefore I think Bradford and I will be fine."

Cali and I say our goodbyes and just as I hang up, my husband and son come over to join me on the blanket. "There's my boys."

"And there are my girls." Bradford leans down and

kisses me on the lips and as he sits down next to me, he kisses my belly. Not wanting to be left out, Alex does the same. He is so much like his father, it's scary at times.

We enjoy some birthday cupcakes and when Alex's eyes begin to droop, we pack up our things and head home. Hand in hand with my boys, we trudge up the beach toward our house. After rinsing the sand off our feet, we head inside. Bradford takes Alex to his room and I begin to unpack the stuff from our beach outing.

I've just finished when a pair of hands slide around my waist from behind and they reach up to cup my sensitive boobs. Dropping my head back, I rest it on Bradford's shoulder while he fondles my tits. "I love your tits when you're pregnant."

"Maybe you'll have to get me pregnant again then?"

"Maybe," he agrees, nibbling on my neck. My body is ablaze right now. Thanks to the pregnancy hormones, the slightest touch sets me off and I'm ready to combust. Spinning around in his arms, I drape mine over his shoulders and kiss him deeply. He slides his hands under my ass and lifts me up. Placing me down on the granite countertop. He slides his hands up underneath my sundress and removes my panties. "You are too good at doing that."

"Mmmhmpf," he agrees. "You know what else I'm good at?"

"What?"

"Eating your pussy, now lie back, wife, and let me feast."

Saluting him, I lean back on my elbows and I watch as he lowers down between my thighs. I can't see what he's doing due to my pregnant belly, but I feel his tongue dart out and lick me from taint to clit. My head drops back and I give myself over to the pleasure and my husband's tongue.

"Sir, please," I pant when he slips a finger inside of me.

"I fucking love it when you call me, Sir."

"Sir, shut up and eat me."

"So bossy."

"It's my birthday, I'm allowed to be. Now less talking, more licking, if you want me to blow you before Alex wakes up, you better hop to it."

"Yes, ma'am." And hop to it he does.

Bradford doesn't get a birthday blow job because right after I climaxed, my water broke and we had to rush to the hospital for me to deliver our little girl. Sophie managed to hold off and just after midnight the following day, she came screaming into this world. Our little girl has a set of lungs on her and I cannot wait to see the woman she grows up to be.

"Sorry, Grandad," the nurse says, just as I finish feeding Sophie, "you need to go now."

"Ummm, he's my husband," I growl at the nurse.

"Ohh, I thought …"

"Well, you thought wrong," I snap at her.

This is a common occurrence for us and it pisses me off to no end, especially during a happy moment like this. Bradford and I may be unconventional but I'm Fern Manning nee Halstead. There's nothing conventional about me or us, but Bradford Manning is mine and I'm never letting him go.

The End!!!!!!

Wanna know how Cali and Kane got together? You can read their story now in Love Me Like You Do.

Calliope

Love blossoms when we least expect it.

I've loved him for as long as I can remember.

I just never anticipated he would ever love me back.

Kane Heatherington is off-limits, but I can't stop thinking about him.

A chance encounter one evening changed our relationship.

Then years later, when I was at rock bottom,

he found me in a place neither of us ever expected to see each other.

Now, he's my boss and the dynamics between us are changing.

Kane is my everything. He's it for me. No one loves me like he does, but

is our love strong enough to survive the backlash from our families?

Kane

Love came to me for a second time.

I never thought it would come again.

Especially from the girl I've known her whole life.

Calliope Fischer is the forbidden fruit, but I can't stop thinking about her.

One night in New York City changed our relationship. Years later we were

brought together again when we needed each other the most.

Now, I'm her boss and the lines are blurring.

Calliope owns me, heart and soul. She's my endgame.

Now I just need to find a way to tell my best friend

I'm in love with his daughter.

DL GALLIE

PLAYLIST

Never Let Me Go - Florence + The Machine
Song for Someone - U2
You and Beautiful - Lana Del Ray
Can't Go Back - Ross Golan
Sleep Like a Baby Tonight - U2
Silhouettes - Of Monsters and Men
Breathe Me - Sia
The Shortest Straw - Metallica
California Love - 2Pac
Girls Like You - Maroon 5 feat. Cardi B
Sweet Nothing - Calvin Harris feat. Florence + The Machine
Broken Ones - Jacquie
Give Me Love - Ed Sheeran
Breath of Life - Florence + The Machine
I Know You - Skylar Grey
Mad World - Demi Lovato
Jar of Hearts - Christina Perri
Flashlight - Jessie J
The Heart Wants What it Wants - Selena Gomez
One More Light - Linkin Park
Hurt Somebody - Noah Khan
Never Gonna Cry Again - Pentatonix
How Did You Love - Shinedown
arms - Christina Perri
Hit Me With Your Best Shot - ADONA
Wannabe - why mona
Metallica - Lux AEterna
Sad But True - Metallica
Welcome Home (Sanitarium) - Metallica
The Unforgiven II - Metallica
Hero of the Day - Metallica
The Unforgiven - Metallica
Bones - Imagine Dragons

Fly Me To The Moon - Frank Sinatra
I've Got You Under My Skin - Frank Sinatra
The Way You Look Tonight - Frank Sinatra
My Way - Frank Sinatra
Love Is Here To Stay - Frank Sinatra
I Get A Kick Out Of You - Frank Sinatra
Just Give Me a Reason - P!nk, Nate Russo

This playlist can be found on Spotify.

Acknowledgments

First and foremost, I need to thank **Alex** and **Sophie** for creating Silverbell and inviting me to be a part of this project, twice. I have fallen in love with this fictional town and I can't wait to read everyone's story. Also a shout out to my fellow Silverbell authors, thanks for joining the journey with me.

Rebecca Barber, you have become one of my most favourite people. I'd be lost without you on my team, feel free to send me chocolate dicks anytime.

My beta babes, **Wench** aka **Tara, Bec, Sarah** and **Rhi;** thank you for helping me make this story everything that it is. You're input and feedback is priceless and I'm so thankful to have you on my team.

Karen Hrdlicka from **Barren Acres Editing**; thank you for everything that you do for me. You've been with me since the beginning and I'm so grateful to have you on Team DL and I cannot wait till I get to squeeze you in person … in August 2023.

Alex; Thank you. Thank you. Thank you for the beautiful, stunning, amazing cover. I'm so in love with it. Both versions.

Lou; thank you for a beautiful interior once again. You are a talented lady and I just love it.

To my husband, **Troy**, and my munchkins, **Piper and Kade**. You all put up with deadline wife/mum and you still talk to me. I couldn't do this without you guys. You three are my biggest cheerleaders and I love you all long-time.

And finally, **you, my reader**. Thank you again for taking a chance on lil old me. My characters and I love it.

Cheers,

Dana XoXoX

Silverbell Shore Books

Careless Whispers - *Alexandra Silva & Sophie Blue*
Love Me Like You Do - *DL Gallie*
Embers of You - *Imogen Wells*
Now and Then - *Katie Rae*
The Shadow of Another - *Lou Stock*
Binding Ties - *Zoey Drake*
The Secrets We Hold - *Kathleen Kelly & Maci Dillon*
My Little Secret - *Rosie East*
Never Let Me Go - *DL Gallie*
Twist of Fate - *Lissanne Jones*

Twist of Fate

LISSANNE JONES

A grieving woman on the run.

A shattered man hiding from the world.

When Beth Adams is forced to take refuge in the resort town of Silverbell Shore, she only means to stay for a few days. But she's inexplicably drawn to the former Navy SEAL who rescues her on the side of the road, so when he offers her a temporary job, she can't turn him down.

Wyatt Kincaid avoids people for a reason. His time in the Navy has left him with emotional scars to match the physical ones. He can't explain what it is about Beth Adams that has him wanting to know everything about her. She somehow has a way of making the carefully constructed walls around his broken heart crumble.

When Beth and Wyatt can no longer deny the attraction between them, they give in to their desire.

A twist of fate brought them together, but when Beth's past catches up with her and threatens to tear them apart, Wyatt will stop at nothing to protect the woman he loves and can't live without.

Books by DL Gallie

STANDALONES

Antecedent

Doc Steel

Oops

Off the Books

Fractured:A driven world novel

Deck…the Balls

Secrets and Sunrises

Always in the Cards

Out of Nowhere

Love Me Like You Do

Never Let Me Go

Seven Nights

Seven Kisses

After the Ashes

* * *

PUCKING NOVELS

I Pucking Hate That I Love You

A Pucking Good Christmas

…and a few pucking more

* * *

FALLING NOVELS

These men make it hard not to fall for them

Falling for Dr. Kelly
Falling for Dr. Knight
Falling for Agent Cox
Falling for Agent Cruz

Falling:The Complete Collection

* * *

THE UNEXPECTED SERIES

When it comes to love, expect the unexpected

The Unexpected Gift
The Unexpected Letter
The Unexpected Package
The Unexpected Connection

The Unexpected series: The Complete Collection

* * *

THE CASTAWAY GROVE COLLECTION

Love has arrived in the Grove

Oasis

Unequivocal Love

Five Words

Broken Rules

…and a few more to come.

The Castaway Grove Collection, Vol 1

* * *

THE LIQUOR CABINET SERIES

Liquor has never been so disturbingly saucy

Malt Me (Book 1)

Tequila Healing (Book 2)

Wine Not (Book 3)

The Final Shot (Book 4)

The Liquor Cabinet: Series boxset

About the Author

DL Gallie writes spicy romance with elements of comedy and suspense. She currently lives in Central Queensland, Australia, her husband and two kids but has lived in many different places around the world and within Australis. She and her husband have been together since she was sixteen, and although they drive each other crazy at times, she couldn't imagine her life without him.

Shortly after her son was born, DL began reading again. With encouragement from her husband, she picked up the pen and started writing, and now the voices in her head won't shut up.

DL enjoys listening to music, drinking white wine in the summer, red wine in the winter, and beer all year round. She's also never been known to turn down a cocktail, especially a margarita.

FIND D.L. GALLIE ON
FACEBOOK ~ INSTAGRAM ~ BOOKBUB

GOODREADS

dlgallieauthor.wixsite.com/dlgallieauthor

dlgallieauthor@outlook.com

Sign up to my newsletter

ROMANCE WITH A SHOT OF SUSPENSE
AND A DASH OF COMEDY